MAR

THE FLORIDA RUN

MARINE C: SBS

THE FLORIDA RUN

David Monnery

First published in Great Britain 1995
22 Books, Invicta House, Sir Thomas Longley Road,
Rochester, Kent

Copyright © 1995 by 22 Books

The moral right of the author has been asserted

A CIP catalogue record for this book is available from the
British Library

ISBN 1 898125 39 2

10 9 8 7 6 5 4 3 2 1

Typeset by Hewer Text Composition Services, Edinburgh
Printed in Great Britain by Cox and Wyman Limited, Reading

1

Nick Russell idled the engine of the *Foxy Lady* and let the boat drift on the placid water. The sun was dropping towards the horizon, flooding the ocean with gold, and he wanted to savour the moment.

As the edge of the molten disc touched the distant horizon, he half expected to hear a loud hiss and to see a plume of steam rise up towards the high, feathery clouds.

Russell had spent his day off in the usual manner, exploring the coral reefs which surrounded the island of Providenciales. Once he had thought that the sense of wonder would gradually wear off, that not even the reefs could keep their magic for ever, but so far there was no sign of any such diminution. The blends of light and colour and movement and mystery seemed just as potent as on the very first day.

The sun slid from sight, and for a few minutes he just sat there, listening to the gentle lap of the water against the hull, and the occasional sound of a car or boat engine drifting across from the direction of the Leeward Marina. The western sky moved from orange to lime green, as the cirrus clouds overhead turned pink against the darkening sky. Above the island the evening star grew more piercing with each passing second.

Russell sighed with pleasure, and then laughed. He engaged the engine and aimed the boat towards the narrow channel known as the Leeward Going Through, which ran between Little Water and Mangrove Cays to the north-west and Providenciales to the south-east. The latter island was known as Provo to almost everyone who lived on it, but even after seven years Russell felt vaguely uncomfortable with the abbreviation – he had come too close to dying at the hands of its Northern Irish namesakes.

That had been a long time ago, though: nearly fifteen years. It was now almost eight since he had worn a military uniform.

Ahead of the boat a lone pelican flew across the channel, headed north towards Little Water Cay. In the distance the lights of the marina were growing brighter against the gathering darkness. At that moment a car started up the slope away from the mooring area, its headlights shining hopefully up at the sky.

Coming here was the best thing he had ever done, Russell thought, and grinned to himself again. The same thought seemed to pass through his brain at about this stage of each journey home from the reef.

But it was true enough. When Worrell Franklin had come to him with the offer of a job his first inclination had been to dismiss the idea. It had sounded great – living in a tropical island paradise, getting paid good money for doing useful and interesting work, able to indulge in all of the outdoor pleasures he loved – but it had also seemed too good to be true. After eleven years in the Marines, the last six of them as a captain with the Special Boat Squadron, Russell had begun to distrust his own good fortune. He had already survived more close encounters with sudden death than seemed natural, and he found it hard to believe that such a run of luck could last for ever.

Even his first meeting with Franklin had been pure chance. A few days before the Argentinians surrendered in the Falklands, Russell had been leading an SBS reconnaissance patrol in the hills above Port Stanley and had just discovered what seemed like the perfect location for an observation post, when a voice came out of the dawn mist, advising him and his men in a Brixton-accented Spanish to lay down their weapons. The SAS, it turned out, had beaten them to it.

In the event the eight men had shared the cramped hide through the hours of daylight, teaching each other regimental slang, listening to each other fart, and wondering out loud whether their respective superiors would ever acquire the skills needed to organize a piss-up in a brewery.

As leaders of their respective patrols, the two men had talked a great deal through the day, and, somewhat to their mutual surprise, had found that they liked each other. They could hardly have come from more divergent backgrounds: Russell was from a merchant banking family and public school, while Franklin was the son of a London Underground guard who had arrived in Britain from Jamaica in 1957. In fact, Franklin had probably been the first black man with whom Russell had exchanged more than half a dozen sentences. Nowadays it was white friends he could count on the fingers of one hand.

Not that it mattered a damn, but it did say something about the way his life had changed. One of the great things about the clinic where he worked was its melting-pot atmosphere, what with Franklin's African wife and the Chinese herbalist and the Puerto Rican doctor . . .

A noise like serrated metal on wood cut through Russell's reverie.

'Shit!' he growled, and instantly cut the engine. It sounded like the keel had scraped a reef, but that was impossible. The *Foxy Lady* was in the middle of the channel, approaching its southern exit. Russell had been through here a hundred times before. There were no reefs, no shallows.

The noise had sounded nasty enough to cut the boat in two, yet there was no sign of damage inside the hull. He would have to take a look at the outside. And right then, he decided. It might make more sense to wait until he was back at the Caicos Marina, but the water wouldn't be so clear, and the *Foxy Lady* was about the only thing he owned in this world. He wanted to know what the damage was.

His determination was frustrated. He had changed back into his wetsuit before he remembered that he had lost his torch the previous week. It would be too dark to see anything under the boat without one.

He restarted the engine and headed for home. The boat wasn't taking any water, and with any luck the damage was considerably less than he had first feared.

Darkness was falling with its usual tropical efficiency, and as he headed south-west, with Long Bay's four-mile stretch of empty sands away to starboard, the heavenly illuminations were gearing up for the night ahead.

After tying up the boat Russell walked down to the office, which was already closed. Fortunately no one had bothered to lock the door, and after a short search he managed to locate a suitable-looking torch. This in hand, he walked back along the slip, past the row of darkened boats. This was the off-season for tourists and part-time residents, and in any case most of the former kept to the island's north coast, where all the new hotel developments were sprouting.

The boats moored here were mostly owned by full-time residents, and came in all sizes and shapes, from yachts to rowing boats, outboards to racing boats, canoes to converted shrimp boats like Russell's own. The biggest craft by far was the *Tiburón Blanco*, the White Shark, which occupied the two moorings next to Russell's. According to the locals the boat belonged to a Cuban-American gangster who owned one of the restored plantation villas behind Long Bay. Russell had never laid eyes on the man, but he had shared a brief conversation with the boat's captain that morning, an Hispanic with a weathered face, hooked nose and longish hair.

The topic of the conversation had been the twenty-foot submersible which was tethered alongside the boat's starboard side. Russell had never seen one like it, and in his years with the SBS he had come into contact with most of the models used by the NATO navies.

'What's it for?' he had asked the man in the captain's hat.

The man had grinned at him. 'We go treasure hunting,' he had said.

'Anywhere in particular?'

'Yes.'

'But that's a secret, right?'

'*Sí.*' The man was still grinning, but Russell didn't get the feeling that there was much enjoyment behind the facial expression. He had restrained himself from asking about the origins of the submersible, thinking that the man might be in a friendlier frame of mind when he returned that evening.

But there didn't seem to be anyone aboard the *Tiburón Blanco*. Russell shone the torch on the tethered submersible. It was actually a submarine in the true sense of the word, with a dry working interior. The propulsion unit was out of sight, under the water at the end furthest from the dock, but he had the distinct feeling the craft was fast, without having any conscious reason for thinking so.

Large front and side windows offered good visibility, and Russell supposed that for anyone searching through the myriad wrecks which littered the local ocean floor it would prove ideal. It looked smart too – the blue-green paint was obviously recent, as was the outsize figure three which adorned the side between the two panoramic windows.

Why had they bothered to number it? Russell wondered, as he clambered back aboard his own, less elegant craft. After donning and checking the oxygen cylinder he adjusted his goggles and dropped himself backwards over the side and into the harbour waters.

It was dark down below, and the powerful beam of light from the torch only seemed to emphasize how much crap there was in the water. After the crystal clarity of the open ocean the waters of the Caicos Marina felt like a microcosm of humankind's treatment of the environment.

He got down to work, methodically scanning the underside of the *Foxy Lady* from the bow backwards, and soon found what he was looking for – a gouge some eighteen inches long. He ran his finger along inside it, and found the cut wasn't deep. Just a flesh wound, he thought with some satisfaction. It wouldn't be hard to put right.

There was nothing to indicate what had caused it, and he couldn't begin to imagine what that might have been. Nothing floating freely in the water could have inflicted such damage. He would have to ask at the office whether anyone else had hit a non-existent reef.

He swam back up to the surface, clambered aboard

the boat, and changed back out of the wetsuit, feeling a huge sense of relief that no real damage had been done. A celebratory drink was in order, he decided, smiling to himself. And maybe Missie would give him a game of chess on her veranda, a bottle of rum within easy reach.

In the old days they might have ended up in bed, but neither of them had been willing to make the relationship as exclusive as the other claimed to want. And though there wasn't much doubt they had enjoyed sleeping together, in time both had come to realize they were better suited as friends.

But first things first, he thought. Some supper and a pint at Suzie's Bar. He locked up the boat, more out of habit than from any sense that it was really necessary, and walked back up to the rack outside the marina office, where the mountain bike which he had acquired secondhand from a homegoing American exile was waiting for him.

It was about five miles to the bar, most of it along the unpaved track which snaked along Provo's southern coast before turning inland to meet the island's one major road – the two-lane Leeward Highway – about a mile east of Suzie Turn. Russell didn't meet a single soul on the track, and treated himself to a spirited rendition of several sixties classics as he leisurely pedalled away the miles. The sea sparkled to his left, low, scrub-covered slopes to his right, and the Milky Way seemed to be pointing his way home. 'To be a rock and not to roll,' he sang, with every bit as much conviction as Robert Plant, though rather less in the way of attention to hitting the right notes.

The mile stretch along the Leeward Highway was more problematic. Lacking any other road on which to practise potential Grand Prix skills, the islanders had turned the road into a formidable exercise of nerve, particularly for cyclists at night. Two trips into the ditch was about par for this stretch, but tonight Russell's luck was working overtime, and only two cars went by, both in the opposite direction, and both travelling at less than Warp 9.

Suzie's Bar was almost empty. Two Hispanic men were sitting at a table near the bar, and a group of obvious tourists sat at one of the farthest-flung tables beneath the two Cuban pines. As Russell approached the bar one of the latter group headed for the toilet, shouting something over his shoulder in German which made his companions roar with laughter.

Russell climbed on to a stool, remembering what an old Frenchman had told him during the previous tourist season – that these days the Germans were becoming as ubiquitous as the Americans had been ten years before. He'd had a theory about it too. This, he reckoned, was the generation of Germans who had been younger than sixteen at the war's end, and who were now retiring, their pockets bulging with the wealth generated by Germany's postwar success. They were the first guiltless Germans since the thirties, the Frenchman had said, and the richest. They were now showing the world the same arrogance their grandfathers had bestowed upon Europe between the wars.

'Mr Nick, sir,' a voice boomed, interrupting Russell's thoughts.

'Mr Jimmy, sir,' he rejoined, mimicking the barman's mock-Sambo act.

They swapped appreciations of the evening and discussed the dance at Downtown on the coming Saturday while the first pint of draught Guinness was religiously pulled.

'I don't suppose I have to ask whether you been out diving?' Jimmy said.

'Nope.'

'You becoming an addict.'

'I hope so. Jimmy, do you know anything about the people who own the big boat down at the Caicos Marina? They've got a small submarine down there now. A guy who looked like the captain said they were going treasure hunting.'

'It's a Cuban owns it – name of Arcilla. He's not often here though. Lives in Miami, I think. His sister lives here most of the time, though.' He raised his eyebrows. 'I hear she has an appetite.'

'She's fat?'

'Not that kind of appetite,' Jimmy said, moving away down the bar to serve one of the German tourists.

Russell turned round idly on his stool, and found the two Hispanics staring at him. 'Nice evening,' he said.

'*Sí* . . . yes,' one of them said, and turned away. The other said nothing, but his eyes seemed to linger on the Englishman, almost like a challenge.

Russell turned back to the bar, and studied the photomontage of fat, bronzed men standing next to fat, dead fish. He had never been able to take fishing seriously himself. He loved the sea too much to use it as a sports field.

'Like I say,' Jimmy continued, materializing in front of him. 'The sister eats tourists. About one a week I'm told, though I expect she sometimes ups or slows the pace, depending on how tasty she finds a particular specimen.'

There was disapproval behind the leer in Jimmy's voice, which Russell didn't find surprising. Afro-Caribbean men might like lives of sexual adventure for themselves, but

9

they expected women to be monogamous. A female who fucked anyone she felt like fucking was almost too threatening to contemplate. Unless she was doing it for money, of course.

'Have you heard about the treasure hunt?' he asked.

'No, but there's always somebody out there looking for treasure. Funny thing is, it's only the people who already have treasure that can afford to go looking for more.'

More tourists arrived – Americans this time – and Russell called Missie on the phone. She would love to see him, she said, and there was a fish stew cooking in the oven. She would even give him a game of chess, though she thought seven defeats in a row should be enough for any man.

He laughed, waved goodbye to Jimmy, and went back to his bike. An hour later he was being fed ladlefuls of steaming stew in Missie's rambling Blue Hills home. Half bungalow and half shack, it seemed to straddle the centuries. Two of Missie's grown-up sons still lived there, while the other two and her lone daughter were scattered across the western hemisphere. Her husband had been lost off a fishing boat in a storm almost twenty years before.

Supper over, they played chess. Missie won both games, and then the two of them sat in silence looking out to sea, sipping their way through the bottle of rum which Russell had purchased on his way through Downtown. Sitting there, he had the momentary feeling that they were like an old married couple, and wondered how that could be when he was only thirty-seven.

He asked Missie.

'That's the big trouble with you folks,' she said. 'You think if something not moving it must be broken or dead.

Hell, I been sitting here peaceful looking at the sea long as I remember. And I ain't broken or dead.'

After one more drink he climbed, somewhat unsteadily, back on to his bike. The three-mile ride home to the clinic was an exercise in keeping on the road, and this he successfully accomplished, eventually negotiating the open gates of the Caicos Research Clinic and Hospital with all the panache of a lion leaping through a blazing hoop. The front door of his bungalow presented rather more difficulty, but eventually he realized it wasn't locked.

From there to the bedroom it was all downhill, and with one last convulsive surge of energy he managed to remove both his shoes.

Three hours later, when the man draped the cloth soaked in chloroform across his face, he came only briefly back to life, before a new and more terrifying darkness swallowed him up once more.

2

Worrell Franklin could feel the sunlight streaming in through the window without opening his eyes. He lay there contentedly, listening to his wife singing to herself in the shower, thinking about the day ahead. He had two classes to take, and a mountain of paperwork to finish, but even the latter failed to douse his sense of well-being. The new computer didn't exactly turn admin into fun, but sometimes it came close.

The noise of rushing water ceased, and he opened his eyes in time to see Sibou enter the bedroom wrapped in a towel. 'Awake already?' she asked, dropping the towel and drying her legs with it.

She was past forty now, and seemed even more beautiful than when they had met, thirteen years earlier in the Gambia. On the wall behind her, now glowing in the sunlight, there hung the brown batik with the stencilled baobabs which they had bought on the Ile de Gorée, off Dakar, all those years ago, on the very day that they had decided to try to turn a love affair into a lifelong commitment. Since both were committed to their professions – she as an overworked doctor in Africa, he as a member of the SAS – their road had not been an easy one. The long separations had been particularly hard, but ultimately worth it. He had saved her life in the Gambia, but she had made his complete in the years that followed.

'Which day is Winnie arriving?' Sibou asked, breaking the spell.

Franklin lifted himself on to his elbows. 'Next Wednesday.' He had to admit he enjoyed his mother's visits. And if only she would stop trying to set up her own School of Nursing in the middle of theirs he would enjoy them even more.

'Great,' Sibou said. 'I've missed her. Maybe this time you can persuade her to come and live here.'

'She won't leave Everton alone in the big city.'

'Everton's thirty-two, with a new wife and enough money to build himself a fortress.'

Which was true. Franklin's younger brother, who had once seemed so firmly mired in Brixton's angry counter-culture, had managed to climb one of the few greasy poles available to him: he had become a highly successful record producer.

'He's still her little boy,' Franklin told Sibou. 'And she's hoping for grandchildren,' he added, and instantly wished he hadn't.

If there was one cloud in their sky it was Sibou's inability to have children.

This time though she just smiled. 'We've also got the second visit from the adoption agency next week,' she said. 'Winnie may find herself with some grandchildren here.'

He got out of bed and took her in his arms. 'I hope so,' he murmured.

'Me too. Now go take a shower,' she said, pushing him away.

He grinned and did as he was told. When he came out she was gone, probably down to the canteen, where they usually ate breakfast with each other and assorted students and staff. Franklin dressed in his usual T-shirt, shorts and sandals and left the bungalow, pausing outside the front door to yawn and rub the remaining sleep out of his eyes. Then he strolled slowly down the path towards the central area.

The clinic grounds spread over several of the island's acres, and had been laid out, largely at Sibou's direction, on the pattern of a similar establishment in the Gambia. Long, one-storey buildings surrounded a large central square of grass studded with ornamental trees, and behind these to the south and east more scrubland had been cleared for staff bungalows and student dormitories. On the west side of the square lay the buildings of the research wing, which was mostly concerned with seeking a reliable detection test for ciguatera fish poisoning, a Caribbean-wide scourge associated with coral reef-derived toxins. The two long-term wards for TB and Aids patients were on the south side, the canteen, nursing school classrooms and daily clinic on the east. The small admin block was just inside the gates, from which a palm-lined lane led out on to the Leeward Highway.

In the canteen Franklin found Sibou working her way through a bowl of fruit salad as she read a newly arrived patient's history. He went for his usual cornflakes, and sliced a banana on top of them. There were about a dozen students scattered round the room, most of them bent over ring files – Nick Russell was probably giving them a test in their first class of the day.

Franklin wondered where his friend was. Nick was usually in the middle of his third cup of coffee by this time.

Still, the clock said ten to eight, so maybe he was already in the classroom setting up the exam. Franklin turned his thoughts back to the classes he was giving

14

that afternoon. Infectious Diseases had never been one of his favourite subjects, but he enjoyed the Emergencies class.

Half an hour later he was searching for a mislaid computer manual when there was an apologetic knock on his open door. He looked up to see one of the students.

'Nick ... Mr Russell hasn't come to class,' she told him.

'Oh,' Franklin said, surprised. He looked at his watch, but only from habit. Nick was never late for anything.

He accompanied the student back to the classroom, and found it full of adults doing their best to relive their adolescence. He asked what the subject was for that lesson, and set them some reading. Back outside, he started off down the path in the direction of Nick's bungalow.

He hoped that he wasn't going to find his friend sleeping off a drunken binge. When Nick had first come to work at the clinic Sibou had been worried by his alcohol intake, but had gradually come to accept that it never compromised his work. Franklin didn't want her worst fears coming true at this late date. Particularly since Nick seemed to have cut back substantially over the last couple of years.

His bungalow was the farthest from the central compound, and one of the most attractive, its veranda shaded by a stand of beautiful Cuban pines. The red mountain bike was leaning against the veranda steps, so Nick wasn't out on that. The screen door was shut, the door behind it open. There was no noise coming from inside, no screaming riffs from Nick's beloved Clapton, Hendrix or Page.

Franklin let himself in quietly, more from SAS habit

than any sense that danger was present. The living-room and kitchen doors were open, and both rooms looked as tidy and well organized as usual. The bedroom door was closed. Franklin rapped on it lightly, received no answer, and edged the door open. The room was full of sunshine, the bed half-wrecked but empty, as if someone had got up in a hurry.

Most of all, though, Franklin noticed the smell.

He stood there for a moment, worry lines prominent on his forehead, before walking over to close the window. Nick's incense jar – a souvenir of his Hong Kong days – was on the sill, and maybe that was the source of the familiar odour. He hoped so.

Franklin left the room, closing the door behind him, and walked back through the village of bungalows to the medical treatment block. Sibou was in her office between the two wards, talking to two of the trainee nurses.

'Sorry to interrupt,' Franklin said, 'but I need the doctor for a few minutes.

'What for?' Sibou asked, surprise in her voice. One of the nurses giggled.

'Can you come with me,' Franklin said, 'it's important.'

'What's up?' she asked once they were outside.

'I'll tell you in a minute. First I want your opinion on something.'

She heard the trouble in his voice, and didn't ask any more questions as he led the way back to Russell's bungalow. Once inside he took her into the bedroom and closed the door behind them.

'What's that smell?' he asked.

'Chloroform,' she said immediately.

Franklin sat down on the unmade bed. 'That's what I thought. I just wanted to make sure.'

16

'But . . . where's Nick?'

'He didn't turn up to teach his first class, so I came looking for him.'

She sat down too. 'You don't think . . . ?'

'Someone drugged him with chloroform and took him away?'

'But that's ridiculous. Why would anyone do that?'

Franklin shrugged. 'God only knows.'

Slightly more than a hundred miles away, Nick Russell was experiencing more than a little difficulty in regaining consciousness. His mind seemed to flicker on and off, like a light with a switch containing a loose connection. And though one voice in his brain was all for trying to keep the light on, others were more interested in losing the headache and the nausea and the vague sense of terror which consciousness seemed to involve.

This battle went on for some time, until the need to throw up forced him into greater wakefulness. Between periods of retching over the side of the bed – an iron cot, he realized, with a thin mattress – he managed to focus his eyes sufficiently to pick out the whitewashed cement-block walls, the small window high up behind the bed, and the bare, white-painted door.

The next thing he noticed was someone coming through the door, carrying a tray. It was a grey-haired black man, and he seemed to be angry about something, though the actual words sounded like gibberish.

No, French. The man was speaking French.

'Where am I?' Russell asked, sounding to himself like a man in a bad movie.

The man either didn't understand him, or didn't care to answer. In fact he was already on his way out of the

17

door. A key clicked loudly in the lock, and then silence enveloped his cell once more.

Worrell Franklin nursed the minivan along the Leeward Highway towards the cluster of new shops and offices which was collectively known as Downtown. The island's only police station was on the other side of this development, only a stone's throw from the newly lengthened airport runway. He wasn't expecting much in the way of help from the local constabulary, but he couldn't think of anywhere else to turn.

Downtown seemed almost deserted, with only a trickle of tourists making use of the banks and new shopping mall. The police station didn't seem much livelier. There was only one officer present – Sergeant Oswald.

Franklin had seen the man before – as he had most of Provo's five thousand inhabitants – but couldn't remember ever talking to him. Over the next couple of hours he came to regret breaking this mutual silence.

Sergeant Oswald, though unimpressed by the short space of time for which Nick Russell had been missing, did agree to visit the scene of the possible abduction. Once there he sniffed appreciatively, and announced that there was definitely a hospital-type smell in the room. 'It is a hospital you have here, Mr Franklin, yes?'

'The smell is of chloroform,' Franklin insisted. By this time the odour was growing decidedly faint.

'It smells like the dentist I once went to,' Oswald decided, before abruptly sinking to his knees and looking under the bed. The missing man was not there. He then looked round the room with a professional air. 'There are no bloodstains, no signs of a struggle. You can think of no reason why anyone should kidnap this man. He has no money, you say?'

'Nothing worth kidnapping him for.'

'That's what I thought. And you say his boat is where it should be . . . ?'

'So the marina man told me on the phone . . .'

Oswald nodded wisely. 'I think you will find he has stayed with some woman friend, and they lose track of the time. It is easy to do when you are young,' he added wistfully.

'And the chloroform?'

Oswald sniffed again. 'I can't smell anything now.'

Franklin couldn't either.

'If he has not returned by tomorrow I will take this further,' the sergeant concluded. 'He was a diver, you say?'

'One of the best.' An SBS Swimmer-Canoeist First Class, no less.

'Even the best sometimes get careless.'

'But . . .' Franklin began, and gave up. He was going to ask how Nick's boat had reached port without him, but decided that there was no point in antagonizing the man at this stage. Maybe there was some less dramatic explanation of the chloroform and the disappearance. Whatever had happened, he had no way of making any sense out of it with the information currently at his disposal. Maybe he could gather some more, and give Oswald's brain something to chew on.

After shepherding the policeman back to his car, and watching it accelerate down the lane to the Leeward Highway like a racing car emerging from the pits, Franklin turned to find Sibou coming towards him, white coat flapping in the warm breeze.

'Well?' she asked anxiously.

'I would have got more joy out of talking to one of the pelicans,' Franklin said.

She sighed. 'I saw who it was. Someone told me he was one of the family appointments during the Saunders administration.'

'A professional blind eye.'

'Something like that.'

Franklin grunted. 'He seemed willing to be helpful. Just not able to be.'

'All he ever has to do is wag a finger at the odd drunken tourist. I doubt if he's ever seen a real crime.'

'He looked under the bed.'

She laughed, but only briefly. 'Something bad really has happened, hasn't it?'

'It looks like it,' Franklin agreed, his face grim. 'I can't see any other explanation. And I don't know what else I can do.'

She put an arm through his, and they stood in silence for a minute.

'Missie,' she said suddenly. 'He often goes to see her after his day out on the reef.'

'She's not on the phone.' Franklin looked at his watch. 'I've got a class in ten minutes . . .'

'I can take an hour off,' Sibou said. 'Give me the keys,' she added, offering up her palm.

Russell's next waking thought was that perhaps he had gone to heaven. A face of such loveliness was leaning over his own, large-eyed, small-nosed, with a mouth that, even pursed with concern, seemed almost angelic. Curls of raven hair were slipping out from their confinement behind the ears. Huge earrings dangled half out of sight.

He became aware of something metal against his skin. It was a stethoscope, not earrings.

'Who are you?' he tried to ask, but only a murmur

seemed to emerge from his lips. He tried 'where am I?'
with somewhat better results.

'L'Ile de Tortue,' she said.

It sounded French. He had a memory of something
else sounding French.

'What's the matter with me?' he asked slowly.

'They used too much chloroform,' she said in French-
accented English.

He closed his eyes. The bike ride home, pissed out
of his skull. The shot of terror in the night. Had that
been . . . ? He opened his eyes again, struggling to keep
the lovely face in focus. 'Where is the . . . the place
you said?'

He saw the surprise on her face. 'It is an island near
the coast.'

'Which coast?' he enunciated carefully.

'The north coast,' she said patiently. '*De Haïti.*'

'I am in Haiti?'

'*Oui*, yes.'

'And who are you?'

'I am a doctor,' she said, but there was a bitterness in
her voice he couldn't begin to understand. 'My name is
Alabri, Emelisse Alabri,' she added, in a tone that seemed
inexplicably defiant.

'Nick Russell,' he said thickly. 'Who brought me
here?'

'No more questions now,' she said, smiling to make
up for the curtness in her voice. It was as lovely a smile
as he could remember, and it seemed to hang in his
mind, before receding slowly into the distance, in a
manner which somehow reminded him of the Tardis.

Sibou had seen the look on Franklin's face as she headed
out of the clinic gates, and spent the next couple of miles

resenting it. Certainly she drove fast, but she had never had a serious accident, unlike her husband, who had driven a rental car into a coconut palm soon after their arrival in the Turks and Caicos. The car's bumper had been bent like a boomerang, its roof severely pitted by the resulting shower of dislodged coconuts. Her worst mishap had been to drive through the clinic's gates while they were still closed, and that could have happened to anyone with as much on their minds as she usually had.

She grinned at herself, and forgave Franklin his scepticism. He was only worried about her, after all.

She turned right on to the Blue Hills turn-off just before Downtown, and a few minutes later was following the road which ran behind the beach north from Thompson Cove Point. Inside the dark line of reef the waters were their usual pristine turquoise; beyond it the ribbon of breakers gave way to the deeper blue of the ocean proper. Every couple of hundred yards a group of white tourists was encamped on the white sand.

Sibou shook her head, and wondered for the hundredth time why the European races were so frightened of being close to each other. Twenty years before, when she had first been a student at St Thomas' Medical School in London, she had gone on to the upper deck of a bus, seen only one passenger, and naturally sat down next to him. He had muttered to himself for a minute, and then got off the bus. Looking back, she had been able to see him waiting for the next one.

She was still smiling at the memory when the first dwellings of Blue Hills loomed into view. This was one of the three pre-tourist settlements on the island, and like the other two it hadn't changed very much. It was more scattered than an English village, more like a random spread of homes on which the road had later been superimposed.

Missie's house was down by the beach. Sibou had been there a couple of times with Franklin, in the days when Nick and Missie were toying with the idea of being a couple. She had liked Missie's no-nonsense personality and felt vaguely guilty for not keeping up the acquaintance over the last few months. She told herself that there was always so much to do at the clinic, and so little time, but knew that was not the real reason. Missie was a mother, and Sibou was still trying to come to terms with the fact that she would never be one.

She left the minivan by the side of the road, and walked down the shaded path towards the house. It was unusually hot, and the moment she emerged from the trees the sun resumed its business of trying to burn a hole through her straw hat.

Missie was on her veranda, kneading Johnnycake dough on a wooden board that was perched across her thighs. She looked just the same as Sibou remembered: a tall, big-boned woman with a long neck and beautiful African head. She was dressed in shorts and a Miami Dolphins T-shirt. Her feet were bare.

Her first reaction to seeing Sibou was a look of surprise, the second a warm smile of welcome. 'Come into the kitchen,' she said, getting up. 'You can pour us some coffee while I finish this.'

Sibou did as she was told while Missie shaped the dough into balls, flattened them out and greased a tray for baking. Once they were in the oven, the two women went back out on to the veranda, where the shade and slight breeze offered some respite from the heat.

Sibou took a deep breath and explained why she was there.

'He sure was drunk when he left here,' Missie said. 'I've still got a headache myself. Maybe he just fell off that bicycle somewhere, and . . .'

'The bicycle came home.'

'That sound bad.'

The two women sat in silence for a moment, looking out to sea. It all seemed completely unreal, Sibou thought.

'He didn't say anything to you?' she asked. 'He wasn't worried about anything?'

'He seem fine. He had a good day on the reef. Hit his boat on something, but he say no real damage. He just the same as ever. He still can't play chess worth a damn.'

'Do you know if he came straight here from the marina?'

'Far as I know. No, wait. He phone from Suzie's, and there was beer on his breath when he come here. He must have stop for a drink on the way.'

Sibou couldn't think of anything else. 'How are you?' she asked Missie.

'I was fine until now.'

They talked for a while about her sons, and the clinic, and Franklin's mother's visit, and the possible adoption. 'You come see me again,' Missie said, 'with some good news, maybe. You can bring your husband if you want to. I happy to see you both, or just you. And I'll keep my ears open for any news of Nick,' she added as Sibou was leaving.

On the drive back down the coast Sibou thought the matter through in her usual logical manner, and realized just how little they had to go on. There was a man missing and a smell of chloroform in his bedroom. They had no idea why anyone should want to abduct him. The whole business seemed as ludicrous as it was chilling.

Back at the clinic she found Franklin in the canteen, nursing a can of Coke. She told him what she had found out, which wasn't very much.

'I'd better check out Suzie's Bar,' was his reaction.

'It won't be open until early evening.'

'Do you know where the guy who runs it lives?'

She shook her head.

He gently squeezed the empty Coke can. 'Well, I guess I'll have to wait.' He smiled ruefully. 'It doesn't feel right, calmly going off to teach an Emergencies class when . . . you know . . . I feel like I should be rushing around, trying to do something.'

'I know. One thing that occurred to me – whoever chloroformed Nick could just as easily have killed him . . .'

'Unless they wanted to kill him somewhere else.'

'Why would they want to do that?'

'Christ knows,' Franklin said, angrily crushing the can. 'Why would anyone want to kill him at all?'

3

Aleksandr Solayev bit down on the Bacon Mega Double Whopper and felt the extra mayo he had ordered dribbling down his fingers and on to the plastic tray. The burger tasted like heaven. He followed it with a handful of French fries, and sat there for a moment, holding the last mouthful between sticky fingers, reluctant to complete the meal. He wondered how the Soviet Union could ever have hoped to win the Cold War.

The last mouthful went down, thrilling his taste buds, and he let the flavours linger on his tongue for a few seconds before reaching out a hand for the triple-thick strawberry shake. It was so thick that he almost pulled a lip muscle trying to suck it up through the straw.

Three children walked past his table, all screaming at the tops of their voices. Their parents followed, apparently oblivious to the noise, and herded the whole brood out of the restaurant, across the parking lot and into a large blue Nissan Maxima. Solayev could still hear the children yelling as the car slipped down the ramp and back on to the interstate.

He belched softly, took another draw on the straw, and examined his surroundings again. The restaurant looked as good as the food tasted. Everything was so pleasant on the eye – the printed menu above the servery, the brightly coloured furnishings, the mosaic floor ... And all of it bathed in the bright Florida

26

sunshine that came pouring through the panoramic windows. There was nothing drab here, nothing grey, nothing . . . like home.

He smiled at the thought that this place was also called St Petersburg. It was a long way from the one he had been born in.

The shake seemed easier to draw on now. He removed the plastic lid to investigate and discovered that the ice-cream around the edges was melting quicker than that in the centre. He gave the whole thing a stir, and tried again. This time less effort was required. Learning to live in America, Solayev decided, would involve the mastering of many such minor techniques.

He began tidying up his tray, and noticed the three unused ketchup sachets. They must have given him four, he realized. Surely no one could use four. And there had been six napkins – he had counted them. Such plenty. It was incredible.

The previous evening, in the motel outside Orlando, he had worked his way through the channels on the TV in his room. There had been cop shows, quiz shows, comedies, music, sports of every kind, people talking about God, people selling jewellery. It had reminded him of the first time his father had taken him inside the special Party shop in Leningrad – there were just too many riches to absorb in one go.

Like the Florida women. All those young girls in shorts. He had a better idea now of what dogs on heat felt like. Well, now that he had all the money at last, some female companionship was one of the things uppermost in his mind. Once he was down in the Keys his new life could begin in earnest.

But not Key West, he reminded himself. At first he had thought the guy was kidding him – a town full of queers! – but someone else had confirmed the story. And looked at him strangely. There were some things about America he would have a hard time accepting. And this unhealthy tolerance of perverts was definitely one of them.

His straw gurgled and struck air. Solayev thought about ordering another shake, his third of the day, but one glance at his waistline dissuaded him. It was partly the light summer clothes, he thought: in Murmansk everyone had needed to dress like a bear, and he had hardly noticed the growing paunch.

But it was also about being forty-five. He had to be careful of his diet now – there was no point in striking it this lucky and then immediately keeling over with a coronary.

He carried his tray to the disposal bin, tipped its contents away, and looked around for someone to say goodbye to. But the woman he had spoken to earlier was gone. He remembered the feeling in the motel room, the sense that the room was too big for just him, and that watching TV was something you did with others. The old Russian habits would die hard, he thought.

He walked out to the car, carrying the brown leather attaché case, and climbed in behind the wheel. He placed the case on the seat beside him and opened it, not so much to check that the money was still in it – the case had never been out of his sight – but simply to enjoy the view. A quarter of a million dollars looked back at him.

He smiled to himself, re-locked the case, placed it on the floor behind his seat, and started the Toyota's engine. The two years he had spent as a naval attaché in Cuba in the early eighties had certainly paid off, albeit in a way that he would never have imagined in his wildest dreams. Back then Raul Ochoa had always behaved as if the sun shone out of Fidel Castro's arse, and in between chatting up girls at Havana's tourist hotels the two of them had argued about the relative merits of the Cuban and Soviet roads to socialism.

Solayev snorted with amusement as he pulled out on to the interstate and headed south out of St Petersburg. The collapse of the Soviet Union had been the first of several big surprises in recent years, but all the others had paled before the sudden appearance of Raul Ochoa at his apartment in Murmansk. Ochoa had not only known the details of the small submarine research programme he had been running, but had also been able to confirm the rumours of the programme's imminent cancellation. Solayev was apparently about to join the rapidly swelling ranks of the post-Soviet unemployed.

But not necessarily, Ochoa had told him. Solayev's government might not want his submarines, but the Cuban knew someone who did. Not his own government, with whom he had come to a reluctant parting of the ideological ways, but a private businessman.

Ochoa also had a plan for getting both Solayev and the submarines out of Russia. There would be a $250,000 fee for facilitating the export process and instructing the new owners in how to use the craft, and then Solayev could begin a new life in the West. What did he have to lose?

Quite a lot, if the new crime-busting KGB had caught him, but the whole plan had gone like clockwork. In Yeltsin's Russia a few dollars bought a lot of silence.

He was driving out on to what looked like an endless causeway. 'The Sunshine Skyway', a plaque announced. Ahead of him the concrete roadway swept across the bay in a graceful curve on its line of cylindrical pilings. A couple of miles away, somewhere close to the midpoint, a strange-looking bridge reared up against the blue sky.

This is America, he thought. This was something that had been built by people who had confidence in themselves and the world. It was like something out of a science fiction novel. As he neared the bridge it became apparent that it comprised two huge stanchions, which rose soaring out of the centre of the highway, and from which were suspended two vast triangular fans of suspension cable.

The genius of simplicity, Solayev thought, and with all the beauty which that implied. He wanted to stop, but as usual there was nowhere to pull over, so he drove on down the causeway, hoping to find somewhere from which to take a photograph.

He had just sighted the lay-by up ahead when a car cut across in front of him and slowed, siren wailing and red light flashing.

Solayev looked at his speedometer. Perhaps he had been a bit over the limit, but only a bit. Still, what did a twenty-five-dollar fine matter to him?

The police car pulled over into the lay-by and Solayev followed. A flicker of doubt passed through his mind, but was quelled by the sight of the uniformed officers emerging from the car. And in any case, cars seemed to be going past all the time.

Both officers seemed to be Hispanic. One leant non-chalantly against the bonnet of the Toyota while the other asked for his driver's licence.

'Was I going too fast?' Solayev asked, his Russian accent still strong.

The officer continued looking at the licence, as if it fascinated him.

'*Es claro*,' the other man said.

The officer returned the Russian's licence, and pulled the gun from his holster. The last thing Solayev saw was the man's brown finger clenching on the trigger.

It was just after six when Franklin arrived at Suzie's Bar, and Jimmy Durham was still in the process of opening up for the evening.

'Mr Worrell, sir,' Jimmy greeted him sardonically. 'Don't anyone in that clinic of yours know that alcohol is bad for you?'

'Only in large doses. Give me a Pils.'

Jimmy retrieved a bottle from the refrigerator. 'Hot day,' he said cheerfully.

'They're all hot,' Franklin said. He might have been born in Jamaica, but he had left for England before he could walk or talk, and contrary to white public opinion, black people were no more imbued with a tolerance of extreme heat than they were with natural rhythm.

'The trick is to sleep by day,' Jimmy confided, drawing a circle with the drops of beer on the bar.

'Right. Was Nick in here yesterday?'

'Yep. Not for long, though. Why – you checking up on your employees?'

'He's gone missing.'

Jimmy's doodling finger came to a stop. 'What – really missing?'

'Looks like it.' Franklin was reluctant to go into the business of the chloroform, though he had little doubt the story would be all over the island before too many more hours had gone by. 'Did he talk to anyone in here last night?'

'Only me. He was asking about that boat moored

next to his – can't remember the name. The one Fidel Arcilla owns.'

'What was he asking?'

'Just that. Who owned it. Oh, and he said something about a submarine . . .'

'A submarine?'

'A small one. You know, the kind they use for treasure hunting. And research. One of those.'

'This Arcilla involved in treasure hunting?'

'Seems like it.'

'But Nick didn't know about him?'

'Nope. I told him about the man's sister. She picks up tourists for a living, screws each one every which way for a few days and then goes back for another.'

Franklin raised an eyebrow. 'And where do they live?'

'The restored plantation villa at the end of Long Bay – the last one you come to on the road. Or the first one on the path from the Caicos Marina. But the man's hardly ever there – spends his time in Miami, they tell me. Just his sister giving it away like there was no tomorrow.'

Franklin grimaced. 'Is that all?'

Jimmy grinned. 'Yep. Total Recall is my second name. Second and third names, I suppose.'

Franklin took a last satisfying swig from the bottle of Pils, thanked his informant, and walked back across to the minivan. Once behind the wheel he sighed loudly, ran a hand through his hair, and started up the engine. A few minutes later he was pulling on to the track which led down to the Caicos Marina, and listening to the minivan's suspension beginning to complain. It was only a four-mile walk, he decided. And the evening breeze was beginning to blow.

His long strides ate up the ground, and not much

more than forty minutes had gone by when he walked down the final slope to the channel's edge. He and Nick had often gone out diving together in the early days – Nick the teacher and he the pupil – and Franklin knew where the *Foxy Lady* was berthed.

But it was fully dark now, the moon yet to rise, and he had to strain his eyes to be sure he had found the right boat. Having done so, the first thing he noticed was the absence of the boat Nick had mentioned to Jimmy. On one side of the *Foxy Lady* a small yacht was tied, one of its sail cords tapping against an aluminium boom in the breeze. On the other side were two empty berths. Arcilla's boat had gone. Treasure hunting, maybe. With Nick on board, maybe.

Franklin clambered aboard the *Foxy Lady* in search of clues.

He found none. The local ocean charts had been generously augmented with felt-tip, but the markings seemed nothing more than a record of Nick's reef explorations. The small cabin below was locked, but Franklin felt no scruples about breaking in. After all there was no need for any damage – picking locks was one of the few skills he had learned before joining the army, from the least reputable of the five uncles on his mother's side of the family.

But there was nothing inside the cabin either. An old Walkman with a Doors tape in it, a couple of private-eye paperbacks, a copy of *Teach Yourself Chess* and a book of tropical fish, and Nick's diving gear.

Franklin re-locked the door, climbed back on to dry land and walked up to the marina office. The man in charge was closing up. He hadn't seen Nick since the previous morning. And the big boat – he seemed reluctant to mention the owner's name – had left before sunrise that morning. Headed west, he'd been told; aiming to do some treasure hunting with their submarine on the Cay Sal Bank.

Franklin thanked him and walked slowly back down towards Nick's boat, wondering what to do next. Then abruptly he reversed course and walked back up to where the footbridge crossed the channel beside the marina office. On the far side he struck off up the path which ran around the headland towards Long Bay.

He had only been walking ten minutes when he rounded a bend and saw the old plantation house, perched on a slight rise above the beach. There were lights burning in several windows, but he could see no movement.

There were two single-storey buildings behind the main two-storey house, and the property as a whole was surrounded by a high wall, along the top of which Franklin could just make out the glint of razor wire. The only break in these perimeter defences was a pair of colonial-style gates, adorned with post-colonial video surveillance equipment.

The plantation house had verandas on three sides of each storey, and as Franklin watched a woman came out through a door on to the upper deck and stood at the railing, looking out to sea. She seemed to be wearing a T-shirt and tight trousers, but as Franklin soon discovered, the trousers were only in his imagination. As she flicked on the lighter for her cigarette, he could see that she was naked from the waist down.

The flare died away, and he stood there staring at the distant silhouette, thinking that a painter or photographer would find it hard to come up with a purer image of loneliness.

* * *

Nick Russell's watch, which he had forgotten to take off in his drunken stupor the previous night, told him it was seven forty-five. The lack of light from the small window high in the wall told him it was evening. Assuming he hadn't been out for two days, it was the evening after the one he had spent with Missie.

He forced himself into a sitting position, and had the distinct feeling his brain was slopping around inside his head. He held his head in his hands and took several deep breaths.

He was still sitting in that position when the key clicked in the door. He looked up suddenly, hoping to see Emelisse Alabri again, and felt his head swim. When his eyes cleared he found a black man standing over him, a gun sticking out of his waistband.

If I was *compos mentis*, Russell thought, the man would be without the gun by now. But he wasn't. And there would probably be other chances to indulge in empty heroics later.

He grinned, and even that seemed to conjure up a desire for sleep.

'You walk?' the man asked in English with a marked French accent.

'I don't know,' Russell said mildly. 'Are we going for a stroll?'

The man smiled. 'Something like that. The commandant wants to see you.'

'I'll be home all evening.'

The man grasped Russell roughly under the arm and pulled him to his feet. His brain rocked to and fro, and settled down once more. Maybe he was getting the hang of it.

'Enough joking,' the man was saying.

It seemed like good advice. Russell tried a couple of

paces and found he could just about walk. The man prodded him in the direction of the door.

Outside he found a short passageway. To the right were more doors, to the left an opening on to the outside world. The man prodded him again, towards the latter.

He emerged from the doorway into a world not that dissimilar to the ones Hieronymus Bosch had painted several centuries before. It was a darkness split by fires, full of reeling shadows, with hanging bodies swaying in the breeze. Bosch had never made movies, but if he had ever needed a soundtrack then the ominous, overlapping rhythms of different drummers would probably have been just what the doctor ordered.

As his eyes gradually focused, Russell could see that the fires were mostly surrounded by people cooking, the shadows were tall palms waving in the breeze, the hanging bodies long garments drying on a line. The drums, though, still sounded ominous.

'Who are the drummers?' he asked his escort.

'Just voodoo priests,' the man said. He sounded bored by the idea.

There were buildings all around them, Russell realized. In fact the place didn't look that dissimilar to the place where he lived and worked. There were several low buildings grouped in a rough square which could easily be hospital wards. Or barracks, he thought, as they emerged from under a group of palms and a tall watch-tower loomed into view against the night sky. It wore a radar dish on its roof, which made the whole structure look like one of H. G. Wells's Martian war machines balancing a plate on its head.

But if it was a barracks, then who were these people

grouped around the fires? They looked more like refugees than soldiers. And in fact most of them seemed to be not much more than children.

Russell began to feel very tired. 'I can't walk much farther,' he said.

'We are almost there,' the man told him, gesturing towards the building directly ahead of them.

What seemed like an hour later they reached the door. Inside the furnishings were smarter than Russell had expected, and had a distinctly military feel to them. It reminded him of the Admin block back in Poole.

The next thing he knew he was coming back to life in a chair, with a new throbbing pain in his head. Since there didn't seem much profit in anyone hitting him again, he assumed he must have collapsed.

'Mr Russell,' a voice addressed him. With a supreme effort he managed to refocus his eyes. The man who had spoken was sitting opposite him, behind an office desk, leaning back in his chair with hands behind his head, legs stretched out and crossed at the ankle. There was more American than French in his accent, but the face, though African, had a Gallic quality to it. The nose was decidedly Roman, the mouth almost thin-lipped, the hair lustrous and wavy. The eyes, though, were what drew Russell's attention. They seemed to be straining at their sockets, as if eager to leap out and devour the world.

For the first time in an often dangerous life Russell had the sense that he was in the presence of evil.

'Who are you?' he asked quietly. The words seemed to boom inside his head.

The man smiled. 'I am Toussaint Joutard. Colonel Joutard. But . . .'

'Of the Haitian Army?' Russell interrupted him.

Joutard didn't seem to mind. 'I am the leader of an

organization known as the Sons of the Motherland. We work closely with the army, of course. Most of the time we share the same objectives.'

His English was perfect, Russell thought, and said so.

'I lived in America for several years.'

Bully for you, Russell thought. The man was probably another CIA-trained fascist gone bananas in his own country. 'Why have I been brought here?' he asked.

Joutard smiled again, but it wasn't the sort of smile which engendered bonhomie. 'You could say this was a job interview . . .'

'I already have a job.'

'No longer. You will either take the job I am offering you, or you will be killed.' His lips creased in response to some inner amusement. 'Either way I shall make an excellent profit.'

The last sentence passed Russell by. 'What have I done to you?' he asked.

Joutard looked at him for a few seconds. 'You don't know?' He laughed. 'Perhaps you don't. It doesn't really matter any more.' He slapped the desktop suddenly with the palm of his hand, and then seemed to examine the backs of his fingers. 'You are an extremely lucky man, Mr Russell,' he said. 'We lose the services of one of our doctors, and, hey presto, here you are. I'm told you're a paramedic, which I assume is a step up from being a nurse. Well, here you'll take another step up – to doctor.'

'I don't have that sort of training . . .' Russell said.

'You will get it here. A man with your experience will have no difficulty learning the techniques required – the operations performed here are simple enough.' He smiled yet again. 'We're not doing brain surgery yet.'

Russell felt a sinking feeling in his stomach. 'What sort of operations are you talking about?'

Joutard told him.

Russell just shook his head.

'Of course, if you refuse you will be killed and your body harvested. Being British, you might think that seems a jolly noble sort of thing to do. But you must also understand that these operations will be performed with or without you, and that the patients' chances of survival will no doubt worsen dramatically if they are performed by people with inferior skills. So it might be more noble to stay, *n'est-ce pas?* And of course if you accept – not that I imagine such matters interest you – you will earn an extraordinary amount of money in a short space of time.' He paused for effect and then looked up and said: 'So you can either leave the sick to fend for themselves or die a useless death.'

Russell just looked at him.

'I will give you until tomorrow morning to decide which.' His eyes moved across to Russell's escort by the door. 'Take him to the late Dr Barlow's bungalow,' he said. 'And tell Dr Alabri I want to see her.'

Franklin got home soon after ten, and found Sibou waiting anxiously for him.

'Where have you been?' she asked angrily. 'Why didn't you phone?'

'I . . .'

'Your best friend vanishes off the face of the earth, and then you take five hours over a trip to Suzie's and expect me not to worry?'

He reached out for her hand. 'Sorry,' he said.

'So I should think.' She burrowed into his arms, and they held each other tight for a while. Eventually she disentangled herself. 'Where have you been then?' she asked.

He told her what he had learned at Suzie's Bar and the Caicos Marina, and of seeing Arcilla's sister. 'When I got back to the marina I had another talk with the guy there. He told me Arcilla has a private helicopter, and that he heard it taking off in the middle of the night.'

'So Nick could have been taken away by air or by boat.'

'Yep. He could be anywhere by now – the Bahamas, Cuba, Haiti, you name it. And we still haven't got a clue why he was taken.'

'Maybe they needed another diver for this treasure business,' Sibou suggested.

Franklin thought about it. 'You could be right there. Though I don't see why they couldn't just hire one. There's enough of them around.'

'I suppose.'

Franklin sat down on the sofa, laid his back against it and closed his eyes. 'I don't know what else we can do,' he said.

She sat down next to him. 'Put pressure on Oswald,' she said. 'If that doesn't work, go to his superiors on Grand Turk.'

'And if they can't find him?'

'I don't know,' she said. It was too much to accept – that a friend could disappear in such circumstances and that nothing could be done to find him.

The late Dr Barlow's bungalow turned out to be as comfortable as Russell's own on Providenciales. The screening seemed to be in good repair, and the air-conditioner, though somewhat noisy, was an efficient enough cooler. There was a refrigerator in the kitchen, a working shower in the bathroom. The furniture was somewhat sparse, but did include a functioning cassette player. The doctor's tastes had apparently been somewhat different from Russell's – Handel rather than Hendrix.

Having concluded this brief tour, Russell sank back exhausted on to the large bed. He could still hear drumming in the distance, and see the reflected light of the fires dancing in the trees outside. It occurred to him that Colonel Joutard had not bothered to warn him against trying to escape.

From what he could remember the Ile de Tortue – or Tortuga, as the English called it – was several miles off the northern coast of Haiti. In the old days it had been used as a base by French and English buccaneers for raiding the Spanish gold traffic which passed through the nearby Windward Passage. Russell had no idea who lived on the island now, or whether the writ of the Haitian Government – such as it was – extended this far. It seemed much more likely that Joutard had turned the place into a semi-private fiefdom.

Escape should be possible. Russell's expertise as a diver was common knowledge on Providenciales, but his background in the Marines and SBS was known only to very few, and Joutard had given no indication that he was aware of this pre-medical career.

Still, as of that moment he was in no condition to walk round the bungalow, let alone make a break for the Turks and Caicos Islands. He would need to be fully recovered from the effects of the chloroform, and to know a lot more about exactly where he was, before seriously contemplating escape. One such attempt, he suspected, was all he was likely to be allowed.

And in the meantime he had Joutard's offer of

employment to consider. Not that there seemed to be much choice.

He wondered if there was anything to drink anywhere on the premises. Levering himself gingerly off the bed, he was halfway to a promising-looking cabinet when there was a rap on the outside door.

Maybe room service, he thought wryly. He tried to shout 'come in', but could manage little more than a loud croak.

Whoever it was seemed to hear. He heard the door open and close, and there she was standing in the doorway of the room, still wearing the white coat. She looked just as lovely as before. But then she had seemed like a ministering angel; now he knew her to be one of Joutard's 'doctors'. And maybe she had been sent to him as a further inducement to sign on the dotted line.

'I thought I'd better check up on you,' she said.

'I'm OK.'

She walked forward and took hold of his wrist, the way he had seen Ching Ling do with patients back at the clinic.

'You do Chinese medicine?'

She concentrated on his pulses. 'Only a little,' she said, taking the other wrist. 'One of my grandmothers was Chinese.'

That explained her extraordinary face, he thought.

'Your pulses are better,' she said. 'You should be back to normal in a couple of days. But you should be in bed,' she added.

'OK, doc,' he said, expecting her to leave.

But instead she stood there, obviously uncertain about something.

Russell found himself wondering what Joutard had wanted with her.

As usual she seemed to read his mind. 'The colonel wants me to persuade you to work for us,' she said.

'With what?' he asked wryly.

Anger flashed in her eyes. 'By appealing to your better nature,' she said sarcastically.

'Not my nose for profit?' he replied in kind.

'I may be mistaken in your case,' she said slowly, 'but nursing isn't usually the sort of career someone enters with money in mind.'

Russell looked at her. 'I may be mistaken in your case,' he said, 'but I didn't think doctors signed on for Joutard's sort of operation with anything else in mind.'

Her whole body seemed to tense, and for a moment he thought she was going to hit him, but then she let it all out in a long sigh. 'How would you know?' she said, looking at the floor.

'Explain it to me.'

She looked him in the eye, and for a moment he felt uncomfortable, as if she was seeing right through him. 'The world doesn't always work the way you want it to,' she said. 'Especially in Haiti. There are two hundred young people here who have no parents, and no matter what I do they will suffer. But I can lessen that suffering; I can see that they lead a healthy life after they leave here.'

'Are you here willingly?'

She shrugged. 'What does that mean?'

'Could you walk out of this place, and take a boat across the strait, and tell the authorities in Port au Prince what is going on here?'

She sighed again. 'You don't understand. There are no authorities in Port au Prince who would care a damn about what's happening here. And even if there were, do you think Joutard would throw his hands up in the air and promise not to do such things again? Of course not. He'd just find another base, another corrupt government.' She shook her head in exasperation. 'This is the Third World in 1994, for heaven's sake – where have you been?'

Exploring coral reefs, was the answer that came to mind. It didn't seem the sort that would appeal to her.

'I'm sorry,' she said, unexpectedly. 'This is not your country, and you have been brought here against your will. There's no reason why you should want to help me.'

'There's no reason why I should want to help Joutard. Except that he'll kill me if I don't.'

She shrugged. 'I'm sorry. If there's some sort of principle at stake here that you think is worth dying for, then there's nothing more I can say. Except that if you do decide to live, then your skills will make a difference to the children here.'

Russell bit back the retort that was on his tongue. 'There's no principle,' he said. 'Nothing that grand. And I have no desire to die, or to be "harvested". I'll work for Joutard. But I'm not going to kid myself into thinking that I'm doing something that's morally acceptable.'

She smiled for the first time, but Russell found it unsettling rather than comforting, for in it he seemed to see his own pomposity reflected.

'Maybe,' she said. 'But after you've been here a while you may decide that morality is just one more luxury no one can afford.'

4

The clear turquoise waters of the Caicos Bank gave way to the deep blue of the ocean trench which separated South Caicos from the Turk Islands. As usual, the eight-seater plane was full, mostly with men in suits. It was only about eighty miles from Providenciales to Grand Turk, but the three intermediate stopovers stretched the journey time to almost ninety minutes.

The pilot began his descent. Franklin looked down at the sea, wondering why he had bothered to make the trip. As far as he could tell the chances of getting any satisfaction from the commissioner were about as minimal as chances got.

But six whole days had now gone by since Nick's disappearance, and he and Sibou had been unable to think of anything else. Making use of his SAS skills in clandestine observation, Franklin had spent several days and nights practically staking out the Arcilla villa, but had come up empty. The sister – whose name was Tamara – seemed to rise around noon, stare at the sea for most of the afternoon, and go out drinking in the evening, usually at the Club Med-Turkoise bar on Grace Bay. Once she had brought a man home with her, and perhaps had sex with him. If so, the encounter didn't seem to have been mutually satisfactory. He had left at two in the morning, looking angry.

She was presumably in charge of the place, but the

man who did what work there was to be done was a Jamaican named Freddie Bartholomew. He collected supplies, acted as a resident watchdog, and lived in one of the converted outbuildings. He did most of his drinking at home, usually with two other equally underemployed cronies. They looked like the sort of men who would be hired by someone expecting trouble. Two ferocious-looking Rottweilers only emphasized the atmosphere of potential siege.

Arcilla himself had not been seen on the island for at least a couple of weeks. Still, Franklin was convinced that the Cuban was responsible, one way or another, for Nick's disappearance. The problem lay in finding a single shred of evidence to that effect. He had gone back to Oswald and asked him to find some pretext for searching Arcilla's home but, not surprisingly, the policeman had refused. Franklin was told what he already knew – that there were no substantive grounds for obtaining a search warrant, and that where prominent citizens like Arcilla were concerned, Oswald was not going to act without such grounds. He was sorry about Franklin's friend, but there was nothing more he could do. Some crimes just remained unsolved. It was the way of the world.

But it was not the way of his world, Franklin thought, to give up looking for a friend who had inexplicably vanished.

The police station was the taxi's last stop. It lay behind the oldest building on the island, Guinep Lodge, which was being turned into a maritime museum. The adjoining building had not as yet been rebuilt following its torching on the last day of 1985. The unidentified arsonist's intention had probably been the destruction of financial and other records, and the attack had spawned an official British government inquiry. Where the police were at the time had never been established. 'Incorruptible' was not a word which came easily to mind where the local force was concerned. At least not in those days.

Maybe things had changed, Franklin thought, as he pushed through the double doors of the police headquarters. There was no one visible, so he pressed the bell.

The commissioner himself appeared in a doorway.

'Worrell Franklin?' he asked.

Franklin nodded.

'Come through,' Missick said, lifting up the counter.

Franklin took a seat in the man's office, which seemed unusually bare. There were no paintings, photographs or posters – just cream walls, an uncluttered desk and a bookcase full of what looked like bound reports.

'Cigarette?' Missick asked, pushing forward a carved wooden box full of Marlboro Lights.

'No thanks.'

Missick lit one for himself. 'So how can I help you?' he asked, in a tone that suggested help was unlikely to materialize.

Franklin doggedly went through the story of Nick's disappearance, and outlined his suspicions.

'But there is no evidence linking Arcilla to your friend?' Missick asked when he was finished.

'He talked about him that evening.'

'He probably talked about other people too. That hardly counts as evidence.' Missick sucked in his lower lip and blew smoke down towards his desk. 'I'm not saying you are wrong in your suspicions, but . . .' He shrugged. 'It's not only that you have no evidence. You have no motive either.'

Franklin offered the notion that Arcilla needed a diver.

'Divers are ten a penny in the islands. Why would he need to kidnap one?' The commissioner took another drag on the cigarette and waved it around in the air. 'People do not like to think they are mistaken about their friends, but have you considered the possibility that your friend staged this disappearance because he had a better offer from elsewhere? Maybe even an offer from Fidel Arcilla.'

'That's crazy,' Franklin said, his voice rising. 'If Nick had wanted to leave the clinic there was nothing stopping him. And the idea of him spreading chloroform around his room to deceive us is just crazy.'

Missick shrugged again. 'Then I don't know what to suggest. But you must see the situation from our point of view. A man has disappeared. There is no evidence that he was abducted, save perhaps a smell which has long since gone. Assuming he *was* abducted, there is no evidence linking him with Arcilla, save an apparently innocent piece of chit-chat in a bar. And in addition to that I find it very hard to imagine that he is being held captive anywhere in these islands. They are too small and too open and everyone knows what everyone else is doing. If your friend has been abducted, then I think he has passed outside my jurisdiction. Of course, I can pass on his details to my colleagues in the Bahamas and Haiti and the Dominican Republic, but unless he has used his passport to gain entry . . .'

'His passport is still at the clinic.'

Missick shrugged for the third time. Three shrugs and out, Franklin thought to himself. He felt as helpless as he could remember. Only those long-gone Brixton summers spent worrying about his kid brother came even close.

Franklin got to his feet. He had been bound to try, but this trip had been as fruitless as he had expected.

He shook hands with Missick and left. There were two hours to burn before the return flight on the inter-island shuttle, so he decided to go and look for lunch somewhere on Front Street.

In the office he had just left Alden Missick was direct-dialling a number in Miami Beach and asking for '*el jefe*', the boss.

Arcilla came on the line. '*Qué pasa?*' he asked, almost playfully.

'The man from the clinic – the Englishman – he has been here. But I think it was his last throw. I think he has realized that there is nowhere else for him to go.'

There was a short silence at the other end. 'OK. *Es bueno*. But I want you to keep an eye on him, just in case.'

That evening Franklin and Sibou went out for an expensive meal at the Club Med-Turkoise. Tamara Arcilla arrived alone when they were halfway through the entrée, and was given a table no more than ten feet away. It was the first time Franklin had seen her up close, and the first time his wife had set eyes on her.

'She's beautiful enough,' Sibou commented.

'On the outside,' Franklin added.

His wife gave him an amused look. 'You're not comfortable with the idea of a woman just picking up men for sex, are you?'

'Not particularly.'

'But men picking up women for sex is OK?'

'No ... well ... it seems more natural that way round. And yes, I know, it shouldn't. But it does.' He stole another glance at the Cuban woman. Probably in her early thirties, she was slim, but not model-slim. There was an Hispanic lushness about her body, from the slightly rounded calves up past the prominent hips, narrow waist and full breasts. Her dark hair tangled down past her face, often hiding one dark eye from view. She was wearing a simple white dress and deep crimson lipstick.

She was beautiful, Franklin agreed. But not happy. She was eating the starter too slowly, drinking the wine too fast.

'If you can tear your eyes away,' Sibou was saying, 'I've had an idea.'

'What?'

'Why not contact your old friends in the SAS?'

'What could they do?'

'I don't know,' Sibou admitted. She wanted to give him some hope, even if it only served to soften the blow. 'I thought there was some unspoken rule about looking after your own,' she said.

'Up to a point, maybe. But it doesn't apply to ex-members of the Regiment. And anyway, Nick was in the SBS, not the SAS.'

'Have you got any contacts there?'

'Not really.' But maybe it wasn't such a bad idea, Franklin thought. The Regimental CO at Hereford, whoever he was, might know someone in the Foreign Office. Might be owed a favour, or something like that. Maybe it was worth a shot . . .

'Look,' Sibou said, 'your mother's arriving tomorrow . . .'

'You're right,' Franklin said with a smile. 'I'll give Joss Wynwood a call when we get home.'

'There's a name from the past,' Sibou murmured.

Wynwood and Franklin had been the two junior members of the three-man SAS team sent to the Gambia in 1981 to help restore President Jawara to power after a left-wing coup. The final act of Franklin's first trip to Africa had been to save a local doctor from being raped and killed by a local psychopath. The same doctor who was now eating a chicken salad across the table from him.

Franklin and Wynwood had seen active service again the following year, as members of a four-man reconnaissance patrol on the Falklands. Both had been present when Nick Russell and his SBS boys had stumbled into their observation post.

Since Franklin's departure from the SAS in 1986 he had only seen Wynwood once, for a short drink in a London pub a couple of years later. Since then they had sent each other the occasional postcard, but that was all. Wynwood was still in the SAS, as far as Franklin knew. His last news of the Welshman, which had come via another old comrade, was of a promotion to senior sergeant of the Counter-Revolutionary Warfare Training Wing.

Back at the clinic an hour or so later, Franklin punched out the number on their bungalow phone, and listened to the ringing at the other end. Sibou had suggested waiting until morning, but there was no knowing where Wynwood would be during the day. At three in the morning he should be in bed.

'Wynwood,' the familiar voice said sleepily. In the background a female voice was asking who it was.

'Joss, it's Worrell Franklin.'

'Well, that's nice. I wait ten years for a call, and here it is – in the middle of the night.'

'It's urgent.'

'I suppose you've run out of Weetabix.'

Franklin grinned. 'Yeah. But that's not the reason for this particular call.'

'Shit. OK, let me take the phone through into the living room, so my friend here can get back to sleep.'

'Your *friend*?'

'We've been very friendly for some time now. We've even been thinking of honeymooning in the Turks and Caicos. At your expense, of course. How's Sibou?'

'Fine. She says hello.'

'OK, I'm stretched out on the sofa now. You can tell me all about it. If I start snoring, shout.'

Franklin took a deep breath. 'You remember Nick Russell?'

'The SBS captain.'

'Yep. He works here, or at least he did. He disappeared a week ago.'

'He what?'

Franklin went through the whole story one more time.

'Sounds bad,' Wynwood said, after he had finished, 'but how can I help?'

'Who's the CO at the moment?'

'Barney Davies still. They're putting him out to pasture soon, which'll be a pity.'

'You like him?'

'Yep. He's got a brain *and* a heart. Rare qualities in an Englishman.'

'Good.' Franklin found himself missing Wynwood's company. It would be great to see him on Provo . . .

'You want me to take this business to him,' the Welshman was concluding.

'I thought it would be worth a shot. Maybe he knows someone useful at the Foreign Office, or he can put some pressure on somewhere else. Maybe MI5, for fuck's sake. This is still British territory, even if the money's all American. London still has the final say, at least theoretically.'

'I'll do what I can, Frankie boyo. Now give me your number so I can get back to you.'

Franklin read out the endless digits. 'Any idea when you can see him?'

'Tomorrow. Or should I say this morning.'

'Thanks, Joss. And I'm glad you've finally found a real friend,' he added sardonically.

Seven hours later Wynwood was rapping on the office door of his Commanding Officer in the Stirling Lines barracks of 22 SAS Regiment. 'Enter!' came the cheerful reply from inside.

Lieutenant-Colonel Barney Davies was sitting behind his desk, a mug of tea in one hand and the *Daily Mirror* open in front of him. To one side sat a plate containing crumbs from a recently devoured rock cake. The CO smiled up at Wynwood, and gestured him into a seat. 'I can't believe these people,' he said, looking down at the paper. 'Isn't there anyone in the royal family who thinks about something other than sex?'

'The Queen Mum,' Wynwood suggested.

'Under forty, I meant.'

'Prince Harry?'

Davies grinned. 'I suppose you're a republican,' he said.

'Certainly not,' Wynwood said. 'If Wales has to be ruled by foreigners, I'd rather it was Germans and Greeks than the English.'

'Figures. So what can I do for you this morning?'

'I've had a distress call from the Caribbean. You remember Worrell Franklin.'

'Of course. It was a real loss to the Regiment when he called it a day.' He grimaced. 'We don't have so many ethnic-minority members we can afford to lose them, particularly when they're that good. And no,' he added, seeing the look on Wynwood's face, 'I don't think of the Welsh as an ethnic minority.'

Wynwood laughed.

'So what sort of distress is Franklin involved in?'

Wynwood told him, and got much the same response from the CO as he himself had given Franklin.

'I'll call a few people, but I don't hold out much hope,' Davies said. 'From what you say it looks as if checking out this Arcilla would involve tracking boats and helicopters across the Caribbean, not to mention investigating his businesses in the States. All of which would add up to a major operation, probably costing millions. No one in Whitehall is going to sanction that sort of expenditure just to find one missing ex-Marine.'

Wynwood looked glum. 'I know,' he said. 'But I can understand how Frankie feels.'

'So can I. I'll do what I can.'

'Thanks, boss.'

Once Wynwood had left, Davies ordered another mug of tea and thumbed through his unofficial list of useful official numbers, and noted several of them down. But the man who should be making most of the calls, Davies decided, was Russell's ex-CO. He called up his opposite number in Poole, the officer currently commanding the Special Boat Squadron of the Royal Marines, Lieutenant-Colonel Neil Colhoun.

The two men had not run into each other for several years, but not from any design. They had first met during planning for the Falklands campaign, and Davies had taken an immediate liking to the Scot, despite his stereotypically dour exterior. The liking had deepened with the discovery that, lurking beneath the forbidding mask, there was a warm and affectionate man with an almost impish sense of humour.

'Barney!' the familiar voice answered. 'So how's the competition doing?' he asked drily. 'Still working on those press releases?'

It was a standing joke among the SBS that their brethren in the SAS were prone to glorying in the spotlight of publicity. Though this, with rare exceptions, was far from the truth, the SBS did tend to be more concerned with preserving their anonymity.

'Paranoia is still rampant in Poole, eh?' Davies riposted.

'Aye. There's a rumour going round that the navy's going to be one of the prizes in the new National Lottery.'

'No one would enter,' Davies said.

Colhoun laughed. 'What do you want?' he asked.

Davies told him about Russell's disappearance and Franklin's call.

'You say Franklin was one of your best,' Colhoun said, all trace of flippancy gone. 'Well, Nick Russell was one of ours. He did a brilliant job in Hong Kong for us. Too good, really. He found something that moved him more than soldiering.'

'What was that?' Davies asked.

'Medicine. At least that's the precise answer. But caring for people in the widest sense. He spent almost two years working undercover in the refugee camps there, both Chinese and Vietnamese. His cover was as a medic, of course, and the cover gradually became more important than what it was covering. Not that he did less than a perfect job in both respects, you understand. But once it was over, it was the caring he missed, not the intelligence work. And when your lad offered him a job which allowed him to do both, and carry on a love affair with the sea, then we'd lost him.'

'Not the sort of man to just walk out on a job.'

'No. So what's next? The Foreign Office, I suppose.' Colhoun sounded about as enthusiastic as Davies felt.

'Brits missing abroad are their responsibility. And if you stress the former-hero angle, and find someone sympathetic, then maybe something will get done.'

'Aye, but what? A polite request to the local police commissioner. This doesn't sound like a situation where doing something will be cheap or easy.'

It was the same conclusion that Davies had reached himself. 'We can only try,' he said.

'For us there is only the trying; the rest is not our business,' Colhoun quoted.

'Bill Shankly?' Davies asked.

'T. S. Eliot.'

'It must be easier to find time to read on boats,' Davies suggested. 'How about we talk again this evening?'

'Fine,' Colhoun said. 'We can share our experiences of rejection.' He put the phone down and looked blankly into space for a moment, thinking about the last time he had seen the missing man. It had been at Russell's farewell party in a Hong Kong restaurant, the night before he flew back to England.

He exhaled noisily, got up and walked across to the window. The autumn sun was shining on Poole harbour, the myriad boats bobbing at anchor in the sluggish sea. In his time as the Commanding Officer of the SBS Neil Colhoun had lost several men, most of them in actions which had never received any publicity. In some cases even their wives had not been told all the circumstances of death.

That was bad enough, but somehow it seemed even

crueller to lose a man in such suspicious circumstances after he had left the SBS. There was no reason why men who had been through all the dangers implicit in such service should expect a quiet life thereafter, but it seemed like a fair arrangement to Colhoun. He went back to his desk and reached for the telephone.

For the next couple of hours he sought out potential sources of support in the Foreign Office, at the Admiralty, in the intelligence services, even at Scotland Yard, restricting himself to people who might be able to exert influence behind the scenes. Those capable of making a public stink – contacts in the press and politics – he decided to keep in reserve.

Everyone he spoke to was sympathetic, although in their voices he could hear echoes of his own pessimism. There was no point in exerting influence for its own sake – it had to be exerted in favour of some sort of action, and there was no chance of the Government sanctioning anything really meaningful. Not for one man.

By lunchtime Colhoun felt thoroughly depressed, and the feeling hung over him for the rest of the working day. It was only once he got back home, and found himself back in the usual mix of family problems – a sick dog, a tap that kept dripping, a son who wasn't doing enough homework – that Nick Russell's disappearance, and his own impotence in the face of it, was edged to the back of his mind.

He and Jenny were just sitting down to watch *Between the Lines* when the telephone rang. The caller announced himself as Robert Jacklin.

'Yes?' Colhoun said in an irritated tone, not recognizing the name.

'Junior Minister at the Foreign Office,' the man said smoothly. 'The problem you called about today . . .'

Colhoun's hopes rose. 'Nick Russell.'

'Yes . . .'

'Have you heard anything?'

'No. But there are . . . well, we would like you to attend a meeting tomorrow morning. Here in London, of course.' He gave Colhoun the time and place, and then abruptly said goodbye.

The SBS boss went back to the TV, wondering what devious reason the Foreign Office might have for actually helping someone.

5

The meeting place turned out to be a typically nondescript conference room somewhere in the bowels of the Whitehall government machine. Though machine was perhaps the wrong word, Colhoun thought, as he took his seat at the polished table with its glasses of water. It was more like an organism. One prone to torpor and sudden bursts of spite.

There were four other persons around the table. All men, of course, now that the Medusa had been exiled to the House of Lords. Robert Jacklin, who had called him the previous evening, was obviously in charge. He was a tall, saturnine man with thinning hair, glasses and a rather oily smile. He was also, as Colhoun had discovered from his morning *Times*, one of the rising stars of the ruling Conservative Party.

Jacklin looked anxiously at his watch and began by introducing the meeting's participants to each other. The two men across the table from Colhoun were Brian Findhorn and Gerald Branson, representing, respectively, MI5 and MI6. Findhorn looked like a TV policeman, Colhoun decided, vaguely harassed, overtired, on the verge of a belligerent outburst. Branson looked a bit like his famous namesake, fresh-faced, ex-public school, with a mouth not quite large enough for his teeth.

Another representative from the Foreign Office occupied the end of the table to Colhoun's right. His name was Hilary Smith, and he didn't look much more than twenty. He was nervously fiddling with the knot of his tie and brushing back an obstinate forelock of blond hair from his blue eyes.

The seat next to Colhoun was empty.

Jacklin looked at his watch again. 'I have another meeting in an hour,' he said, 'so I think we must start . . .'

The door behind him swung open to reveal a large, uniformed man with a mass of dark, tangled hair.

'Sergeant Wynwood?' Jacklin said. 'At last.'

'My train was half an hour late,' Wynwood explained. 'I blame impending privatization,' he added mischievously.

Jacklin had the grace to smile back. 'Maybe we can argue about that another time. Gentlemen,' he said, looking round the table, 'we are here to solve a puzzle, or perhaps just get a clear idea of what the puzzle is. Each of you has one of the pieces.' He smiled at everyone, as if expecting applause.

Colhoun remembered the newspaper article raving over his recent performance at the party conference.

'Sergeant Wynwood,' Jacklin was saying, 'if you could start the ball rolling by telling us what you know of the disappearance in the Turks and Caicos Islands.'

Wynwood went through what Franklin had told him, and as he spoke Smith took minutes in an impressive-looking shorthand. Colhoun wondered when the Foreign Office would discover the cassette recorder. Perhaps as they sat there, Q was inventing one in the basement below, unaware that they were on sale down the road at Dixons.

After Wynwood had finished, Colhoun was asked to give an appreciation of Russell. He did so, thinking that if he had been called all the way to London just for this, he would be exceedingly angry.

Jacklin then turned to the man from MI6. 'Eight days ago,' Branson began, reading from a notebook, 'a man was found murdered in his car in Florida. The car was sitting in a lay-by near Tampa Bay, and the man had been shot once through the forehead. His wallet had been stolen, and the detectives could find no identification. There was no luggage in the boot. There was, however, a novel in German in the man's jacket pocket, and a German–English phrasebook on the seat beside him.'

Branson looked up. 'So, at first glance the victim looked like one more European tourist who had been robbed and killed in friendly Florida. But the police didn't have a name for the victim, and when they tried to trace him through the car registration it turned out the plates had been stolen only the day before in Miami. So they either had a German tourist who was also a car thief, or something more mysterious. They started backtracking the dead man's journey.'

Branson looked around the table, just to make sure everyone was paying attention. Colhoun found that he was enjoying himself.

'There was one other clue,' Branson went on. 'An empty milk-shake container from the Burger King chain. The police started checking out the various franchises up and down the man's probable route, and soon got lucky. The man had stopped in a restaurant only ten miles to the north, and the woman who recognized his picture said he had told her he was a Russian. "From the other St Petersburg," she remembered him saying. And he had been carrying a brown attaché case.

'Now, since the man had eaten lunch there around noon and was travelling south, the police worked on the assumption that he had started out that morning from a point some three or four hours' drive to the north or west, and checked out all the hotels in that area for departing guests with Russian-sounding names. There were seventeen of them to choose from, and the dead man was eventually recognized from his photograph in one of the Disneyworld hotels. The name he had registered under was Aleksandr Tretchkin. According to US Immigration he had first arrived in the US some three weeks earlier.'

Branson paused, took a sip of water from the glass, and went back to the notebook. 'The FBI were called in, and eventually the CIA ran a photograph of the dead man through their computer at Langley and came up with a different name – Aleksandr Solayev. Solayev, it turned out, had been a commander in the Soviet Navy, a former military attaché in Havana, and one of the top names in naval craft design at the Naval Research Academy in Murmansk. He had specialized in miniature submarine and submersible technology.'

Hence the connection, Colhoun thought. This was getting interesting.

'US Immigration had one other useful piece of infor-mation,' Branson went on. 'Three days after arriving in the US, Solayev had left again, on an American Airlines flight to Providenciales in the Turks and Caicos Islands. He returned to Miami ten days later.'

Branson closed his notebook with a triumphant flour-ish.

'And all that from a strawberry milk shake,' Wynwood murmured.

'Your turn, Brian,' Jacklin told the MI5 man.

Findhorn had only a crumpled sheet of paper to compete with Branson's notebook, but in any case he hardly looked at it. 'The address Tretchkin – Solayev – gave the authorities on Provo was Fidel Arcilla's villa on Long Bay, so I think we can assume he had some connection with the submarine which Russell told the barman about. Our best guess is that it's a Soviet craft which the Russian somehow or other procured for Arcilla. Afterwards, either to keep the Russian's mouth shut or simply to avoid payment, Arcilla had him killed.'

'What do we know about this man?' Jacklin asked.

'I'm coming to that. First off, he's a British citizen, even though he was born in Cuba and lives mostly in the States. He became one in 1984, probably with the help of his friends in the Turks and Caicos government, the same ones who were implicated in the 1985 drug business . . .'

'Which business was that?' Colhoun asked. He had a vague memory of some Caribbean politicians being charged with drug smuggling, but no more than that.

'In 1985,' Findhorn said patiently, 'three members of the then government, including the Prime Minister, were arrested during a trip to Miami by the US authorities, and charged with conspiracy to import narcotics into the United States. What they had actually done was receive payment for turning a blind eye to drug runners using the islands as a refuelling stop. A lot of minor officials had also got in on the act, and great chunks of the administration had been compromised. The big three went to jail, and another three ministers were forced to resign the following year, allegedly for various improprieties, but basically for being part of the whole crooked set-up. The islands were governed from Whitehall in all but name for a couple of years, and since then things have slowly got back to normal. The Americans wanted a tougher

law-enforcement system worked out between themselves
and the locals, but the islanders were still feeling a bit
too sensitive for that sort of interference, so the Yanks
had to make do with access to local bank records for
their drug investigations. Which brings us roughly up
to date.' He looked round the table. 'And back to Fidel
Arcilla. He was undoubtedly one of those involved in the
smuggling operation back in 1985, though no evidence
was ever discovered against him.'

'He seems to specialize in leaving no traces,' Wynwood
remarked.

'He does. The only evidence was against the original
three politicians, and as I said, they went to jail. We
managed to get rid of a few more of their cronies by
political means, but gangster-businessmen like Arcilla
are only susceptible to the law. We had nothing on
him, and he had spread enough money around, both
in Florida and the islands, to buy himself a lot of useful
friends, not to mention legal advice. A few years ago he
even sued the Florida Drugs Enforcement Agency office
for harassment and won.'

'What's his background?' Colhoun asked.

'We don't know that much. He was born in Cuba in
1959, about three weeks after Castro took the place over.
Which is probably why his parents named him Fidel. He
left Cuba in 1980, during the Mariel boat-lift, and took
up . . .'

'What was the Mariel boat-lift?' Jacklin asked.

'The Americans had been demanding that Castro
allow people to emigrate from Cuba, and for about six
months he obliged them. He also used the opportunity
to get rid of a few thousand convicts and mental patients.
Arcilla was one of the convicts and, not surprisingly, it
didn't take him long to get involved in the drugs trade.

Within a couple of years he was an important player. The FBI have been sending us information on his activities during the last few years. They want us to put him away.'

Finally Colhoun saw where this was all leading.

'What it all comes down to,' Findhorn concluded, 'is that the Americans smell more trouble. They think Arcilla is probably putting together another major drug operation, and using British territory as a base. They want us to either get in there and sort things out, or let them do it . . .'

'Needless to say, Her Majesty's Government prefers the former option,' Jacklin interjected.

Like Grenada, Colhoun thought sourly. 'I don't suppose you have any information on this Russian submarine's range,' he asked.

'No,' Findhorn and Branson answered simultaneously. 'But we have people looking into it,' Branson said. 'Inside Russia,' he added, as if expecting congratulations.

'Good,' Colhoun said. 'Because generally speaking, such craft have a very short range. Considerably shorter than five hundred miles, which, I believe, is roughly the distance between the Florida Keys and the Caicos Islands.'

'Maybe Arcilla has retired from the drugs business,' Wynwood suggested. 'Maybe he really is going after sea treasure. I should think it's a pretty competitive field, and Arcilla doesn't sound like a good loser. Maybe Nick Russell just saw something he wasn't supposed to.'

'Perhaps,' Jacklin said. 'We just don't know. So our first job is to find out.' He looked round at them all. 'We can't send police down there – it would cause too much of a political stink. If we learned anything from '85 it was that the islanders prefer their own corrupt officials to officials from London.

Whoever we do send will have to be sent under-cover. That might sound like a job for intelligence, but in this case we've decided that certain factors make this inadvisable.' Jacklin looked straight at Colhoun. 'Because of the submarine angle, and the probable need for qualified divers, it has been decided that the SBS should handle at least the preliminary portion of the investigation.' He paused, as if he expected Colhoun to say something.

The SBS man simply nodded at him.

'Splendid. I would like a plan of action submitted by the end of the week if that's possible?'

'Certainly.' You can have it tomorrow, Colhoun thought.

'Your primary objective,' Jacklin continued, 'is to find out whether the Turks and Caicos Islands are again being used for drug-trafficking purposes. If you discover the answer to that question is yes, then we can go on from there.'

'I understand,' Colhoun said. He was already turning his mind to the question of whom to send.

'I think the four of us – excluding Sergeant Wynwood here – should meet again at the same time next Monday,' Jacklin concluded. He turned to Wynwood. 'Sergeant, thank you for coming,' he said, and offered his hand with what looked like genuine warmth, before disappearing out the door.

The intelligence men followed him, skipping down the stairs side by side. Colhoun and Wynwood descended at a more leisurely pace.

'You'll probably need an SAS adviser on this trip,' Wynwood suggested.

Colhoun grinned at him. 'And what sort of adviser would that be?'

'Oh, you know. How to do things, when to do them. What to do once you've done them.'

'We do all that ourselves. But I might consider buying you a drink if you're good.'

'I'm good.'

They found a pub just past the National Gallery, in the lanes behind Leicester Square tube. Colhoun asked Wynwood about Franklin, and heard the story of their week together in the Gambia. 'He's a nice man, and a straight one. You remember in the old movies when they say someone's a real white man – well, that's Frankie, except that he's black.'

'And a good soldier.'

'No doubt about that. I think becoming a good soldier was one of the few things he found easy in life.'

'I'll need his phone number on the island,' Colhoun said, 'but if you could call him tonight and let him know . . .' The SBS man stopped to think for a minute, and took a sip on his pint. 'If you told him a couple of your friends were arriving on the island in a few days, and would like to contact him, would he catch on?'

Wynwood looked surprised for a moment, then nodded to himself. 'I suppose the clinic lines might be bugged,' he agreed. 'But don't worry, I'll make sure he gets the message.'

After the two men parted, Neil Colhoun walked up Long Acre to Stanfords map shop. There he purchased the best map and most comprehensive guide to the Turks and Caicos Islands he could find. It might be that official sources would come up with something better, but experience had taught Colhoun not to be optimistic in such matters. On the journey back to Poole he read the guide book and then sat watching Hampshire go by, wondering how many men to send.

By the time the train pulled into Poole Station he had decided on two. It was off-season in the Turks and Caicos, and the resident population of Providenciales was only about five thousand. A larger group of men might be noticeable. And if it turned out that more were needed, then more could always be dispatched.

As for the two, they more or less chose themselves. This was a far from purely military mission, and his men would be up against an enemy whose tentacles stretched through several countries. They would probably not be able to trust the local authorities. What Colhoun needed was a pair of soldier-diver-detectives, men who embodied the highest aspirations of the Special Boat Squadron. 'Not by strength – by guile' was the SBS motto, but sometimes both were needed in equal amounts. On land, at sea and in the deeps.

Back in his office he asked for the service files of Captain Callum Marker and Lieutenant Robert Cafell, albeit more from a desire to be thorough than from any real need. Colhoun knew all his men's military records off by heart, and as much about their personal lives as a commanding officer needed to, given that his was the responsibility for sending them out on such dangerous missions.

The Poole classroom that was used for the film test was, as intended, overheated and lacking any compensatory ventilation. Even Callum Marker was having trouble staying awake, and he, unlike the twenty or so Marines with their eyes glued to the screen, wasn't struggling into the fourth day of the SBS pre-selection course.

On the screen an open lorry was being loaded with green oil drums by three men, while a fourth man sat on the wall to one side, smoking a cigarette. A selection of red, green, yellow and black drums were gathered in the road in front of him. Once the greens were loaded the idle man joined one of the others in beginning to unload them again, while two men rested on the wall. One of these then joined the two workers to load up the red and yellow drums. This accomplished the yellows were removed by all four men and replaced with a mixture of blacks and greens by three of them.

And so on. The suspense was hardly killing, but there was no doubt the film offered a good test, not only of the applicant's powers of observation and concentration, but also of his determination to succeed. These men were midway through their fourteen-day nightmare, and had already yomped through most of Dorset with fifty-five-pound bergens on their backs, spent nights under piles of wet leaves which lacked a Michelin rating, and enjoyed long, kit-encumbered night swims in the waters of Poole Bay. Before entering this classroom none of them had slept for forty-eight hours.

Those who got through the fourteen days would be given a further fifteen weeks of assorted tortures to endure. The lucky ones who graduated would move on to eleven weeks of 'trade' training, which included all the advanced techniques and skills required of a fully-fledged SBS Marine. He would learn signal skills, beach reconnaissance, demolition and sabotage, anti-terrorist drills. He would parachute into Arctic seas. His diving, canoeing and weapon-handling skills would be further honed. And at the end of it all he would graduate as a Swimmer-Canoeist Third Class, and be graciously granted leave to serve an eighteen-month probationary period as a member of the SBS.

After that he would be expected to go for Swimmer-Canoeist Second Class, and then First Class, and then the Senior Command Course.

It was a hell of a long climb, Marker thought, as he watched the sea of blinking eyes and yawning mouths in front of him. Thirteen years earlier he had sat in this same room, watching this same dumb film. A lot had happened in the intervening years, including his ascent of the SBS totem pole. The Falklands, the North Sea oil rigs, Hong Kong. He must have seen a thousand movies. He had met and loved and lost Penny.

He closed his eyes for a second, and heard the rattle of the ancient projector change gear. The film was over. He got up, turned on the lights, and started handing out the question papers.

'I was waiting for the naked lady to leap out of the drum,' a tired voice complained.

Marker smiled. 'I'm sure most of you will spend your lives waiting for a naked lady,' he said sympathetically. He placed the last question paper on the last desk and walked back to the front of the classroom. 'You have fifteen minutes,' he said. 'And remember to put your names on the paper.'

At the end of the allotted time he had to nudge three of the examinees awake. Most of the collected papers were covered with barely legible scrawls.

Marker unloaded the projector as the Marines filed out, en route to a shorter rest period than the one they were expecting. Only about a quarter of these men would be accepted for further training, but there was certainly no shame in not being one of them. Marker remembered a visitor from the SEALs – America's SBS equivalent – who had watched the training programmes slack-jawed in awe.

Maybe they were too hard. Marker himself thought so, and having passed them all he felt able to say so. Good men were having good days and all the luck they needed, while better men were making one mistake and failing.

He locked up the projector in the cupboard, and wondered yet again whether to press for something truly revolutionary like a VCR. But you could hardly move around Poole these days without someone moaning about how tight money was, so it probably wasn't worth the hassle. He reluctantly picked up the pile of exam papers and headed for the door.

Outside the day had greyed over, and the wind was rustling the waters of the harbour. It was going to rain, Marker decided. Maybe he wouldn't go into Bournemouth that evening. Maybe he'd stay at home, cook himself something nice, and watch TV. Sooner or later he had to get used to her not being there.

A couple of buildings down from the projection room, Rob Cafell was sitting at a drawing board, pencil between his teeth, studying the sketches he had made over the last half hour. He was alone in the room, and about the only thing in it which looked even vaguely military. Any unwitting outsider who stumbled in through the door would be forgiven for assuming he was in an art college.

Strictly speaking, Rob Cafell had no right to be there. The room was the preserve of the Marines' Illustrators Branch, whose remit included the supply of maps and plans from aerial photographs, and any three-dimensional models of terrain, installations and vehicles which the Corps might meet in the course of fulfilling its military duties. Few solo activities pleased

Rob Cafell more than drawing maps or making models, but unfortunately officers were barred from the Illustrators – supposedly too busy learning how to command – and the time he spent there could only be his own. He had helped out the regulars often enough on urgent projects for no one to mind his using either the premises or the modelling supplies.

That afternoon he had begun planning a model of the sister freighters recently converted for the shipment of high-grade plutonium from British and French reprocessing plants to Japan. The two vessels had originally been American, but a Belfast shipyard had converted them for their new role, strengthening the hatches and removing cranes, converting a high proportion of previous cargo space into extra fuel capacity, creating more accommodation for armed guards, and upgrading all the ships' electronics. The problem for the modeller, as was usual where asymmetrical craft were concerned, lay in providing a clear enough picture of the ships' innards without destroying all sense of what they looked like from the outside.

There was a very good reason for this particular job – if one of these ships was ever hijacked by terrorists the model's availability for planning purposes would save a considerable amount of time. But Cafell didn't really need the excuse. He loved the whole process, from the research through the planning to the manufacture and the painting – all of it. He had always been good with his hands – it saved him using his brain, his mother had always said – and he had been making models of ships as long as he could remember. Both his parents' house in Plymouth and his own flat in Poole were filled with them. His innocent invitation to 'come up and see my Dreadnought' had long since passed into local legend. And still made him blush whenever he thought about it.

That had been a long time ago, he told himself. Almost ten years. He was over thirty now, and these days felt almost as comfortable with women as he did with men. He had always felt comfortable with his date for the evening, but then Ellen had always been a friend before. It was probably going to be a bit strange for both of them.

He looked up at the clock, and realized he should be on his way. But the sketches caught his eye again, and he started thinking about the problems an assault group would have in surprising terrorists on one of these ships. If the terrorists had any sense at all, it would be bloody difficult. There was every chance the plutonium would end up in the ocean.

Maybe his mum was right, Cafell thought. They should just ditch nuclear power altogether. His dad, who until recently had captained one of the Royal Navy's nuclear submarines, had other ideas.

It was time to go. He packed the sketches away in the drawer he always used, and opened the door just as a young Marine was raising a hand to knock.

'Lieutenant Cafell, sir,' the young man said. 'Lieutenant-Colonel Colhoun wants to see you.'

'Now?'

'Yes, boss.'

Cafell and Marker reached Colhoun's door at almost the same moment.

'Any idea what this is about?' Cafell asked.

Marker shook his head and rapped on the door.

'Yes,' Colhoun said.

Inside they found the CO poring over a map of the

Turks and Caicos. Underneath it was a larger scale map of the seas to the south and south-east of the continental United States. It looked promising, Marker thought.

'I've sent for tea,' Colhoun said, sitting back down in his famously tattered leather chair. At that moment an orderly arrived with three mugs of steaming tea and a plate full of Kit-Kats.

'If only the enlisted men could see this,' Marker said wryly.

Colhoun smiled at him. 'I've got a job for you two,' he said. 'In the sunshine.'

'Sounds ominous,' Marker said, but the sudden sense of inner excitement belied his tone of voice.

'Either of you two remember Nick Russell?' Colhoun asked. 'He left us in '86.'

'Only by reputation,' Cafell said. 'Before my time.'

'I knew him by sight,' Marker said. 'Curly-headed guy with an innocent-looking face, like Rob here.'

'That's Russell,' Colhoun agreed. He reached under the maps and extracted two copies of the minutes of the meeting he had attended that morning, which Hilary Smith had faxed through to him an hour or so earlier.

The two SBS officers started reading, and Colhoun watched their curiosity deepen as the pages turned. The two of then looked so dissimilar, the CO thought, and not just in the obvious sense. Certainly Marker was dark, wiry and brown-eyed, Cafell big, blond and blue-eyed, but that only touched the surface. It was all in the facial expression, Colhoun decided. Next to Cafell's open, trusting face Marker's looked almost haunted. They were almost like Lenny and George from *Of Mice and Men*, he thought, only in their case the differences were those of temperament rather than mental acumen. Both these men were supremely competent.

'Comments?' he asked, once they were both finished.

'Just the two of us?' Marker asked.

'For the moment.'

'So basically, we have to check out this Arcilla's boat, submarine and chopper? If he's running drugs he has to be using one or more of them.'

'Right.'

'But none of them are on the island at the moment.'

'That's true. And it may not be drugs. He could be laundering drug money. He could be hunting for treasure.'

'We might find the *Santa Lucia*,' Cafell suggested.

'The what?'

'It's one of the most famous of the Spanish galleons which have never been found. It was carrying more than ten million in gold when it went down south of the Keys.'

'I might have known you'd be up on this stuff,' Marker murmured. 'We'll be needing a boat of our own, not to mention a submarine and access to either a chopper or a light plane.'

'There's a frigate permanently on patrol in the Caribbean,' Colhoun said, 'and the base in Belize has Kleppers and submersibles. I'll get on to the Admiralty tomorrow, and try and persuade them to do a little chauffeuring for us. If that's not on, then we'll have to fly them out from here somehow. As for a boat, you can hire one on Provo according to this' – he indicated the guide book – 'and hiring one will look less suspicious. It's not going to be easy slipping you a submersible and a couple of canoes without getting the whole island talking.'

'With any luck we won't need them,' Cafell said. 'Look at the range we've got here. It's over five hundred miles to the nearest US coast – they can't be running a small submarine there from the islands.'

'And they sure won't be canoeing that sort of distance,' Marker added thoughtfully. 'What about weaponry?' he asked Colhoun.

'No firearms are allowed on the island. And since you're going in as tourists . . .'

'We'll have to be extremely cunning,' Marker completed the thought.

'We'll get you handguns at least.'

'We'll need a couple of MP5s, a couple of harpoon guns,' Marker insisted. 'And some stun grenades might come in handy. Arcilla and his chums don't sound like nice people.'

Colhoun smiled. 'I'll do what I can,' he promised.

'What about the Yanks?' Cafell asked.

'If the trail leads into their territory – and the way they see it their territory includes just about anything within two hundred miles of their coastline – then we'll have to come to some sort of arrangement with the US Navy, Coast Guard and Customs Service. Shouldn't be a problem – they're the ones who want us to do something about Arcilla.'

'So when do we leave?' Marker asked.

'I don't know yet. There's no great urgency – if Russell's still alive he's not likely to be in imminent danger. But there's no point in hanging around, either. So as soon as everything's in place . . .'

'One thing, boss,' Marker said. 'There's nothing in these minutes about rescuing Nick Russell.'

'I know. If he's still alive, then Russell may have struck it lucky. Because there's no way Whitehall would have agreed to send out a rescue mission just for him. As it is . . .'

'We consider him an SBS priority,' Marker said.

Colhoun nodded. 'Any more questions, gentlemen?'

There were none.

'Well, start clearing your personal decks then. Callum, I'd like a word with you.'

Marker looked surprised but sank back into his seat.

Cafell paused in the doorway. 'Nine o'clock tomorrow morning in the mess?' he asked Marker.

'Fine.'

Cafell shut the door behind him.

Colhoun sighed and looked out of the window. Thanks to the grey sky it was almost dark already. 'I don't want to butt in on your personal business,' he began.

'But you're going to anyway.' Marker smiled. 'That's OK. I've got no secrets from myself.'

'I imagine you're going through a rough time.'

Marker shrugged. 'Sounds about right. Beats being in Rwanda though.'

Colhoun persisted. 'A job like this might be a good way of drawing a line under the past. Or it might be you're not ready to do that, and the past might get in the way of the job.'

Marker raised an eyebrow. 'Did you rehearse that, boss?' he asked.

Colhoun smiled in spite of himself. 'I just want you to think about it for twenty-four hours.'

'OK, but there's no need. I miss my wife, no doubt about that. But it won't get in the way. And I don't think I believe in drawing lines under anything. You can hide the past away, but you can't get rid of it. And if you do hide it away, it just makes it easier to repeat your mistakes.'

Colhoun simply nodded.

Marker smiled at him, got to his feet, and took his leave.

The CO leaned back in his chair, going over his earlier thoughts on his pairing of the two men. With any luck they were not only different, but almost complementary. Two sides of a single coin – probably the best currency he had.

6

The sound of the approaching helicopter jerked Russell out of his doze. He lay there with his eyes closed, trying to bring back the dream. Emelisse Alabri had been walking along the street, looking back over her shoulder as if she thought she was being followed. He supposed it had been himself doing the following. Strangest of all had been the location: the local shopping street in Twickenham, where he had grown up.

The helicopter was landing now, on the area of cleared ground which was otherwise used as a baseball diamond. It was the fifth such arrival in the ten days Russell had been on Tortuga, but he had no idea of who or what was being brought in or taken out. He supposed it might be a good idea to find out, but he seemed unable to shake off the mental lassitude which had afflicted him ever since the chloroforming. The causes of this might well be in part physical, but, even if so, Russell had no doubt they were also partly psychological. The more he found out about his new home, the more despairing he felt.

As yet he had not been obliged to do anything more than familiarize himself with the medical procedures. Emelisse had escorted him around the camp, showing him the dormitories where the orphans slept and the dusty space beneath the coconut palms where they went to school. She had not bothered to point out the security features, but then there had been no need to. The walls were real enough, and so were the Kalashnikov AK47s carried by the T-shirt-wearing guards. The atmosphere was not oppressive – two Kalashnikovs had provided the goalposts for an ongoing game of football – and in a way this made things seem even more depressing. The dreadful normality of the whole place made Russell almost want to cry.

After the camp, the hospital had been a revelation. Here everything – technical equipment, instruments, clothing, furnishings – was spotless and new. Nearly all of it was American-manufactured, and as far as Russell could tell no expense had been spared in procuring the best. Even the small outpatient clinic, where Emelisse did her best to function as a normal doctor, was well equipped, presumably as part of the bargain she had made with Joutard's devil.

The guided tour had taken place during his third day in the camp, and he had not seen much of her since. One day she had come by with some books in French, and pointed out sections which she said he should familiarize himself with. The books had all been printed in Paris, and one bore the inscription 'for Emelisse, with love from Jean-Pierre, August 17, 1983.' Russell had asked her if she had ever been to France; she had told him that was where she had studied medicine. He had wanted to ask her more, but the look in her eyes had not been encouraging.

He tried to remember what she had been wearing in his dream. He had only ever seen her in the white coat, and he didn't think it had been that.

His watch said it was almost five o'clock – another hour and he could go in search of food. He got up and removed the Rachmaninov tape from the cassette recorder, and looked through his deceased predecessor's collection once more. Brahms, he decided. If he stayed *chez Joutard* long enough he might even grow to like the stuff.

It was time he gave some serious thought to getting out of the bloody place. He couldn't believe escape from the camp itself would pose any serious problems, but getting himself beyond Joutard's reach probably would. The first thing he needed was a precise fix on where he was, and work out a few options for . . .

The rap on the outside door was swiftly followed by the appearance of Emelisse in the living-room doorway. 'Time to go,' she said.

'Where?'

She was already halfway out of the door. 'To work,' she said over her shoulder.

He hurried after her. This was the moment he had been dreading. Even if everything went right, and he found he could do what was needed, there was still the overwhelming sense of wrongness. As they walked briskly across the camp towards the hospital he told himself once more that a single kidney operating at fifty per cent of its full capacity could perform all the blood-cleaning operations necessary to a normal healthy adult.

It might be true, but it begged more questions than he had answers for.

He followed Emelisse in through the hospital doors, feeling like he was stepping out of one world and into another. These rooms, with their shiny machines and sterile furnishings and efficient air-conditioning, belonged to the rich man's world. It was only a freak of geography that had placed them here. That and the warped logic of global supply and demand.

Two young Haitian women were already scrubbing up

in the washroom, chattering to each other in a language Russell didn't understand. They couldn't be much older than fourteen, he decided, and the pale-blue smocks they were wearing made them look like boarding-school girls getting ready for bed.

One of the other two doctors – the only other European in the camp, an overweight Frenchman named Bodin – was examining himself in the mirror. Seeing Emelisse appear behind him he muttered something sarcastic under his breath. She ignored him, and he turned to leave, casting red-rimmed eyes in Russell's direction as he did so. The Englishman could smell brandy on the man's breath.

He and Emelisse scrubbed their hands with the iodized soap, tied each other's smocks, and went through into the room set up for surgery. The line of four parallel operating tables made it looked like an updated set for the TV series *MASH*. On three of them naked bodies were laid out on sheets. On the far table the last doctor, a bald, middle-aged Hispanic man with a small thin moustache, was already at work.

'Forty minutes,' he told Emelisse. She nodded. 'We'll start in ten,' she told the others.

'Why not now?' Russell asked.

'So that we all finish at roughly the same time,' she said.

That made sense. Russell looked across the room, and suddenly realized that though the two unattended patients were hooked up to tubes, needles and various monitoring sensors the one on the far end was not.

'What's Calderón doing?' Russell asked Emelisse.

'Harvesting,' she said coldly. 'The boy died a couple of hours ago. The helicopter brought in the body.'

'Harvesting what?' Russell asked.

'Kidneys, corneas and as much bone tissue as he can manage in the time.'

'Why not the heart and the liver?' Russell asked, though he thought he already knew the answer. Somehow it felt better talking than simply watching.

'The time factor, I assume.' She seemed nervous too. 'They wouldn't survive the journey.'

'How long does a heart last?'

'I don't know exactly. Six hours? Something like that.'

'And kidneys?'

'More like thirty-six.'

That made sense, Russell thought. Unless they were flying them into the US, which would surely be too risky. Of course, for all he knew the organs were being supplied to some private clinic on another island.

'Why bone . . .' he started to ask, but his voice dried up. Across the room the Puerto Rican doctor had just lifted the kidneys from the dead boy, still with the main vessels attached, and was carrying them across to the table nearby, where a pan of cold solution was waiting to wash off the blood. He then placed the kidneys in a clear plastic box about ten inches square, one of four in a row which sat on a slightly larger box surrounded in blue casing. These were perfusion machines, whose task was to pump cool preservative through the detached organs until they were transplanted into another patient.

Four boxes for four doctors, Russell thought. If the time factor was tight, then the more operations they could perform simultaneously, the more profit per delivery.

And the more lives could be saved, said another voice inside his head. More people with their sight restored. All

Americans, no doubt. All rich by the world's standards. But human beings nevertheless.

The doors behind swung open, and two trolleys were rolled in, each carrying an unconscious young Haitian. One was a boy, one a girl. Russell guessed they were both about sixteen.

They were transferred on to the operating tables, the cotton shifts they were wearing undone and left hanging down towards the floor.

The Frenchman and one of the nurses took up position on either side of the boy, leaving the girl for Emelisse and the other nurse. Russell stood behind the doctor's shoulder, and set himself to concentrate on something for the first time in ten days. He was about to receive his first and last lesson in safely removing a kidney from a live donor.

Emelisse lost no time, making the major incision with an electric scalpel that cauterized the blood vessels as it cut through the thin layers of fat and muscle. Then she used retractors to ease the kidney into view from its position behind the liver in the abdominal cavity.

So far it all seemed pretty straightforward, Russell thought, and said so.

'It is not a difficult operation,' she said. 'But it does require care. One little mistake and you can traumatize an artery or abrade the renal vein. The patient can die, particularly with the sort of after-care we have here.'

She asked the nurse to wipe her brow, and took a long, searching look at the pulsing kidney and the area around it. 'See here,' she told Russell, 'we have to clamp these, cut through them here and here, cut through the ureter exactly here, lift out the kidney and then suture everything back together again.'

'Just a plumbing problem,' he said, more lightly than he felt.

He watched her do it all. After the kidney had been removed and placed in its clear plastic box she began the delicate work of restoration. She had good hands for such work, he thought. Nimble, steady hands. There was no doubt that it was tiring work, but she only stopped once to flex her fingers before the final stitching together of the original incision.

Glancing across at her, Russell saw the skin stretched tight across her cheek-bones, the lips drawn rigidly together. It was as if she had drained the tension out of her fingers by pouring it into her face.

Midway through the process the nurses had carried out the three boxes and their four kidneys, and as the last stitches were threaded Russell heard the helicopter taking off into the night. He looked down at the face of the unconscious girl and felt as if he was seeing it for the first time.

Emelisse either followed his gaze or read his mind. 'When they remove organs in America the surgeon never sees the donor's face,' she said.

'I think this is better,' Russell said.

She looked at him, and for the first time her expression towards him seemed to soften slightly. Then she turned away and told the nurses to take over. They re-wrapped the girl in her cotton gown and wheeled her away on a trolley to join the boy in the recovery room.

Emelisse and Russell undid each other and washed once more.

'Will you have a drink with me?' he asked.

She shrugged. 'Why not.'

Outside, darkness had long since fallen, but the breeze from the sea had not yet picked up, and the air seemed hot and sticky. A huge yellow moon had just emerged above the palms in front of them, and drums resounded from across the camp.

'I always hated World Music,' Russell murmured.

'They're burying the boy,' she said, starting to walk towards his bungalow. There was nothing accusatory in her tone, but she had a knack of making him feel in the wrong.

'What's left of him,' he said.

'If people have souls, I expect his managed to get wherever it was supposed to go.'

He sighed and changed the subject. 'Why bone tissue?' he asked. 'Is it worth that much?'

'You must be kidding,' she said. 'Fresh powdered bone sells for about $200 a gram. That's four times more than the street value of cocaine.'

'*Powdered* bone?' He suddenly remembered the noise he had heard through the wall during the operations – it had sounded like a coffee grinder. 'What's it used for?'

'Mostly replacing skeletal areas that have had to be removed, usually because they're cancerous. Lengthening deformed spines. Dental work. There are hundreds of uses.'

'How long does it last?'

'I don't know. Long enough, obviously. Calderón has an expensive toy next door for freeze-drying it.'

'What brought him here – just greed?'

'Mostly, but not just. Curiosity. He's a researcher at heart.'

'So was Mengele.'

She sighed. 'Calderón was disbarred in Puerto Rico.'

'What for?'

'He hasn't said. Illegal abortions would be my guess.'

'And Bodin – what's his excuse?'

They had reached his door. He reached to push it open for her, but she beat him to it.

'Take a seat,' he offered, as she walked into the main room ahead of him. 'What would you like to drink? Comrade Joutard has supplied me with rum, whisky and beer. Haitian beer, I'm afraid.'

'Whisky,' she said.

He poured two glasses and took one over to her. She was slumped on the sofa, eyes closed, looking utterly exhausted.

'You need some sleep,' he advised.

She half smiled. 'Tell me something I don't know.'

He sat down opposite her. 'What about Bodin? Where does he come from?'

'Martinique, he says. He's just a pig. I've always had the feeling that he's wanted by the police, but he's never admitted it. He just drinks and lusts after the girls. So far, the boys have been pretty good at protecting them.'

'That reminds me,' Russell said. 'I thought organs for transplants had to be tissue-matched, or the chances of rejection got too high.'

'The ones we send are tissue-matched. All the boys and girls here have been typed. The two we operated on today are good matches for the recipients, whoever they might be.'

'You mean there's a shopping list?'

'You could call it that.'

He stared into his glass for a moment, then raised his head. 'And what about you?' he asked. 'Were you struck off? Are you on the run?'

'You know why I'm here.'

'I don't know how you got here. How come your English is so good? Were you born here?'

'In Port au Prince. My mother was French, my father

87

is African. Our family wasn't socially acceptable, but we had plenty of money. I went to medical school in Paris, and while I was away my mother died. My father moved to America with my two brothers, and I joined them there. I worked in a Boston hospital for four years.'

'Why did you come back?'

'There's one doctor to every three hundred people in Boston, about one to every six thousand here.'

It was the sort of answer Sibou would have given him. The two of them obviously had more in common than being beautiful. 'So how did you get tied up with Joutard?' he asked.

'That's a long story,' she said, looking at her watch and getting wearily to her feet. 'And maybe I'll tell you it some other time. Right now I should be looking in on the two children.'

'You and Dr Bodin.'

'Dr Bodin is not a great believer in post-operative care.'

'Do you want any help?'

'No. But thanks for the drink.'

The screen door slammed shut behind her. Russell poured himself another glass of Joutard's whisky and sat back down again. The drums seemed to have fallen silent, and the only sounds from outside were the chirping of the crickets and the hum of a distant conversation. He wondered where the helicopter was now, and where it was headed. Somewhere out there four people who spent a lot of their life on dialysis machines were about to get another shot at normality. Two more people would probably get the chance to see again. As for the bone . . . well, that was worth four times its weight in cocaine.

If he tried to escape there was no chance she would

come with him. And if he failed he might well end up on Dr Calderón's table, minus both kidneys and corneas, his bones compacted for transport in a jar.

Russell wondered if they'd play the drums for him. As if in answer, the mesmerizing rhythms started up again somewhere in the darkness outside.

Four days after their summons to the CO's office in Poole, Callum Marker and Rob Cafell found themselves between flights in Miami Airport, with three hours to waste before their connection departed for Providenciales. Cafell had bought himself a paperback history of the SEALs in Vietnam, and was devouring it with his usual single-mindedness, apparently oblivious to the fact that the plastic seat on which he was sitting had been designed by either a Martian or a sadist. Marker, meanwhile, was prowling through the waiting and shopping areas, reminding himself that there were few places on earth he hated more than modern airports.

It was because they were the negation of travel, he thought. He and Cafell had come five thousand miles and everything looked the same, smelt the same. The same products were on sale, even the same foods. 'Home of Whopper values' one sign told him. That just about summed it up.

Cheer up, he told himself – you'll soon be eating conch stew beside the shining sea. At least that was what the brochures had promised them.

The wait seemed endless, but at least the American Airlines flight was called on time. The plane was only two-thirds full, and both men managed to grab window seats, from which they watched Miami Beach and the setting sun fall away behind them. Within a few minutes they were flying over the Bimini Islands, and soon after that the first of the Bahamas. The ocean below seemed crowded with boats.

They flew east into the approaching night. Not much more than an hour later their plane was touching down on the runway of what seemed an almost deserted airport. Marker felt a sense of pleasure walking down the steps on to the tarmac – it was so much nicer than being sucked into a terminal building by one of those telescopic corridors. A hundred yards away the lights of the two-storey terminal building beckoned, but in every other direction there was only darkness. Benidorm it wasn't.

The two men went through passport control, and then collected their luggage before going through customs. The officer simply waved them through, which rather devalued all the effort they had put into creating an inspection-proof hide for the handguns inside their diving gear.

Outside, a line of taxis, and only taxis, was waiting. Marker, who had done some overland travelling in South-east Asia during stints in Hong Kong and Brunei, recognized a monopoly when he saw one, and cheerfully accepted the quoted price for transport to their hotel.

'That's a fortune,' Cafell muttered behind him.

'You want to walk five miles?' Marker asked. They had now been up for about eighteen hours, and he felt exhausted.

'Not a lot.'

'Well, get in then.'

They both got in, leaving the driver muttering about how much gear they had. He then leaned against his bonnet for a while, presumably hoping for more passengers, but eventually accepted that none was coming.

The drive took about twenty minutes, and offered little indication of what the island looked like. They passed through two small shopping centres but the rest was darkness, until the taxi breasted a low hill and a shimmering ocean filled the windscreen. The Coconut Cove Hotel – one of the newest on the island – sprawled along low cliffs above a wide, sandy beach, and a grove of the relevant palms stood just beside the men's allotted cabin.

Inside it the rooms were clean and pleasantly furnished.

'You can have the bedroom,' Marker said. 'I'll take the convertible couch here.'

'You want to watch TV in bed, don't you?'

'Privilege of rank.'

By the time they'd unpacked it was gone eight. They walked up to the hotel restaurant, looked at the menu, and realized that they had already had enough meals that day. A pint in the bar seemed like a better idea, but even that was hard to finish.

'I'm going to call it a day,' Marker decided, with two inches of beer still waiting. 'Gonk is calling,' he added, using the Marine slang for sleep.

'We're not going to call Franklin tonight?' Cafell asked, after looking round to make sure no one was in earshot. Feeling a trifle paranoid, he reminded himself who they were probably up against, and how easy it would be to get seduced by the atmosphere of this place into relaxing their guard.

'We'll call him tomorrow,' Marker said. 'Take the day to get acclimatized, and see him in the evening.'

'I hope he has some ideas,' Cafell said, 'because we haven't.'

'Speak for yourself,' Marker countered with a grin.

'If all else fails we can always use you as bait. You see *Jurassic Park*?'

'No.'

'Well, everyone remembers the goat.'

It was only about five in the morning when Marker woke up. Ten in the morning in England, he reminded himself.

His partner seemed to have adapted more quickly. Marker had to pass through the bedroom on his way to and from the bathroom, but Cafell didn't stir, unless an almost melancholy whistling sound counted as such.

Marker dressed, left a note saying he'd be back by nine and went out. The sun was rising above the island, and he managed to coax one of the kitchen staff into supplying him with a premature cup of coffee. Down by the hotel's small jetty a number of boats were tied up – rowing boats, paddle boats and canoes. They had to be there for the use of guests, Marker told himself. None of the rowing boats had any visible oars, but someone had been carelessly kind enough to leave a paddle in one of the canoes.

Murmuring mental thanks to this unknown benefactor, Marker stepped in and cast off. The water was smooth and, as became increasingly apparent with the brightening light, almost unbelievably clear. Once he was out a couple of hundred yards Marker just let the canoe drift, and watched the sun rise across the low hills of the island, turning the waters to a shade of turquoise which any kingfisher would have envied.

After all the hustle and bustle of the last few days, and particularly the frenetic boredom of ten hours' flying the day before, sitting in the gently bobbing canoe felt like the most relaxing massage for the soul anyone could have devised.

He had always felt calmed by the sea. Calmed and comforted. Often challenged, but never threatened. Ever since he was a small boy Marker had cherished the feeling that the sea was his real home.

He had grown up in north London's Highgate, or at least that was where the house the family called home was situated. Both his parents were actors, and fairly successful ones at that, if almost continuous employment could be so called. Neither was famous, although both by now had the vaguely familiar faces of people who had been playing small parts on TV for the best part of thirty years. During Marker's childhood most of their work had been in the theatre, and he had been packed away to boarding school as soon as he was old enough. His most abiding memories of the time were the long summer holidays spent beside the sea, at the resorts where his parents were appearing. The evenings had been spent backstage, the days with the sea, swimming or sailing with his father.

Public school had been an isolating experience. He was tough enough for the school thugs to give him a wide berth, but uninterested in either academic work or team sports. It was only in the Navy cadets that he discovered challenges of lasting interest, and the school had at least shown the sense to encourage his already prodigious skill as a swimmer and diver.

At fourteen, after seven years at the school, he had been brought back to London by his parents. Their work was now almost exclusively in TV or the capital's theatre, and at last the house in Highgate became something of a home. Marker was sent to the local comprehensive, where he found a world utterly different from any he had previously known. His school work didn't improve much, but he found his new schoolmates a much more interesting bunch than the ones he had left behind. For a time other loves like music and films and girls vied with the sea for his attention, but when it came time to leaving school there was no real conflict in his mind. Marker's ambition was to work at sea, and of all the options he considered, joining the Marines seemed the one with the most potential. And once that was decided, he knew he would settle in the end for nothing less than the best – the SBS.

First, of course, he had needed to make the grade as a Royal Marines officer. Marker could remember the first day as clear as yesterday, clearer in fact. He had arrived at the training centre in South Devon on a sunny September morning, and realized that most of the other young men around him were much more nervous than he was. Even some of the ones who had come straight from university had looked lost and lonely. Not for the first or the last time, Marker had appreciated the edge his childhood had given him when it came to self-reliance.

But, as he had found out much later, there had also been a price. The inner-directedness which made him such a proficient SBS officer also made it hard for him to share his life. In one of their final rows Penny had told him she had only stayed for the sex. Their bed was the only place in which he knew how to give of himself.

She had probably been right, Marker thought, as the canoe drifted slowly out from shore. He had been selfish – there was no doubt of that. She had wanted them to have a child, and he had wanted to wait until they were permanently settled in one place. He hadn't wanted to do to his own children what his parents had done to him.

Penny had understood, but that was all. She hadn't

agreed. And now she was gone. And he was sitting in a canoe on a turquoise sea feeling sorry for himself.

'Fuck a pig,' he muttered to himself, and took charge of the canoe's direction again, turning it in a long arc back towards the shore.

He found Rob Cafell halfway through breakfast, and helped himself from the self-service buffet.

'Cabs offer tours of the island,' Cafell told him, 'or we can hire a four-wheel drive. Some of the roads are not exactly built yet, apparently.'

'Hiring a car sounds better. Can we do it from here?'

'No, but the place is only a mile or so away.'

'Good.' Marker looked at his watch. 'And Franklin should be reachable by then.'

'I'm ready to go.'

'Yeah, yeah,' Marker said, scooping up the last of the tropical fruit salad. 'But you're too good to be true.'

They collected the documents they needed and started up the road which led inland from the cove, declining several offers of a cab. It was hot — probably over twenty-five degrees already, though it was not yet eight-thirty — and there wasn't much in the way of shade. The rolling terrain was covered with vegetation, but mostly in the form of scrub. In the open countryside trees were few and far between.

Leeward Rent-A-Car was situated on the other side of the island's main highway, at its junction with the road from the hotel, and was just opening for business as they arrived. Marker left Cafell and the owner picking a vehicle, and went inside to use the phone. He dialled the clinic's number and asked to speak to the administrative secretary.

'Worrell Franklin speaking.'

'Mr Franklin, the consignment of textbooks you ordered from London has arrived.'

Franklin smiled to himself. 'Great. I'll collect them this afternoon.'

'You know where to come?'

'Yep, thanks.'

'Thank you,' Marker said, and hung up.

Outside, Cafell was signing papers on the bonnet of a four-wheel-drive Subaru.

Within minutes they were on the highway, heading east.

They spent the next four hours exploring the island, from the Leeward Marina opposite Mangrove Cay at one end to the secluded, west-facing beach at the other. They briefly visited a conch farm, the ruins of an old slave plantation and a nature reserve. The only road they didn't venture on to was the one which led down towards Arcilla's house on Long Bay. There was no point in offering the enemy a free memory of their faces until they had a plan of action.

In the afternoon they hired a boat from one of the diving services on Grace Bay and tested their equipment on the undersea wall west of Provo, where the shallow waters of the island shelf abruptly dropped into the thousand-fathom depths of the Caicos Passage. Spectacular formations of rock and coral hung over the edge of the wall, and both men caught glimpses of sharks and rays cruising in the shadows. It all seemed a long way from Poole Bay.

'Some people have to pay for all this,' Cafell said, as they stripped off their wetsuits before taking the boat back in.

For Franklin the day passed by at a snail's pace. He

had only had one class to take, but, much to the amusement of his students, twice found his attention drifting helplessly away from the subject in hand.

Soon after five he left the clinic. The Coconut Cove was only ten minutes away by car, but he had decided on walking, and by a roundabout route at that. It might well be no more than paranoia, but several times over the past week he had felt that he was being followed.

After receiving the welcome but surprising news from Joss Wynwood, Franklin's first reaction had been to sit and wait for the reinforcements to arrive. But this, he had quickly realized, would look suspicious. If he didn't keep up his campaign of harassment against Sergeant Oswald and the authorities, then the opposition might get the idea that he had something else up his sleeve.

Now, striding purposefully down the dirt road which reached the northern coast some two miles west of the Coconut Cove, he was eager to meet the SBS men who had been sent out from England. He still had little idea of what any of them could do to find Russell, but over the past few days he had decided there must be more at stake in this matter than he knew. And that meant that the SBS men should have as much to tell him as he had to tell them. And then maybe between them they could build up a wider picture and come up with a suitable plan of action. He hoped this was true, because the only plan he had managed to formulate on his own was not one with which he felt at all comfortable.

Reaching the beach, Franklin walked down to the sea, took off his shoes and paddled around in the shallow water for several minutes, keeping one eye on the road he had arrived by. No walker appeared, and no car. If he was being followed, then it wasn't with much thoroughness.

Darkness fell as he walked the two-mile stretch of beach, and the lights of the hotel grew brighter with every moment. In the bar he spotted the two men straight away, sitting with their cans of Heineken and reading a week-old *Daily Express*. He would have known them without the prearranged signs, simply from the fact that they both looked so fit.

When they got up to leave he waited a minute, and then followed them out to the beach. Half a mile to the east, when all were sure that they weren't being followed, the two SBS men stopped and waited for Franklin to catch up.

They introduced themselves, and sat down with their backs against the abandoned hulk of a rowing boat. A large and lonely sapodilla tree towered above them, black against the sky. To left and right the empty beach stretched away into the darkness.

After Franklin had confirmed that he had no fresh news of Russell, they briefed him on the wider reasons for their presence.

'Have you been keeping an eye on Arcilla's house?' Marker asked.

'Not really. I've been up there a few times, but I can't spend my life in a hide. I've got a job to do. And my mother's visiting from England,' he added with a rueful grin. 'But we've got some friends up on Long Bay, and the guy at the marina isn't what you'd call close-mouthed. Arcilla's helicopter has made a couple of trips to who knows where; the last one was the day before yesterday. After dark both times, which sounds a bit suspicious. The boat hasn't been back . . .'

'The boat's anchored between Muertos Cays and the Dog Rocks on the Cay Sal Bank,' Cafell told him. 'It's a region of shallows between Cuba and Florida,' he added.

'Since it's one of the prime drop sites for drug planes, the US Coast Guard checked the *Tiburón Blanco* out a few days ago. The identity of the owner didn't exactly inspire confidence, but they can't arrest a boat for sitting in international waters. And unless it's waiting a hell of a long time for a drop, it's probably doing what it says it is – treasure hunting. There are lots of known wrecks there, and quite a few more which no one has ever found. The *Santa Lucia* . . .'

'I don't think Worrell needs a run-down of famous wrecks,' Marker interrupted. 'Has Arcilla been here himself?' he asked Franklin.

'Not as far as I know. And there's no reason to think he's skulking in his villa. His sister's behaviour hasn't changed. Neither has the caretaker's.'

'We're waiting for a complete run-down on Arcilla,' Marker said. 'Maybe that'll give us some ideas. But the way I see it at the moment, the only thing of Arcilla's on this island is his house. We have to get into it, one way or another. The question is how.'

'I've been thinking about that for ten days now,' Franklin said slowly, 'and there's not much doubt what the easiest way into it is. In all the hours I've watched the place I've seen three strangers go through the front gate – and all of them have been picked up by Tamara Arcilla at the Club Med-Turkoise.'

Cafell laughed. 'You're not suggesting one of us gets himself picked up . . .'

Franklin shrugged. 'I don't like it, but . . .'

'The things a man must do for his country,' Marker murmured.

'Is she beautiful?' Cafell wanted to know.

'Yes, she is,' Franklin admitted.

'I know we're both devastatingly good-looking,'

Marker said, 'but what makes you think she'd pick one of us out of the crowd?'

'It's the low season,' Franklin said, 'and there's not much of a crowd.'

'I don't know,' Cafell said. It didn't feel right, though he wasn't sure why. James Bond did it all the time, and probably charged condoms to expenses.

Marker was looking out to sea, trying to think of an alternative. 'What about a break-in?' he asked.

'You have a look at the place tomorrow,' Franklin said. 'It wouldn't be difficult to get in, but to search the place thoroughly without getting caught . . . There's always people there. And with the woman, well, there's always the chance she'll let something slip in conversation.'

'Or talk in her sleep,' Cafell offered.

'What's her taste in men?' Marker asked.

'All the ones I've seen her with have been dark.'

'I'm afraid it's up to you then, boss,' Cafell said. 'Of course I'll give you detailed advice . . .'

Marker didn't laugh. He could hear Penny screaming, 'I only stayed with you for the fucking sex.' There had to be some other way to do this.

7

This is not going to work, Marker thought to himself. There had to be about twenty available-looking men spread around the Club Med-Turkoise dining room, and probably the same number again in the bar next door. Knowing Tamara Arcilla's predatory m.o. might give him an edge, but forty to one was still long odds.

He lifted the glass of wine to his lips, took a modest sip, and put it down again. Another couple of drinks and his ability to think straight would follow his inhibitions into limbo-land.

He wondered where the inhibitions came from. Before Penny he had stalked his way through enough parties and pubs in search of women to screw. In Hong Kong he had occasionally gone with a street whore. What was the line from the song? – 'times I was so lonesome I took some comfort there.' Lonesome? Horny, more like it. Sex for its own sake was hardly a crime, and he was only sitting at this table because that was the way Tamara Arcilla seemed to like it.

So why was he agonizing about it? Nick Russell's life might depend on him screwing this woman. Maybe other people's too. He told himself to stop being so bloody moralistic, and took a larger gulp of the claret, just as the waiter appeared at his shoulder suggesting coffee. He raised his head to say yes just in time to see the woman enter.

He immediately knew it was her, and the signal from Franklin, sitting across the room, merely offered confirmation. At least she didn't look like Penny, he thought. Almost the opposite in fact. She had those classic Spanish cheek-bones which in some faces seemed unbearably haughty but which in hers were more than offset by the full lips and tumbling hair. The eyes were deep and dark, but Marker was too far away to read any expression they might hold.

She was wearing a simple red cotton dress which made the most of her figure, and walked with an easy grace. Inside his head Marker heard a familiar schoolboy saying, yeah, I'd like to give her one.

He sugared his black coffee and looked at his watch. According to Franklin she never ate more than a starter, before moving through to the bar.

Marker waited patiently, drinking the coffee more from a sense of duty than pleasure. At first he tried not to stare at her, but then realized that it was hardly a suspicious thing to do – most of the men in the restaurant were finding it hard to keep their eyes off her. Occasionally she would look up and catch someone, and a slight smile would crease her lips. It occurred to Marker that with a brother like Fidel Arcilla she would probably have been allowed little control over her own life. Maybe here, in the choosing of sexual partners, she was exercising the only power she had. Like a female Sultan she was visiting her harem to pick out a man for the night.

Suddenly she was getting to her feet and walking out, hips swinging slightly, the dark hair dancing on her bare shoulders.

Marker followed her out of the restaurant, hoping that she followed her usual pattern and went to the ladies, before gracing the bar with her presence.

She did, and Marker quickly took in the situation at the bar. There were only four stools unoccupied, in two pairs of two. Of the four seats adjoining these, one was occupied by a woman, two by middle-aged Americans and one by a handsome young West Indian. Marker took the seat next to him, and hoped she didn't change her usual habits and take a table.

He ordered a drink and waited, feeling more than a little ridiculous. If she was on a power trip, he told himself, then she would have to choose him. He couldn't afford to show any interest in her until she had made the decision. He took a diving school leaflet out of his pocket and begun to study it.

The scent of her perfume was the first thing he was aware of. It was a subtle, lovely, expensive smell. He looked up to say hello and found her eyes already on him. Franklin had told them of his feeling that she was lonely at best, seriously disturbed at worst, and maybe, Marker thought, he was seeing something that wasn't really there, but in that moment her dark eyes seemed to hold a sort of quiet desperation. A stab of pity went through him, just as the smile lit up her face, and drove the bleakness of the eyes away.

'Hi,' he said, smiled, and went back to his leaflet.

'If you're interested in diving you should try the Laurel Canyon,' she said.

'Oh, where's that?' he asked.

'On the West Wall.'

He half turned back to the leaflet, then looked up again. 'Can I buy you a drink?' he asked, in a tone that was mixed politeness and kindness. His parents would have been proud of him, he thought.

'Thank you,' she said, with another smile.

Marker was finding it hard not to stare at her. Her legs

103

were crossed and the red dress had ridden up, exposing beautiful brown thighs. When she leant forward to put an elbow on the bar more square inches of brown breast came into view.

'Do you live here?' he asked.

'Uh-huh. I have a house over on Long Bay. How long are you here for?'

'Two weeks. We arrived the day before yesterday.'

'We?'

'A friend and I. A male friend. We belong to the same diving club in England.' Which was almost true, Marker thought.

'I like the English,' she said. 'Mostly because they are not American,' she added, smiling. 'Tell me what you do when you're not diving.'

They talked for the next hour, working their way through several drinks in the process. She talked about the islands, and asked Marker about England and himself, but the occasional attempts he made to get her to talk about herself all fell on stony ground. She never refused, just deftly changed the conversation back to safer territory.

After an hour Marker was beginning not to care. He was not drunk, but neither did he feel any intense urge to organize his thoughts. Most of all he wanted sex with her, wanted it more strongly than he could remember wanting sex with anyone for years, Penny included. And he didn't want to think about why.

It was hard not to, though. He told himself it was a primal urge, and that was all there was to it. It was the same urge which had given him such rock-hard erections looking at *Playboy* centrefolds when he was fourteen. It had nothing to do with love or affection or home or anything like that. He just wanted to fuck her, and not because of any desire to extract information from her. He just wanted to fuck her.

And it seemed she wanted to fuck him.

'I'd like a walk on the beach,' she said abruptly.

'Great idea,' he murmured.

There were a few couples on the beach in front of the hotel, but the two of them hadn't walked more than a hundred yards when the sand stretched away empty into the darkness. She put an arm through his, and he felt a shot of electricity pass through him, then a slowly rising sense of excitement. She leant across to kiss him lightly on the lips, as if she was announcing that he had won that evening's prize.

They walked on in a silence broken only by their feet in the sand and the distant swish of the waves on the reef. After about half a mile she pulled them to a halt, and turned to face him, her back to the sea. 'I feel like a swim,' she said, kicking off her shoes. She slipped her shoulders out of the straps, let the dress fall, and stepped out of it. 'Unhook me,' she said, turning her back to him. He did so, and she dropped the brassière neatly on the dress.

'Aren't you coming?' she asked, pulling down the lacy knickers.

She walked into the sea. Marker watched her for a moment, silhouetted against the sky, and then took off his clothes and followed her in.

She swam well, and they were fifty yards or so out from the shore when he caught her up and roughly pulled her into his arms. The water was only about four feet deep, and they found themselves standing in it. She returned his kiss hungrily, almost too hungrily, and pushed her body hard against his. The stray thought went through his head that if there were perfect relative heights for doing it standing up then his and hers qualified.

'Not here,' she said. She sank back into the water and started swimming back towards the shore. He followed, thinking that a few seconds earlier he had been trying to insert himself, without a condom, into a woman who probably slept with two hundred men a year.

She had more sense. 'If you don't have one I do,' she said.

'I have one,' he said, reaching into his trouser pockets for the packet he had bought earlier that evening.

'Give me,' she said, holding herself against him and kissing him again. 'And lie down on your back.'

He did as he was told, his mind spinning off into the distance as she sat astride his knees and took the condom out of its packet. Then she leant forward and took his penis briefly in her mouth, as if she was lubricating it for him. Marker felt he would come on the spot, and frantically tried using his mind to bring his body under control.

She was easing the condom over his throbbing cock, and then holding it in one hand as she gently lowered herself on to him.

'Don't move,' he groaned, and he thought he saw the glint of teeth in her shadowed face as she smiled. Her head was surrounded by stars, and she begun to hum with pleasure as they lay there locked in a stillness that seemed to have no end.

It was almost one in the morning when Marker let himself back into their cabin at the Coconut Cove. He found Cafell and Franklin watching Robert Mitchum and Jane Russell trade innuendoes in an old movie.

Cafell reached forward and turned the TV off. Marker sat down on the couch and closed his eyes. Either he was getting paranoid, or the looks on the faces of the welcoming committee had rather too accurately reflected the way he was feeling.

'Any luck?' Cafell asked. He could tell Marker was not feeling too good about things, but had no idea what to say to make him feel better.

'I scored, if that's what you mean,' Marker said.

Cafell and Franklin said nothing.

Marker opened his eyes. 'Sorry,' he said. 'No's the answer. I didn't get taken to the house.'

'Then where . . .'

'The beach.'

'It's kind of a traditional place around here,' Franklin said. He and Sibou sometimes went to a secluded beach at the western end of the island. And the very first time they had ever made love had been on the one behind the Atlantic Hotel in the Gambia. The memory still made him smile inside with happiness.

'Did she say anything useful?' Cafell asked.

'Nothing. The woman talks about everything but herself.' Marker got up and went to pour himself a glass of water. 'I didn't want to push too hard,' he added, as much to himself as the others.

'Sure,' Cafell agreed. He couldn't remember seeing Marker like this.

'Did you arrange another . . . ?' Franklin began.

'Date?' Marker laughed. 'Yeah, tomorrow night.' He sat down again. 'Maybe this time I'll get invited home.'

'We can always drop this approach,' Cafell said.

'We haven't got any others,' Marker said flatly.

'OK,' Cafell agreed, 'but . . .' He wanted to ask his partner what it had been like, and wondered if his motives amounted to anything more than mere voyeurism. Then again, talking about it might be the best way of ridding Marker of whatever it was that was troubling him . . .

Maybe later, Cafell decided. 'We got the report on her brother,' he said.

Marker looked a bit more cheerful. 'How did it get here?'

'Would you believe by special plain-clothes courier? A Yank flew over with it from Miami, and pressed it into my grubby hand.'

'What's it say?'

Cafell retrieved it from the table. 'There's not much more in the way of hard fact than we had already, but some of it's interesting. He lived in Cuba until he was twenty-one, and he seems to have had problems with the authorities there from about the age of six. Castro's regime set up political neighbourhood-watch-type things called CDRs – Committees for the Defence of the Revolution? Well, young Arcilla managed one hundred and seventeen black marks on his social-behaviour record before he was fourteen. And of course once he really got into his stride, well, then the real trouble started. Black marketeering, ration swindling, simple theft, and eventually murder. He was sixteen when he knifed a boy who he caught in bed with his sister . . .'

Christ, Marker thought. She would have been twelve.

'He spent four years in prison in Havana,' Cafell continued, 'and then he was one of the thousands of misfits Castro managed to dump on the Americans with the Mariel boat-lift. He got his sister out a year later – no one knows how.'

'What happened to his parents?' Franklin asked.

'No information. I guess they're either dead or still in Cuba. Anyway, Arcilla signed on with one of the Cuban crime factions in Miami, probably just as extra muscle. But he obviously has brains – he also got involved with the largest and most right-wing of the exile organizations . . .'

'And they make the Nazis look like Social Democrats,' Franklin muttered.

'He seems to have used his criminal life to do favours for his political chums, and in return he got both money and a degree of protection.' Cafell looked up. 'Of course it wouldn't say so here, but he may even have been doing jobs for the CIA, which would give him a pretty long rope.'

'Any definite drug connections?' Marker asked.

'I'm getting to that. In 1983 he bought the house here on Provo, and a year later he was given British citizenship. The Americans don't know why . . .'

'Neither did the Foreign Office,' Marker said. 'It must have been some local fix. Makes me wonder why we can't just revoke his citizenship and leave it to the Yanks.'

'That wouldn't help us find Nick,' Franklin said quietly.

'Right,' Marker agreed.

'He was a known associate of the three island politicos who got sent to jail for helping drug smugglers, but not a known *business* associate. There was no proof against him then, and there never has been. He hasn't been arrested since his departure from Cuba. He even survived a heavy tax investigation in 1988. He is suspected of involvement in the drug trade, if only as a money launderer, but that's all it is – suspicion. He's extremely rich and getting richer all the time, but . . .'

'If you're rich you have to work really hard not to get richer,' Marker said gloomily.

'It has to be him, doesn't it,' Cafell said. It was half statement, half plea for reassurance.

'Yeah,' Franklin said quietly.

'Who else?' Marker asked. And the only way to reach the man was through his sister, whose perfume was still lingering in his nostrils.

Despite their late night the vestiges of jet lag ensured that neither Marker nor Cafell found it possible to sleep beyond seven. This was particularly bad news for Marker, whose head seemed to be vibrating in an unpleasant manner. 'You're not doing any diving today,' Cafell told him, but he needn't have bothered: Marker knew from painful experience how dangerous diving with a hangover could be.

So when they took the boat out that morning it was Cafell who ventured down into the magical kingdom of the reef, leaving the senior man to gaze out across the open sea and brood over the happenings of the last twenty-four hours. And the last year.

Before he had met Tamara . . . He smiled to himself. Who was he kidding? He had not *met* her in any significant sense – they had fucked, that was all.

He started again. Before he had *fucked* Tamara he had entertained the thought that, however else the experience would affect him, it might at least drive Penny out of his mind. Draw a line under the past, he thought wryly, remembering what Colhoun had said. Well, the boss had been wrong. Somehow the pain of losing his wife seemed even more intense in the cold light of day.

He didn't know what to do about it, and for someone who had made his living overcoming mental and physical challenges that was a hard thing to admit. He knew that in a way it was just a question of grief – learning to accept the loss from day to day. But when the lost one was dead there was no small voice wondering if she would ever come back to you.

He sighed and tried to turn his mind back to work. If Tamara's past habits were anything to go by there was a good chance he would be invited back to the villa that evening, and he would have to make the most of the opportunity. If he was unable to discover anything either incriminating or worth following up, then there seemed no point in hanging around on the island.

An involuntary pang of regret accompanied this thought.

'Fuck,' he muttered to himself.

Russell lay on his bed, a book face down across his chest, watching a mosquito carefully checking out his screen for a possible entry point. Emelisse had just dropped by with the news he had been dreading for days – in not much more than an hour he would be extracting his first kidney.

He covered his mouth with cupped hands and stared at the ceiling, where faint, flickering shadows from fires outside were dancing. Get a grip, he told himself, and abruptly levered himself into a sitting position on the side of the bed.

A drink was what he wanted. In fact he found it hard to remember wanting one quite so much. He also knew that having one would be the worst thing he could possibly do.

Where had all that training gone, he wondered. The self-discipline, the ability to centre oneself, to feel the stillness spreading out from that centre. In Hong Kong he had studied several of the martial arts, and got more than a little interested in the philosophies which underlay them. In some strange way – which seemed less strange as his knowledge increased – his Marine and SBS training had been the perfect preparation for such studies. After all, lying in an inch of water in a soggy hide above Port Stanley for three days presented a man with a pretty stark choice – he could either go mad or start making use of his inner resources.

Which was exactly what he needed to do now, he decided. But he seemed to have lost the knack, to have allowed his mental muscles to get flabby over the years.

He walked through into the main room. His stomach felt the way it always had as a child sitting in the dentist's waiting room. Then he had tried to distract himself with thoughts of some future treat.

It had never worked.

The only thing in this place which might stop him thinking was Emelisse Alabri. The evening he had witnessed his first operations – the evening she had come to his bungalow for a drink – had marked a watershed in their relationship, and by extension in Russell's attitude towards his captivity. She hadn't suddenly started treating him as a friend, and as often as not her instinctive reaction still seemed suspicious rather than trusting, but since that night he had the feeling she had decided to give him the benefit of the doubt. His offer to help at her clinic had been accepted, and now each morning he assisted her in dressing wounds, taking vital signs and dispensing drugs from the surprisingly well-stocked pharmacy. After the last patient disappeared they would usually drink coffee together and reminisce about their pasts. His, of course, had been offered in a somewhat censored version. She had been surprised, and he thought probably somewhat disappointed, to learn that he had been in the armed forces at all, without him regaling her with tales of life in the SBS.

As for Emelisse, she had brought herself to speak freely about her years in France and America, but her life in Haiti, both as a child and now, was still something she rarely referred to.

Russell was not sure whether he could now consider himself her friend, but she didn't seem to have any others. There didn't seem to be a sexual partner either, and occasionally he had found himself thinking about her in that way. The loveliness which had taken his breath away at their first meeting had become something he almost took for granted, except in those rare moments when something caught her by surprise and she let her guard down. Then he wasn't at all sure how he felt about her. Protective maybe, almost fatherly. And sometimes he had felt the beginnings of a desire which he didn't think had anything to do with sex, but for which he could imagine no other outlet.

As the days went by he had also learnt more about the camp. The three doctors – four, if he counted himself – were left pretty much to their own devices, subject to their all being available at short notice for collective surgery. Otherwise Bodin kept to his bungalow and bottle, Calderón to his laboratory, and Emelisse to her clinic and the orphans. Joutard's thugs were always around, but after a while it was possible to think of them as moving parts of the scenery, with about as much brains as the palm trees.

He had not seen Joutard since their one and only meeting, but occasionally he could hear Elvis Presley's voice coming from the colonel's living quarters. According to Emelisse, Joutard never allowed anyone else to be played on his 'boombox'. This, though bizarre, was almost comforting, rather like the situation as a whole. If it hadn't been for his dread of this particular moment, Russell might have thought he was getting used to his captivity, even accepting it.

Twenty-seven minutes had passed since her visit. He took a deep breath, and left the air-conditioned bungalow for the steamy heat of the Haitian evening. As usual, it was like walking out into an oven.

The drums were silent. Maybe the voodoo gods were having an evening off. The groups of mostly young people sitting outside also seemed subdued, as if they knew something bad was going to happen.

Stop it, Russell told himself. You didn't put yourself in this position. You can only do your best.

He found the other three doctors in the theatre ante-room. Emelisse and Calderón were scrubbing up, Bodin sitting on a chair with his eyes closed. There was no powerful smell of brandy on his breath this time, but the Frenchman was obviously the worse for something.

As before, the unconscious donors were laid out naked on parallel tables. This time there were four of them. The other three doctors took the same tables as before, leaving Russell the one which had previously been unoccupied. He wondered if he should ask to have his name engraved on it.

There were two males and two females, all of them aged between adolescence and young adulthood. The girl Russell was to operate on appeared to have fully developed breasts and hips, and seemed every bit as physically mature as the nurse who would be assisting him. He looked at her, wondering if life in Joutard's orphanage was worth the sacrifice of a kidney. But then if the alternative was prostituting herself for pennies on the streets of Port au Prince maybe it was. That shouldn't be the choice, though.

'I'll do the first incision for you,' Emelisse said, 'and then you're on your own. Any questions, ask me.'

Russell watched while she opened the patient and showed him once more how to expose the kidney. Then she was gone. He looked at the nurse, who gave him an encouraging smile that lacked a couple of front teeth.

He started work with the scalpel, and his brain started rerunning its film of the previous week's operation. Now that the moment was here he felt exactly that sense of inner stillness which he had thought was lost. He remembered the sergeant at Poole telling them: 'You'll never lose this fucking training, so get it right.'

It was easier than he had expected. A couple of times Emelisse appeared at his shoulder, looked, and merely nodded. He took five minutes longer than the others, but as he stitched up the original incision he felt a sense of achievement which ranked with any he had ever known.

They met as arranged in the Club Med-Turkoise bar, and spent another two hours drinking and talking about nothing in particular. Marker had been interested in how different she would be now that they had consummated their acquaintance, and was surprised, at least initially, by the answer. She was exactly the same.

After a while he thought he could see why. Each date had to be a seduction; each time they had to start and end in the same place. It was as if she was condemned to life on an ever-repeating emotional loop.

And of course there were only so many times she could repeat it with each man.

Changing the location would help. Soon after ten she

leaned over and ran a hand up his thigh. 'Would you like to see me home?' she asked.

'I'd love to,' he said, and wished that he didn't mean it quite so much.

She let him drive her dark-green Range Rover, directing him east along the Leeward Highway and then down the long, bumpy and unlit track which ended at the gates to the Arcilla compound. A strong source of light somewhere within was throwing a halo into the sky.

She leant over and sounded the horn as they approached, and they waited. Longer than usual, Marker guessed, as she honked again. Almost immediately the gates swung open for them. Marker noticed the video surveillance cameras and the discreetly positioned electronic sensors.

'Why all the security?' he asked casually. 'Is there a lot of crime on the island?'

He thought he saw a glimmer of a smile before she answered: 'It's just to keep my boyfriends in. They never escape until I want them to.'

It occurred to Marker for one ludicrous moment that Nick Russell was chained up in one of the outhouses as a sex slave. The thought was driven from his mind by the sight of the brilliantly lit helipad on the other side of the compound.

'Do you have a helicopter?' he asked, sounding impressed.

'My brother does. Just pull up here,' she said, indicating the front of the main house. It was an old colonial mansion which had been lovingly restored, with perhaps half a dozen rooms and an all-round veranda on each of its two storeys. Two other, more recent, buildings were connected to the mansion's rear by glassed-in, covered walkways.

116

Marker could only think of one reason for such an arrangement in such a climate: it offered safe passage between the buildings at night, when guard dogs were loose in the compound.

As if to confirm these suspicions, Tamara looked at her watch before opening the car door.

On the veranda she turned, put her arms around his neck, and kissed him the way she had the night before on the beach, rubbing her pubis against him. He felt a surge of desire, and buried his lips in her neck, even while a voice inside his head was telling him she had stopped here on the veranda, where they were clearly visible from the other buildings, for a purpose.

It doesn't matter, he told himself. Whatever games she was playing had nothing to do with him, or the job he was supposed to be doing.

It was hard to draw the distinction, with her hand inside his trouser pocket, stroking him.

'Let's go inside,' she said finally, and led him in by the hand.

The interior of the villa was decorated in a mixture of modern and classic Spanish colonial styles. It was both tasteful and somehow sterile, like a museum without visitors. There were few signs of ongoing life – no magazines or books or dirty cups or toys. The only thing of interest to Marker was the portrait of Fidel Arcilla above the mantelpiece. He looked like a cross between a political visionary and a captain of industry, which was perhaps the effect intended.

'Who's that?' Marker asked.

'My brother,' she said shortly.

'Oh, does he live here?'

'Only for vacations. He lives in Miami.'

'What does he do?'

117

'He's a businessman. What do you think of my picture?' she asked, reaching down behind a sofa and lifting up a similar-sized portrait of herself. The artist had rendered the lovely curves of her body with even more generosity than nature, but her face had been painted as that of an innocent child. Marker remembered Oscar Wilde's *The Picture of Dorian Gray*, in which a man's face had retained its innocence through life while his portrait had changed to reflect the ugliness growing in his soul. This seemed like an attempt to do the opposite, to hold on to something in a painting which could not be held on to in life.

The fact that she had pulled it out from behind the sofa suggested that her brother was the one with the fixation. For the second time in their short acquaintance Marker felt moved by a terrible pity.

'It doesn't do you justice,' he told her.

Tamara laughed, put the painting back, and took his hand. 'Do you need another drink?' she asked.

'No . . .'

'Then let me show you my bedroom,' she said.

It was as lovely as she was. The furniture comprised a rocking chair, an old Victorian dressing-table and a large bed without head or tailboards. A wooden fan whirred lazily above. Through the open doors which led out to the veranda Marker could see and hear the ocean.

They undressed each other this time, and stood naked in each other's arms for a long time before taking to the bed. Then, as if to make up for lost time, they made love in what seemed a ferocious haste, coming together in a violent arching of limbs and digging of fingernails. They sat outside on the veranda for a while, and then went back to bed and made love again, this time slowly, lingeringly, savouring each sensation until hunger drove them over the brink once more. For half an hour after that Marker struggled to stay awake, until he was sure she was sleeping soundly. Then he eased himself out of the bed, pulled on his trousers, and started to explore the house.

He quickly realized that his chances of finding anything useful were very slim. For one thing he had no idea what he was looking for; for another he could see no reason why Arcilla should leave anything incriminating in a house he only ever used for vacations. The elaborate security might indicate otherwise, but it could easily reflect nothing more sinister than habit on Arcilla's part.

And there was always the risk of his getting caught. He had decided against wearing a gun on the grounds that Tamara's hands would almost certainly have detected it at some point during the evening, and he was far from certain that his unarmed combat skills would suffice to overcome the combination of Arcilla's thugs, the dogs and the wall. Getting caught might be the quickest way to find out what had happened to Nick Russell, but it didn't seem the most sensible.

Of course they might believe he really was looking for the toilet. And that pigs could fly.

It took him ten minutes to go through all the rooms in the main villa. There was a safe behind the portrait of Arcilla which might contain something useful, but he could only have opened it with some C4 explosive. There was nothing else in the house that seemed even remotely suspicious. To all intents and purposes the place seemed set up as somewhere for the idle rich to idle in, and nothing else.

He went back upstairs to check that Tamara was still sleeping, and then down to the door which led out to the covered walkway. In the dark he could detect no alarm sensors, either around the doorway or inside the walkway, and there was no way he could turn on a light.

'Sink or swim,' he murmured to himself, and started forward. No alarms went off, no men came bursting through doorways waving guns. Marker was almost down at the end when he saw two dogs running towards him across the dark compound. They almost threw themselves at the glass, spattering it with flecks of drool, and then stood staring at him, feet restlessly pawing the ground, teeth bared, eyes full of yellow hatred.

But they didn't bark. They couldn't – someone had seen to that. No one would ever hear these dogs coming. They weren't there to provide warning of intruders, they were there to finish them off.

Marker had never liked dogs much. He took a deep breath, opened the connecting door to the next building, and eased himself through it.

The rooms seemed to house the staff, all of whom seemed to enjoy snoring. One door was open though, revealing an empty bed. Either two of the staff were sleeping together, or one of them was up and about.

Confident that he wouldn't be tripping any alarms, and not wanting to attract the dogs' attention again, he took the next passageway at a faster pace, noticing as he did so the light glimmering from one of the windows in the building he was approaching.

Prudence dictated that he check out that room first. He eased his way silently down the passage until he reached the door which was leaking a ribbon of light. Muted Spanish music was audible inside. Putting his eye to the keyhole, Marker could see the back of a seated man, and beyond him a modern radio transmitter. On the edge of his field of vision a silverish glow suggested video screens, presumably those for monitoring the compound. From the man's posture Marker thought it likely he had allowed himself to doze off, confident that any message from the helicopter would wake him up again.

The SBS man started searching through the other rooms in the building. No one lived here – that was for certain. The floors were mostly bare earth, the walls unpainted plasterboard. Several of the rooms were empty, but the largest contained a neat pile of boxes. Marker investigated the contents, and found tinned food, bottled water and sundry general supplies. On the other side of the same room there was a stack of assorted fuel drums, several of them containing marine oil. Twin doors gave on to the empty helipad.

It was all consistent with a regular airlift to resupply an underwater treasure hunt on the Cay Sal Bank. And there was no sign of drugs or guns or any other contraband which Arcilla might be smuggling into the United States.

Tamara Arcilla had led them nowhere, he thought. In his case, in more ways than one.

The silence was suddenly broken by the distant sound of an incoming voice on the radio. Hoping he might hear something interesting, Marker walked quietly and swiftly back towards the radio room, but the message must have been a short one, and the door swung open when he was only about six feet away from it. He flattened himself against the wall of the passage and prayed the man would walk the other way and not look back.

He did, and disappeared into what Marker remembered was the toilet. The sound of piss hitting water confirmed as much.

Marker backed into one of the empty rooms, waited until the man had resumed his position in the radio room, and then retraced his steps through the walkways and buildings to Tamara Arcilla's bedroom. She was still asleep.

He climbed back in beside her, feeling a sense of emptiness which seemed as apt as it was irrational. She stirred and turned towards him, her face almost angelic in the soft, grey light.

Marker let exhaustion carry him into sleep, but not for long. He lay there listening to the sound of decelerating rotor blades, and realized that it been the helicopter's return which had woken him. His watch said half-past three.

When he woke again the sun was already streaming into the room. A hand encircled his neck and gently pulled him into a sleepy embrace.

8

Russell woke to find her face leaning over his in the darkness, and for a moment he thought time had taken him back to their first meeting. But on this occasion her hand was urgently shaking his shoulder. 'I need your help,' she said, seeing he was awake.

'Why, what . . . ?'

'One of the two girls is critical,' she said.

His heart sank. 'Not mine?' he said stupidly.

'No, not yours,' she said impatiently, as he reached for his shoes. 'That bastard Bodin's.'

One voice in his head was thanking God that he was not responsible while another asked bitterly what difference it made. The girl didn't care, that was for sure.

They walked briskly across the silent compound. The first hint of light seemed to be showing in the eastern sky, which meant it had to be around five-thirty. Russell wondered why she had woken him rather than one of the nurses or the vastly more experienced Calderón.

As so often, she seemed to read his mind. 'The last time this happened we had trouble,' she said. 'A boy died and his brother went berserk. A guard shot and killed him. I don't want any of the kids to know about this until they have to. So you're my stand-in nurse.'

They reached the medical building. The girl was lying wrapped in a sheet on one of the operating

123

tables, hooked up to an intravenous drip. Her pulse was almost non-existent.

'Are you going to open her up again?' Russell asked.

'There must be internal bleeding,' Emelisse said. 'I've got no choice. Go and get scrubbed up while I watch her. And be quick.'

He was back out in a couple of minutes, but it no longer mattered. Emelisse was sitting, hands entwined above her head, on the adjacent table. Her eyes seemed cast in stone.

'Is she dead?' Russell said unnecessarily.

'Yes.' She looked at him for a second, then at the dead girl. 'Can you go and wake Calderón,' she said.

'OK,' he said doubtfully. 'What do I tell him?'

She smiled bitterly. 'That there's a fresh corpse for him to harvest – what else?'

What else indeed. He hovered for a moment in the doorway, not wanting to leave her.

She was unwrapping the sheet.

'What are you going to do?' he asked. It sounded the stupidest of questions.

'I'm going to open her up again and find out how that bastard fucked up,' she said in a brittle conversational voice.

Russell went for Calderón. The birds were singing up a storm in the trees now, and he found the doctor already awake, reading an AMA journal and drinking a cup of freshly brewed coffee. The news of the girl's death produced no obvious reaction, except perhaps a flicker of academic interest.

'What was the cause of death?' he asked, as they walked back across the compound.

'Eme . . . Dr Alabri is finding out,' Russell told him.

This produced a quickening of Calderón's pace.

When they reached the operating room Emelisse was back on the adjoining table. This time Russell thought he detected a watering of the eyes. The dead girl lay open on the operating table. 'Take a look,' she told Calderón. 'The bastard forgot to suture one of the arteries. Or just couldn't be bothered.'

Calderón looked, and nodded. 'I'll talk to him,' he said.

'I should save your breath,' she said. 'He'll probably get a bonus for donating the girl's bones.' And with that she strode out of the operating room, eyes blazing.

At twelve-thirty the next day they were eating lunch on the outside terrace of the Ocean View hotel. Marker watched her pick at her chicken salad, and wondered why his own appetite seemed to have deserted him. In the background he could see Franklin lurking, waiting for his signal.

That morning, after they had made love for the fourth time in ten hours, she had announced that she was flying to Miami that afternoon. She didn't know when she would be returning to Provo. She didn't seem to care either.

His implied dismissal had produced a multitude of conflicting emotions in Marker, uppermost of which were relief and an absurd sense of rejection. He had asked her to have lunch with him in reaction to the latter, and it was only later that he had devised the plan which he and Franklin were now about to put into operation.

She had accepted the invitation, but probably only as a convenient way of filling her time. Now, sitting there in dark glasses, she looked as unapproachable as any film star, and it was almost impossible to imagine that less than six hours earlier he had been engaged in passionately kissing almost every inch of the body encased in the tight black dress.

How could feelings so strong mean so little? Because memory was what preserved the meaning, and someone inside her had decided never to remember.

Marker stared out across the tranquil lagoon, inwardly sighed, and scratched his right ear. Almost immediately Franklin was towering over their table, eyes full of anger. He brought his face down to a position only a couple of feet from hers. 'I know your brother kidnapped my friend,' he told her, his voice low and menacing, 'and I'm going to prove it if it's the last thing I do. He may think he has important friends on Provo, but by the time I'm finished the people who live here will know exactly what he is. And all about his whore of a sister.'

'Hey, mister,' Marker said, getting slowly to his feet. 'You take your mouth somewhere else.' Tamara was silent. She seemed to be almost rigid in her chair.

'Her brother kidnapped my friend,' Franklin repeated belligerently, speaking louder this time. 'Or killed him.'

Marker looked across at her, as if inviting a denial. She just shook her head and looked down.

'If you're so sure, then take it to the police,' Marker said curtly. There weren't many people on the terrace, but they were all looking in his direction. 'Now get the fuck out of here.'

Franklin looked at him, as if wondering whether to knock him over. 'Her brother has the police in his pocket. And she's probably had them all in her knickers.' He turned back to her. 'You tell him,' he hissed.

She said nothing.

'You enjoy bullying women?' Marker asked, but the big man was already walking away through the tables.

Marker pulled his chair closer to her and sat down. 'What was all that about?' he asked gently.

'I don't know,' she said. A lone tear welled up in her right eye. 'I want to leave,' she said suddenly, and reached for her handbag.

'I'll come to the airport with you,' he said.

'No,' she said, almost violently. 'I don't want you to. Leave me alone.'

There was nothing he could do. She walked briskly off the terrace, her heels clicking on the stone, every eye following her. Marker watched her go, and then went in search of Franklin and Cafell. He found them in a dark corner of the bar, and took a pint over to join them.

'No joy,' he said. 'If she does know anything she's either too scared or too loyal or too crazy to tell anyone. The whole business has been a fucking waste of time.'

'With the emphasis on fucking,' Cafell added slyly.

Marker didn't laugh.

'But we have found out something,' Cafell went on, pulling a crumpled sheet of paper out of his pocket.

'What's that?' Marker asked hopefully.

'It's some intelligence from the Yanks. The helicopter touched down on the floating helipad next to friend Arcilla's boat at 22.58, and lifted off again at 00.24 hours. You said the helicopter arrived back here at around 03.30, which would figure. It's a 520-mile trip, and the 365F Dauphin has a cruising speed of about 184mph. So around three hours for the journey.'

'So?'

'Don't you see. We watched the damn thing leave before you went off to meet the lady. At 18.30.'

'It took four and a half hours to get there and only three to get back . . .'

'Deduction – they must have put down somewhere else. And not for fuel: the Dauphin has an operational range of 547 miles, fully loaded.'

Marker and Franklin looked at him.

'Why would someone supplying a treasure hunt do that?' Cafell insisted. 'They're either stopping to pick something up or drop something off. And since you didn't find anything at the villa, the odds are they're picking something up.'

'From where?'

Cafell pulled a tattered map from his hip pocket and spread it out in front of them. 'That's an interesting question.'

'Give us an interesting answer.'

'OK. Half the Bahamas are between here and the Cal Say Bank, and there's Cuba too.' He pointed them out on the map. 'A stopover on either wouldn't be much of a detour. Of course, Cuba guards its airspace pretty thoroughly, but who knows what connections Arcilla might have there. Castro had one of his own generals shot a few years ago for involvement in the drug trade.' Cafell looked up. 'But I don't think so. My money's on here,' he added, plonking a finger down on the map.

'Haiti?' Marker and Franklin exclaimed in unison. 'Why?' Marker asked.

'It's just a hunch. Maybe they're smuggling voodoo dolls.'

'OK,' Marker agreed. 'But let's assume it's drugs. The chopper leaves here, picks them up – maybe in Haiti, maybe somewhere else – and then delivers them to the *Tiburón Blanco* along with the supplies.'

'It's a perfect cover,' Franklin murmured.

'And that would explain why they do the resup at night,' Marker added. 'If anyone did challenge them they could always dump the drugs in the sea and have a perfectly legitimate reason for being in the area.'

'And they must be using the submarine for the last leg of the journey,' Franklin interjected. 'From what I hear the US Coast Guard and Navy have made it pretty hard for smugglers to gain entry by air or sea. On the surface, that is. Arcilla obviously had the bright idea of going in underwater.'

'You mean, while the submarine's supposed to be down below Arcilla's boat looking for treasure it's really running a shuttle service to Florida?' Cafell asked sceptically. 'You'd think the Americans would have twigged the possibility of something like that when they checked out Arcilla's boat.'

'Maybe our allies have a blind spot,' Marker suggested without much conviction. 'But if they weren't using the submarine, then how . . . ? There's only one way to find out,' he said, 'and that's to check out the boat ourselves.'

'Makes sense,' Cafell agreed.

Franklin looked first at his watch and then at the others. 'I guess this is where I'm sent back to work?'

Marker grinned. 'And your mother. It's been a pleasure working with you – that was some performance you gave us out there on the terrace.'

'You can nominate me for the SBS Oscars when you get home.' He downed the remaining half inch of beer. 'Don't get me wrong – I like what I do here,' Franklin said, 'but occasionally I miss the rush – know what I mean?'

Marker just nodded.

'And if you need any jobs done around here you know where I am.'

'Thanks,' Marker said. 'And if I were you I'd watch your back for a while. I don't think Arcilla is the kind of man who likes being bad-mouthed in public. And to judge by her reaction today I should guess the relationship between the two of them is probably borderline pathological. And we don't want a phone call saying you've disappeared leaving only a whiff of chloroform in the air.'

'I'll be careful,' Franklin said. 'I got too much to lose these days.' He gave them a final smile and strode out of the dark bar, disappearing into the sunlight outside.

'Nice guy,' Cafell murmured.

'Yep.' And a happy one, Marker thought. Franklin had told them that morning that he and Sibou had passed the first hurdle in being accepted as adoptive parents.

'I think it's time we reported in,' Cafell said.

They drove back along the coast to the Coconut Cove. Marker extracted the PRC 319 radio from his luggage and put it on the table. 'So what do we need to tell them?' he asked, reminding himself that their activities to date hardly came under the heading of standard procedure.

'A description of the foreplay,' Cafell suggested.

Marker smiled, but the memories that came to mind were not comforting.

'Just tell them what we have,' Cafell said. 'Or what we suspect. A chopper based here is picking up contraband and delivering it to Arcilla's boat. As

130

far as we know the contraband never touches British soil. OK?'

'Right.'

'We need to investigate the boat. And for that we need a boat of our own – one that's capable of carrying a submersible. And probably US permission to fish in their waters, so to speak.' He looked at Marker. 'Why don't you just let me take care of it?'

Marker grinned at him, picked up the radio and walked outside. He had already earmarked the patch of bare ground in front of the coconut palm grove as a perfect spot. It was only visible from the direction of the beach, and that was empty save for one couple soaking up the sun a hundred yards away.

He hunkered down on the sandy ground and arranged the two tuning antennae, pointing them up into the north-eastern sky and searching out the correct frequency. Then he unfolded the tiny keypad, typed out his identification code, and used the burst-transmission facility to send it. After receiving an acknowledgement he typed out his report and sent it, ending with a request for further instructions at 09.00 hours the following morning.

That should give Colhoun plenty of time, he thought, packing up the set once more. Time to persuade the Foreign Office that the operation should continue despite the slightness of the Provo connection, time to persuade the Admiralty to cough up a submersible, and maybe even time to enlist American help. Not too much help, though. He and Cafell didn't want bit parts in a SEAL operation.

Lieutenant-Colonel Neil Colhoun had just reached home

131

when the phone rang with the news of Marker's transmission. He listened as the duty officer read it to him,
then asked him to go over it again, slowly, as he took
notes. Ten minutes later, attempting to decipher his
own writing in the 'office' he and Jenny shared, he
reached the familiar conclusion that it was time they
got a fax machine.

Two things struck him immediately. One, if Marker
and Cafell were right in their suppositions then the British connection, though negligible, was also vital. Two,
they were no nearer to discovering the current location
of Nick Russell or the reason for his disappearance.

The importance of a third point occurred to him.
Arcilla's treasure hunt was taking place in international
waters. Even if anyone argued with Britain's right to
board his boat in search of a missing national, no one
would be in a position to do anything about it.

He sat there for a few more moments, rehearsing the
arguments he was about to make, and then dialled the
first of two London numbers.

Fidel Arcilla leaned back in his chair and stretched his
arms above his head. It was gone five in the evening,
and he had spent most of a long day on the telephone.
The slew of real-estate deals and political courtesy
calls had all been necessary, but the excitement such
activity had once generated in his breast had long
since vanished. Making money was just too easy these
days, and Arcilla increasingly found himself drawn into
ventures that were unusual and uncertain enough to
provide him with the challenge his older concerns
lacked.

The article he had just finished reading in *National
Geographic* was a clear case in point. He smiled to

himself and picked up the internal phone. 'Juan, come up for a moment,' he said in Spanish.

His secretary came through the door a few seconds later. 'Read that,' Arcilla told him, passing over the article.

Juan Lozano sat down in the leather sofa, crossed his legs and began reading. He was a thin, handsome Cuban in his early forties, the son of first-generation exiles. His brain was almost as quick as Arcilla's, but he feared he lacked the same imagination.

'Orchids?' Lozano said, looking up with a smile.

'There is a market.'

'I can see that. When people are prepared to pay $10,000 for one rare flower ...' He shrugged. 'It's incredible.'

'It's logical. This is why I give contributions to the environmentalists. Every time they pronounce a species endangered the value of a live specimen goes through the roof. It doesn't matter whether it's an orchid or a parrot.'

'You're interested in parrots as well?'

'No, just orchids. There's something classy about orchids.'

'You want me to look into it.'

'Yes. Find out who the players are, and whether the market is as good as the magazine says. Journalists have been known to exaggerate,' he added wryly.

'If you want a real challenge, how about whale smuggling?'

'One day.'

Lozano left, and Arcilla got to his feet. That was enough for one day – there was no point in being a millionaire and working yourself to death.

He walked through into the bedroom and took off

the tie he habitually wore for work, even in his own home. He examined himself in the full-length mirror, and saw much the same man he had seen for fifteen years. He was thirty-five now, and things would soon begin to change – his jawline would slacken, and his shiny black hair would begin to thin. Neither was an appealing prospect.

There was always cosmetic surgery. And there were good political reasons for spending money on the preservation of a youthful image. Look at the Kennedys, he told himself. Neither of them had been as good-looking as he was. It couldn't be many more years now before Castro was finally swept away, and then he would need every card he had to reach the top of the pile.

He walked across to the glass doors which led out to the roof garden. Carmen was stretched out in her bikini beside the pool, reading some romantic junk. He wondered why he didn't like clever women – it was not as though he had ever felt threatened by their intelligence. His sister had been clever as a child, but she didn't have the temperament to feed her intelligence, to make use of it. She was arriving that evening, he remembered.

Carmen's body reminded him of Tamara's. Not that he had seen his sister fully naked for many years. In the year before they had sent him to prison, when he had been sixteen years old and she nearly thirteen, they had enjoyed sex together quite often, but once they were both safe in America she had never let him touch her again. He had accepted it, though sometimes he wondered why. Maybe it had been his age, but there had been an intensity about the times with her which he had rarely found again.

Carmen, on the other hand . . .

'*Jefe*, Freddie is on the line from Provo.'

Arcilla walked back into the office, picked up the phone, and listened to what Bartholomew had to tell him, a look of faint amusement on his face.

'Do you want me to teach the man a lesson?' Bartholomew asked.

'No. Not yet, anyway.' Arcilla had just heard the door slam downstairs. It was probably Tamara. 'I'll get back to you,' he said, and put the phone down.

He went downstairs. Tamara was pouring herself a drink in his den, having already turned on the TV. He turned it off again.

She sat down in the massage chair her brother used to relax himself.

'I've just had Freddie on the phone,' he said. 'What did the man say to you?'

She looked at him coldly. 'You promised me,' she said. 'Nothing on Provo,' you said. 'Nothing.'

'I know. I'm sorry, but it couldn't be avoided. It was a one-off, I promise. Now tell me what he said.'

'He said you kidnapped his friend. Or killed him. Did you?'

'He's working for me now. Is that all?'

She smiled. 'And he called me a whore.'

Arcilla's eyes narrowed. 'Who was the man you were with?' he asked.

'One of my tricks,' she said.

'Tamara!'

'Except that you're the only one who has ever paid me,' she added.

Arcilla couldn't decide whether to hit her or try and offer comfort, so he did neither. 'Who was he?' he asked again.

She shrugged. 'An Englishman.'

'What was his name?'

'Marker.'

'Is that his family name or his given name?'

'I don't know. I never asked.'

'I don't expect you know much about him, do you?'

She smiled at him. 'No, I don't.'

He sighed. 'How long are you staying this time?' he asked.

'A few days, a few weeks . . .'

'I'll see you at dinner,' Arcilla said, and went off in search of Lozano. The secretary was in his office, tidying his desk. Arcilla told him what had happened on Provo.

'The man was just spouting off,' Lozano said quietly. 'His friend has vanished, and there's nothing he can do about it. If you take any action against him that will only add weight to his accusations.'

It was what Arcilla had already decided. 'I agree,' he said, walking across to the open window. Two storeys beneath him Calle Ocho, the main business street of Miami's Little Havana, was already lit up against the night. He remembered seeing the street for the first time, a few days after his arrival from Cuba, and thinking he had found paradise.

'But?' Lozano was asking.

His secretary knew him well. There was something not quite right about this business with Tamara. 'I don't know. Probably nothing.' He looked down at the street again, smiling to himself.

Marker and Cafell had an early-morning swim, took breakfast in the hotel restaurant, and got back to their cabin in time to set up the PRC 319 for the expected transmission from Poole.

'Proceed investigation of Arcilla boat,' the message proper began, once Marker acknowledged he was receiving. 'American help in pipeline. Will RV Miami Airport, off 14.30 departure Providenciales. Tickets waiting at airport. Stated requirement en route from Belize, ETA Florida Straits noon Sunday. Offshore rendezvous necessary. Good luck.'

Marker acknowledged once more, and the operator in Poole signed off.

'The old man's been busy,' he said.

'Good job too,' Cafell said. 'So far all I've done is take a holiday. It's been nice, but . . .'

'I get the drift,' Marker said. All he had done was tangle up his own emotions. 'I don't know about you but I fancy a couple of hours on the reef before we leave.'

'Suits me.'

They took their hired boat out one last time, but instead of exploring the reef they decided, on the recommendation of the marina boss, to visit one of the new wrecks, an eighty-foot cargo carrier which had gone down in sixty feet of water less than ten years before. It had been several years since Marker had explored a wreck, but the experience was much the same as it had ever been. Some men find mountain scenery reminds them of how unimportant their own lives are; Marker felt the same way about underwater wrecks. They were nearly always strangely haunting, as if the sea, having once reasserted its power over those who had been foolish enough to challenge it, had draped the sunken craft with living things in an effort to make it feel more at home.

Marker returned to the surface, feeling more at peace with the world than he had going down.

They returned the boat to the marina, packed and ate lunch in the hotel restaurant, then drove up to the car-hire firm, where Marker managed to convince the owner to collect his car from the airport in return for a small bonus. Once there they picked up their tickets, and Marker read a two-day-old *New York Times* while Cafell ploughed happily on through his Tom Clancy novel.

The flight was uneventful and on time. At Miami Airport they hadn't yet reached Immigration when an Afro-American naval lieutenant pulled them to one side, confirmed who they were from their passports, and told them to accompany him. Several empty corridors, a flight of steps and a ride across the tarmac later, they arrived beside a waiting McDonnell Douglas OH-6A 'Cayuse' helicopter. The officer handed Marker an envelope.

'These are your hotel reservations for tonight . . .' he began.

'Where?' Marker asked. 'Where are we going?'

The American looked at him blankly, then laughed. 'Don't you know? Key West. End of the line. Like I said, these are your hotel reservations. Tomorrow morning at eleven someone will collect you from your rooms and take you to a meeting with Vice-Admiral Baskin. OK?'

Marker put the envelope in his pocket. 'OK. Thanks.'

'My pleasure.'

The pilot was waiting in the cockpit, and they seemed to be in the air before they were settled in their seats.

The flight took less than an hour. First they passed over an endless grid of suburbs, then a vast expanse of bare grassland in which stands of trees stood out like islands. And then they were out across the ocean, with the hundred-mile chain of the Florida Keys marching along to their left, the serene waters of Florida Bay directly beneath them.

The Cayuse touched down on the Key West helipad shortly before five in the afternoon, only thirty yards or so from the car which was waiting to take them to their hotel. As they drove across the island towards the old town area the streets became increasingly distinctive, with beautiful old clapboard houses peeking out from behind an abundance of gorgeous tropical vegetation.

A couple of men walking hand in hand reminded Marker that much of the town's recent notoriety rested on the size of its gay population.

Rather disappointingly, their hotel turned out to be a modern six-storey concrete block wedged between the old town centre and the Coast Guard base. Both were visible from their fourth-storey balcony, as was a crowd of apparent revellers on the sea-front promenade almost directly beneath them. Marker asked the navy driver, who had helped them with the diving gear, what was going on.

'It's just the sunset,' he explained.

'The sunset?' Marker asked disbelievingly. The sun was indeed setting, but presumably it did that every night.

'It's a local thing,' the driver explained. 'Every evening people gather to watch it down there. Locals, tourists, everyone. When I was first posted here I thought they must be nuts. But when you think about it, it's kind of a cool idea.'

Marker and Cafell looked at each other.

'When in Rome,' the driver said. 'Anyway, I'll be back at nine in the morning, OK?'

'Sure, thanks.'

'So shall we go join the sun-worshippers?' Cafell asked once the driver was gone.

'Of course.'

They took the lift down and joined the throng, most of whom seemed to be sipping or gulping cocktails. The sunset was certainly spectacular, and when the last slice of brilliance slipped behind a distant island the crowd burst into applause.

Marker found himself thinking about Tamara Arcilla, and the smell of her hair in his face.

9

Having finished breakfast, Marker and Cafell had almost three hours to kill before their meeting with Vice-Admiral Leo Baskin. As a quick glance through the tourist brochures in the hotel lobby made clear, there were plenty of sights to see in Key West, but none that appealed to both men in equal measure. They agreed to meet back at the hotel ten minutes before the time arranged for their collection.

There was in fact only one place that Marker really wanted to see, and he spent half an hour gradually working his way towards it through the grid of sun-drenched streets. The houses and luxuriant vegetation were a feast for the eyes in themselves, and the rising heat didn't encourage haste. By the time he reached Tennessee Williams's house the sweat was lining his brow.

The playwright's former home was a modest affair, a single-storey white clapboard structure fronted by a white picket fence. The garden hosted several species of palms and palmettos, including a towering fan-shaped Traveler's tree. The house was occupied, and there was no sign or plaque to advertise its famous former owner, only the street number quoted in the guide book.

Marker had loved all the films made from Williams's plays, from the still-famous ones like *A Streetcar Named Desire* and *Cat on a Hot Tin Roof* to those that had

141

been almost forgotten, like the original *Glass Menagerie* with Jane Wyman and the young Kirk Douglas. The man had understood something about people. How something pathetic could also be noble, maybe. He was a merciful writer, Marker decided.

And a gay one, he thought, as he took a different route back towards the town centre. It was ironic that he and the seriously macho Ernest Hemingway should be fêted in the same place.

Hemingway's house was as distinguished as Williams's had been modest: a lovely two-storey mansion in Moorish-Spanish style. And it had been turned into a museum. Marker took the guided tour, and saw six-toed cats, hunting trophies, Papa's taste in furniture, and the study in which he wrote *For Whom the Bell Tolls* and the original *To Have and Have Not*. Marker had read the latter after loving the movie, and had to admit the movie was better.

Not much more than a five-minute walk away Rob Cafell was pursuing his different interests. Having already been round the Key West Lighthouse Museum, and admired the view from the newly restored tower, a hundred and ten feet high, he was now entering the portals of the oldest house in the town, a raised white clapboard building which was home to the Wreckers Museum.

Wrecking, as he had already learnt at the Lighthouse, had once been Key West's main dollar-earner. In the late eighteenth and early nineteenth centuries the poorly charted shallows and reefs of the Florida Straits had claimed ships almost weekly, and fortunes had been made by those able to salvage the cargoes. Not surprisingly the locals had not been enthusiastic lighthouse builders, and when the first major installation had been lost in a hurricane the celebrations had probably been audible in New York.

The museum rooms contained ship models, painting and ordinary household artefacts from that era. In one room a 'House-Wife's Guide' sat on the table, in another an old sailing ship's medicine chest. On the wall of the passageway had been pinned a collage of press cuttings to do with wrecks. Cafell was fascinated by all of it, and was only driven out into the back garden by the promise of more exhibits.

It was a lovely garden in itself, with well-groomed lawn and flower-beds surrounded by a variety of tropical trees. At the bottom a large shelter housed an illuminated map of local wrecks. Cafell pushed one of the buttons, and lit the spot where the *Santa Margarita* had gone down in 1554 with a cargo of gold today worth $17 million.

One day, he thought, he would really like to do some treasure hunting. Not for the treasure, but for the hunting. And the history.

He sat down on a wrought-iron garden seat and admired the garden. His mother would love this, he thought. She had always said the garden kept her sane through her husband's long absences. He thought about his parents, and how hard they were finding the process of adapting to his father's retirement. The old man's only forte these days seemed to be getting in his wife's way. Like she said: 'You would think a man who had spent half his life on submarines would know how to move around in a confined space.'

Cafell smiled to himself. They would be all right once the dust settled.

It was almost ten-thirty. He reluctantly lifted himself

out of the seat and went back inside. After signing the visitor's book and saying goodbye to the museum keeper, he walked slowly back down Duvall Street. The number of gay-looking men was quite noticeable, mostly because they all seemed to want to dress like stereotypes. Cafell was rather glad they did. It made the place seem different. Not better or worse – just different. And he liked that.

Back at the hotel he found Marker changing into a fresh set of clothes, and decided to do the same himself. On their way down to the lobby he wondered out loud whether the Americans would be expecting uniforms.

'Probably,' Marker agreed.

Their chauffeur was early, and by eleven o'clock they were being waved through the gates of the US Navy Trumbo Annexe. The car drove down between a barracks block and a docked frigate before pulling up outside an art deco-style office building. Once inside they were left in a plush waiting area, where they drew enough curious looks to make them feel like goldfish in a bowl.

After about ten minutes a young lieutenant came to deliver them to Vice-Admiral Baskin's office. The latter was not much older than they were – around thirty-eight, Marker guessed – with an open face, blue eyes and close-cropped blond hair. The man with him, a moustachioed Hispanic named Jiménez, wore the uniform of a commander in the US Coast Guard.

They all shook hands.

'So,' Baskin began, 'what can we do for the British SEALs?'

Marker smiled. 'We like to think of the SEALs as the American SBS,' he said.

Baskin grinned back. 'OK, so everyone thinks they're

144

numero uno. Now, business. Your bosses in London have asked us to fix you guys up with a boat that can tow one of your submersibles. Which is fine – we've got you a real doozy.'

'Great,' Marker said.

'And we reckoned you wouldn't want to be hauling it up and down in the elevator at your hotel, so we've found you somewhere more convenient to stay.' He beamed at them. 'It's kind of suitable, in more ways that one. It's in Marathon, which is on Key Vaca, one of the middle keys, about fifty miles east of here. Closer to where your friend is treasure hunting. The house has cable TV, gym, swimming pool – you name it. There's a dock for the boat. And it's private – the neighbours are a long way off. The place used to belong to one of the Colombian cartels, but it was confiscated when the police busted the small fry whose name was on the deed.'

'Sounds ideal,' Marker agreed.

'That's OK then. Next item. Jorge?'

The Coast Guard man came to life. 'London asked us about a week ago for a discreet check on the Arcilla boat. Because of the discreet tag, we decided not to put it under continuous surveillance, but we've had a surface watch in force on and off for several days and through most of the nights. And we filled that out with aerial and satellite recon, so we don't think we can have missed much. And' – he entwined his fingers in front of his chest – 'it *looks* like they're doing what they claim to be doing.'

'What about the submarine?' Cafell asked.

'It's there. And it stays there . . .'

'Are you sure?'

'It was the first thing we looked for. For the obvious

reasons. We don't know the exact maximum speed it is capable of, but even at twenty knots – which I am sure you will consider outside the range of what is possible . . .'

The SBS men nodded.

'Even at that speed it would need ten hours to make a round trip to either US coastal waters or the Bahamas, and the longest interval between sightings which we have is four hours.' He shrugged. 'So you see . . .'

'Could it be meeting up with another boat?' Cafell asked.

'It could, but what would be the point? Why use a submarine at all if you don't intend to use it where it really matters, in coastal waters?'

The argument seemed unanswerable.

'What about the helicopter?' Marker asked.

'It only paid the one visit, on the Thursday night, which you already know about. It was there for about an hour and a half, sitting on the floating helipad they have out there, unloading supplies and taking on fuel.'

'And then it headed back towards the Turks and Caicos?'

'Yes.'

'A mystery,' Cafell murmured.

'Maybe you boys'll have to pay a visit to Mr Arcilla's boat,' Baskin said with an easy smile.

'Maybe,' Marker agreed. He had the unpleasant feeling that Baskin saw him and Rob as mercenaries on loan from the British government. Well, he would take the goodies that were on offer, and as long as their interests coincided he would play the grateful ally, but should those interests ever diverge then the Americans would find out that the SBS were not for sale. 'One more thing,' he said. 'We were briefed on recent history as far as the local drug traffic's concerned, but if you could give us some idea of the current state of play.'

Baskin deferred to Jiménez, who thought for a moment before speaking. 'It's hard to say,' he admitted. 'Superficially, we're going through a good patch. We're using more aggressive tactics, and the interdiction rate is the highest it's ever been. I'm not saying we manage to check out every boat or plane that enters our waters or airspace, but these days at least the bastards know they're taking a big risk when they try. Of course this has meant a shift in the most-favoured routes, and now more stuff is coming in across the Mexican land border . . .'

'You put a finger in one hole, and the stuff comes out of another one.'

'Something like that.'

'What about the local politics?' Marker asked. 'Haiti, for example.'

'What about it?' Baskin asked defensively.

'Is there any evidence of official involvement in the drug trade – by the military, maybe?'

'None that I'm aware of,' Baskin said. Jiménez just shook his head.

Marker had the feeling he was stepping on toes, though he couldn't see why. For several months the Americans had been threatening to invade Haiti and restore the exiled President Aristide, and the notion that they had no intelligence of what was going on inside the country was ludicrous.

Maybe they knew too much, he realized. Maybe there were political reasons why they needed Haitians whom they knew to be involved in illegal activities. That's all we need, Marker thought – to discover that the CIA are behind Arcilla. He dismissed the thought. The Americans – or at least some of them – definitely wanted Arcilla dealt with.

'Any other questions?' Baskin was asking cheerfully.

Marker looked at Cafell, who shook his head. The four men got to their feet and shook hands again. 'And of course we have a car for you,' was Baskin's parting shot.

The young lieutenant who had escorted them to Baskin's office was waiting outside to show them their new means of transport. As they walked round the back of the building he handed over the keys to the SBS men's new home, car and boat, and a sheet of paper containing names, contact numbers and wavelengths for when the need arose. The car was a bottle-green Nissan Bluebird.

The lieutenant travelled with them as far as the base gate, and told them that if there was anything else they wanted they only had to call and ask.

'This is what I call hospitality,' Cafell said, as he checked one of the maps which had been provided for the quickest route to their hotel. 'And you're supposed to drive on the right,' he reminded Marker, as a taxi went honking past, missing the Nissan's wing by inches.

They picked up their gear at the hotel, and drove east out of Key West along a wide road lined with junk-food outlets, miniature golf courses and discount warehouses. A sign told them it was forty miles to Marathon.

It was a beautiful day, with fluffy white clouds sailing across the sky to their left, and the sun shining down out of a clear blue sky to their right. The prominent mile markers on the single highway were not only there to indicate distances travelled, but also, as Cafell soon discovered, formed the crucial element in any address on the Florida Keys. 'See,' he explained to Marker, 'there's a restaurant advertised here and the address is just "45.3". Everything is on the same highway, for a hundred miles.'

'It's not what you'd call beautiful, is it?' Marker observed.

'According to the guide book it gets better as you travel east,' Cafell told him.

'Good.'

They were traversing the fourth or fifth key by now, and so far the sea had been mostly hidden behind bushes, run-down buildings and the huge concrete poles by the side of the highway which carried both power lines and telephone wires.

Suddenly they were on a long bridge, sweeping out across a wide channel, with panoramic views of the bay and straits to either side. The next key was more the way Marker had imagined them. The highway was lined with palm trees, the neon motel signs adorned with crowns of bougainvillaea and hibiscus. Boats bobbed at anchor behind bait and tackle shops, and there were tantalizing glimpses of white-sand beaches lapped by turquoise water. The only possible catch was evident in one of the neon names – the Hurricane Resort Motel. Marker remembered the hurricane in *Key Largo*, one of his favourite films.

'We're coming to the Seven Mile Bridge,' Cafell said, and a few seconds later they were on it. Double yellow lines divided the road between its beige concrete walls, making it seem like an old-fashioned racing track. A hundred yards or so to the left, the old railway bridge ran a parallel course. The two structures seemed almost to hang in space, somewhere between the sea and the sky.

'Key Vaca's next,' Cafell said. 'Look for 47.7.'

They were hardly off the bridge when the turn-off appeared. It was no more than a rough track, winding down from the highway through a stand of royal palms and past two other entrances before ending at the gates of Buena Vista.

Cafell got out and unlocked the gates for Marker to drive through.

The house was a modern, white-painted, one-storey building with a sun terrace. Steps led through more palms to where a picnic table had been placed near the water's edge. A hammock hung between two of the palms.

Close by, the upright arm of a T-shaped jetty ran some thirty yards out into the Florida Straits. A boat was docked along the cross arm. The sixty-foot cabin cruiser, gleaming white with a pale-blue trim, was named the *Slipstream Queen*. It looked fast, Marker thought.

'It'll have to do,' Cafell said sarcastically.

They went aboard. There were two cabins with four bunks each, a lounge area, galley, small bathroom and ample storage space, most of it filled with fishing tackle. On the bridge they found a folder containing Coast Guard charts of the local waters. The boat manufacturer's manual was also prominently in evidence, but as far as Marker could tell the controls all seemed straightforward.

'I wonder why they bothered with the house,' he murmured.

'There's no TV here,' Cafell told him.

They went back ashore and walked up to the house,

noting the drums of marine fuel which had been stacked in the adjoining garage.

'I don't want to be in Poole when the bill for this lot arrives,' Marker said.

The house offered more of the same: crisp sheets, a full refrigerator and drinks cabinet, a massive stereo TV. The two men opened up a huge bag of corn chips, cracked open cans of cold beer, and took it all out to the terrace, where they lowered themselves into reclining chairs, toasted their allies, and considered the next step.

'I've got a feeling our hosts have fucked up over the submarine business,' Cafell said. 'I mean, they've got boats watching, planes watching, satellites watching – it sounds like a case of too many watchers spoiling the broth to me.'

'Broth?' Marker repeated doubtfully.

Cafell threw a corn chip at him.

'Maybe,' Marker agreed, 'but I wouldn't bet on it. Tomorrow we'll go and have a look for ourselves, unless you can think of a good reason for going out there tonight.'

Cafell considered. 'No,' he said eventually. 'I think we should keep a night visit in reserve. Especially since you forgot to ask the Yanks what sort of warning system the *Tiburón Blanco* has.'

'I didn't forget – I already knew. Franklin told me the boat has radar.'

'Then I think our first approach should be as innocent-looking as we can make it. We should let them see us coming. I can be happily fishing, and you can be doing your camp Humphrey Bogart impersonation on the bridge.'

Marker nodded. 'Two men in a boat,' he said.

'We should get a dog from somewhere,' Cafell decided.

Marker grinned. 'Well, while you're out looking for one I'm going to tell the boss what we're planning. Just in case the opposition doesn't buy our innocent routine, and decides to get nasty when there are no witnesses around.'

'Good point,' Cafell agreed through a mouthful of corn chips. 'And while you're at it, you can ask him where the famous frigate's got to. Tell the boss we've seen *Miami Vice*, we know what we're up against, and two handguns doesn't seem like an adequate arsenal.'

Marker went to collect the radio, set it up on the terrace and sent the report, thinking how strange it felt to be using it in such surroundings. He had typed out messages on windswept Norwegian glaciers and in flooded holes on the sides of Falklands hills, but never before in the shade of palms on a rich man's patio.

When he had finished they took the *Slipstream Queen* a little way out to sea, just to find out how she handled. Like a dream was the answer, and a speedy one at that. After tying up the boat, they took a swim. Then, with the light beginning to fade, they walked back up to the highway, crossed it, and found their way down to the shore of the bay. The sunset was as stunning as it had been the night before, and this time graced by the antics of the local pelican, who flew to and fro along the shore in front of them, as if he was auditioning for a part in a tourist board ad.

Back at the house they tried in vain to find something worth watching on one of the TV's sixty-four channels. They then considered microwaving a couple of the TV dinners from the freezer, before deciding that their culinary expectations had been raised by the days on Provo. Relieved at finding an excuse to indulge their restlessness the two men climbed back into the car and headed east once more, Marker at the wheel and Cafell trying to make sense of the guide book.

The road was reasonably busy, causing Marker to wonder how bad it got during the tourist season.

'Seen the film *The African Queen*?' Marker asked.

Cafell shook his head. Marker looked at him with disbelief. 'You haven't!? Well, you should. It's a classic. Anyway it was a boat. They've got the original here. It's on Key Largo, I think. That's another one you should see. Can you see it in that book of yours?'

Within seconds Cafell had found the place. 'Yeah, it's right by the Holiday Inn. But Key Largo's another thirty miles.'

'We've got all night.'

'I'm hungry.'

'I thought you said it was near a Holiday Inn.'

They arrived a little over half an hour later, and found the original *African Queen* tied up at the dock which ran alongside the restaurant's parking lot. It looked smaller than it had in the film, Marker decided, as he tried to imagine Bogart and Hepburn sitting aboard. There was the boiler Bogart used to kickstart. It was all very strange, looking down at a craft which he had only ever seen in the context of an African river, and which now sat in the shadow of a modern hotel, close by a modern highway.

He couldn't have been more than seven when he had first seen the film. Now, staring down at the boat, he had an almost overwhelming feeling that he had lost something, and that there was no way he would ever get it back. This might be the real *African Queen* in one way, but in another it was no more than an echo of the real thing. The film's final scene on the German boat flashed through his mind, and then his marriage to Penny on that rainy day in Dorchester.

He turned away from the boat. 'Let's eat,' he told the waiting Cafell.

Russell lay awake, listening to the steady hum of the air-conditioner and the random song of the cicadas. It was gone three in the morning, and the excess of booze which had put him out like a light had refused to leave him in this blissful state. His mouth felt like someone had filled it with sand, but he couldn't persuade his legs to go and fetch him a long, non-alcoholic drink.

He was feeling sorry for himself. And sorry for himself that he was feeling sorry for himself.

A racking cough erupted in his throat, and finally forced him up off the bed and into the kitchen. He took the half jug of fresh mango juice out of the fridge and drank straight from it. It was far too sweet, but it soothed his throat. Russell wiped his lips with the back of his hand and sat down in the nearest chair.

Another month of this, he thought, and I'll be drinking as much as that bastard Bodin. And probably forgetting to suture some kid's artery.

There was no getting round it – he had to get out of this place. Up until the previous Friday he had been doing a fair job of convincing himself that he had a duty to stay and help Emelisse. An attempted escape, he had kept telling himself, would be selfish as well as dangerous.

The girl's death had not destroyed the argument, but it had certainly weakened it. If he could get away, and expose this place for what it was, there would be an outcry. It wouldn't matter a damn how many influential friends Joutard had in Port au Prince – someone would close him down. And there would be no more teenagers dying on Bodin's operating table.

That was the optimistic view. Russell took another swig of the mango juice, and stared at the wall. A pessimist might predict that Joutard would react to the threat of imminent closure by liquidating all his human assets in one fell swoop. And become the first millionaire bone salesman.

Russell looked at the floor. He couldn't make a break for it without offering to take her along, even though he was ninety-nine per cent certain she would refuse. 'No, make that a hundred per cent,' he murmured out loud. She couldn't leave her orphans to the mercy of Joutard, Calderón and Bodin.

So how could he? 'Self-preservation,' he told the floor. If he didn't escape, then sooner or later he was going to die here. And so, in all likelihood, were the others. If for some reason the boom came down on the enterprise there was no way Joutard was going to be handing out fat redundancy cheques and gold watches for devoted service. In fact the logical way to close this business down was to sell off first the patients and then the doctors, organ by organ, bone by bone. Two birds with one scalpel – they would be making money out of destroying evidence.

No, he was going to get out, or at least have a shot at it. But he wouldn't tell her yet, not until he was ready.

Next morning the *Slipstream Queen* was already twenty miles south of the Keys when the appointed time for the transmission from Poole arrived. This was deliberate on Marker's part – being out on the ocean, away from prying ears, would make it possible to conduct a normal conversation with the CO.

In fact there was not much to say. Colhoun approved of their plan of action, such as it was. 'The next step will be the tricky one,' he advised, 'depending of course on whether you find out anything. If you do, then one of the most difficult decisions we'll have to take is how much to tell the Americans.'

Cafell raised an eyebrow, but Marker immediately knew what he meant. 'Russell's just a name to them,' he agreed.

'Exactly. Assuming he's alive, I want you to have at least one stab at getting him out of the firing-line before our friends go in with all guns blazing.'

'Agreed, though at the moment I have my doubts as to whether we will find out anything.'

'Take it as it comes,' Colhoun said tritely. 'The "famous frigate", by the way, will be waiting for you tonight, from 19.00 hours, at . . .' He reeled off a series of nautical coordinates, which Cafell took down. 'That's about thirty miles west of our friend's treasure hunt,' he added. 'They have a submersible for you, an electric torpedo, a couple of Kleppers, and the guns you asked for. And they're not going to wander far in the next week or so, just in case . . .'

'Our own frigate on call,' Cafell murmured to himself.

After the connection had been broken, he and Marker studied the relevant chart once more. A cross marked the location of the *Tiburón Blanco*. The question was where they should drop their own anchor.

'If we're pretending to be fishermen then almost anywhere will do,' Cafell said, 'but if we're in the diving business, then we should be somewhere above the edge of this reef.' He ran a finger along the undersea contour line.

'Fishing's a better idea,' Marker said. 'If they see us in diving suits they may start looking for us under their boat.'

'OK, then it's just a matter of how far off we want to be.'

'Far enough not to make them suspicious, close enough to be able to see something. A mile sound too far?'

'Slightly. Those binoculars aren't that good. Make it a thousand yards.'

'We don't need to check their nose-picking style.'

'We don't know what we want to check. If we're as careful as the Yanks must have been we'll end up with what they got – which was nothing.'

Marker grimaced. 'Maybe there's nothing to get. But OK, a thousand yards. Which direction?'

Cafell thought about it. 'South is the obvious bet – between them and the sun. But . . .'

'To anyone with a suspicious mind that'll look a bit too calculated.'

'Yeah. West is the next best bet.'

'Let's go with that.' Marker straightened and yawned.

'I'll get the tub moving again,' said Cafell, moving across to the controls. 'Why don't you make us some more coffee?' he added over his shoulder.

Marker eyed his partner's bare back, bare legs, and the hideous Bermuda shorts which filled the space in between. It was as if some deranged fashion designer had finally found the secret of how to use every clashing fluorescent colour known to man in a few square inches of cloth.

'You do look the part,' Marker admitted.
'The dashing captain or the keen fisherman?'
'The rich prat.'

The sun was almost at its zenith when they had their first sighting of the *Tiburón Blanco*, a dot on the distant horizon, in the gap between the thin lines which marked the two Muertos Cays. The two boats were not alone on the ocean: doing a slow 360-degree turn in the stern, Marker counted twelve others visible to the naked eye. True, most of them were in motion, but at least three seemed to be anchored for one reason or another in the shallow waters of the Cay Sal Bank. Establishing a presence within sight of Arcilla's boat would not seem as automatically suspicious as they had feared it would.

Cafell took the boat slowly towards the position they had decided on, as if he was engaged in looking for the perfect spot. As they approached the more westerly of the two small and barren cays the water grew increasingly clear. Even so, Marker, leaning over the side of the boat as part of the same pantomime, could not make out the bottom. The slope beneath them was steep.

It was, Marker admitted to himself, a good spot for treasure hunting. A wreck that had somehow been snagged near the top of this undersea slope would only recently, with the advances in underwater research technology, have become accessible. Maybe Arcilla really had found a fortune in gold.

As Cafell cut the engines he went forward to lower the anchor, and cast a casual glance over the flat blue sea towards the distant *Tiburón Blanco*. No doubt someone on board Arcilla's boat had been watching them ever since they hove into view. And now it was clear that they were staying for a while the observation would become all the more intense.

'If we're not diving today we can have a beer,' he told Cafell.

His partner obliged, returning from the galley with a couple of bottles. The two men settled into canvas seats in the shade of the awning and appreciatively sipped at the ice-cold beers. Marker had his back to the other boat, Cafell his profile.

'Let's hope they don't have a telescopic microphone,' Marker muttered.

'So what's the next step?' Cafell asked.

'We fish for a while. Then you can head indoors and start taking a closer look at them. After half an hour you can come back out with a couple of microwaved meals, as if you've been cooking.'

'Sounds good to me.'

They finished the beers, collected two more cans, and set themselves up in the stern with the simplest fishing rods they could find among the boat's ample supply. Cafell had not fished for many years, and his enthusiasm for the sport was not much greater than Marker's, who had never held a rod in his life.

The fish didn't seem to realize this, and each man caught a sizeable specimen within the first half hour. They threw them contemptuously back into the sea, had another apparent can of beer – Cafell filled two empties with water – and laughed uproariously at non-existent jokes. A couple of bikini-clad beauties, Marker thought, would have completed the impression they were trying to create.

Cafell got up to go inside, and, with a theatrical

drunken stumble, disappeared from view. He walked through the lounge area and into the galley, where the steam vent had been chosen as the best available observation point. He collected the sheet of gauze veil from the table, and wrapped it around the telescope. This would remove the chances of tell-tale reflective flash with hardly any hindrance to his vision. Kneeling on the counter, he made himself as comfortable as possible and applied the telescope to one of the vent's narrow apertures.

At first he could see only empty sea and sky, but a slight shift to the left brought the *Tiburón Blanco* into view. It more than filled the telescope's field of vision, and Cafell could read the name painted on the bow without difficulty. Behind it, the floating helipad hardly seemed to move in the water.

The boat itself was big, but its lines were graceful enough. Examining it from bow to stern, Cafell counted five men in view, all of whom looked Hispanic. Two of them, one wearing a captain's cap, were talking together in the enclosed bridge; another two, both wearing diving suits but bareheaded, were sitting in the stern taking it easy. Beside them, but not apparently part of their conversation, another man sat with a pair of binoculars around his neck and a shoulder holster draped loosely across one shoulder. As Cafell examined him, the man picked up the binoculars and took a cursory look across the water at the *Slipstream Queen*.

Cafell froze, but if the man had seen anything significant he gave no sign of it. He let the binoculars dangle once more against his matted chest and lit a cigarette.

This scene remained basically unchanged for the

next half hour, and Cafell was about to abandon the observation for lunch when a flurry of movement in the water below the other boat caught his eye. Almost immediately a long, dark shape rose up into view – the submarine.

It was about twenty feet long, and cylindrical. Two bulbous growths had been added: one where the conning-tower on a larger submarine might have been, the other at what was presumably the bow end. This was divided into two large convex windows, which gave the whole craft an insect-like air. There were also large windows in the flanks, through which Cafell could see movement.

Four of the five men on deck were now looking down over the side, while the fifth had resumed scanning the *Slipstream Queen* through his binoculars. A hatch swung open in the top of the bulb on the roof, and a man in a diving suit clambered out through it, swung himself down on to the rungs welded into the side of the boat alongside, and climbed aboard. Another man followed him.

The central bulb had to be a small escape hatch, Cafell figured. Hence the diving suits. It was hard to imagine a craft better suited to treasure hunting.

Its two crewmen had disappeared inside the *Tiburón Blanco*, as had the two who had been relaxing. Even the man with the binoculars had vanished. They were all having lunch, Cafell guessed. He clambered down, found a couple of packets to microwave, and went back to the hatchway leading out to the deck. 'Come and take a look,' he said.

Marker followed him through to the galley, lifted himself up on to the counter and examined boat and submarine through the telescope. He was as impressed by both as Cafell had been. 'I'd like to get a closer look at that submarine,' he said. There were no markings to indicate its Soviet origin – only an outsize number three between the two observation windows on the side.

Nick Russell must have had a much closer view of it in the marina on Provo. But what could he have seen to provoke his own kidnapping?

The microwave pinged to announce lunch. The two men sat either side of the tiny table staring at the little plastic trays containing portions of Chicken Mediterranean on wild rice, carrots and broccoli, and raspberry cobbler. Cafell's cobbler had oozed into the chicken compartment during the cooking process.

It didn't taste bad. It hardly tasted at all.

Marker slid his tray into the rubbish container. 'At least there's no washing up,' he said. 'What do you think about paying them a visit?'

'An announced visit?'

'Yeah.'

'What excuse are we going to use? That we want to borrow some sugar?'

'I've heard worse.'

Cafell switched tack. 'What's the purpose of the exercise? What are you hoping to find out?'

Marker shrugged. 'No idea. Something. Anything.' He leant forward, arms on the table. 'At least we'll get some idea of who we're dealing with. If they really are treasure hunting . . .'

'They'll be paranoid as hell. The guy watching us through the binoculars was carrying a gun . . .'

'Suspicious.'

'Not really. If they think they're sitting on millions in gold bullion, then they would be idiots not to lay on some sort of protection for themselves, wouldn't they?'

'Yeah, OK. You don't like the idea?'

'Not a lot. Whatever excuse we make, it's going to look like we're snooping.'

'If we went and introduced ourselves then at least they would know it wasn't the US Coast Guard watching them.'

'I still don't like it.'

Marker sighed. 'Yeah, you're probably right. I'm just getting itchy.'

'I know what you mean. We'd better get back outside.'

They spent the afternoon alternating fishing with sleeping, keeping both a casual watch and an occasional telescopic eye on the *Tiburón Blanco*. The second crew took the submarine back down soon after two, and reappeared three and a half hours later, by which time the sun was falling rapidly towards the western horizon.

The two SBS men upped anchor and set a course towards it. An hour later, as the last light of the day hung like a luminous curtain across the western horizon, they made first visual contact with Her Majesty's frigate *Argyll*.

Half an hour later Marker was climbing up the rope ladder that had been thrown down to him. The captain greeted him warmly and offered the hospitality of the mess, which Marker declined on grounds of security. The shorter the rendezvous was, the less chance it would be observed.

The Type 23 frigate's winch was already lowering the Vickers Pisces submersible, and in the calm sea it only took a few minutes to attach the tow-line from the *Slipstream Queen*. The electric torpedo and Kleppers followed, straight on to the cabin cruiser's stern deck.

All that remained was the transfer of one large canvas bag, the contents of which Marker checked through in front of the captain. The two MP5s with extra ammo were there, and the two harpoon guns. But no stun grenades.

'We don't have much need of them out here,' the captain told him.

'Let's hope not,' Marker said equably.

The bag was lowered to Cafell in the cabin cruiser below.

'Good hunting,' the captain said, as Marker swung himself back over the side. 'And one day perhaps you can let me know what it was all about.'

Marker grinned and disappeared from sight.

Three hours later they were tying up the *Slipstream Queen* at the Key Vaca dock, having already manoeuvred the Vickers submersible around to the shore side of the jetty arm. Though hardly hidden from prying eyes, it could not be seen from either the open sea or the adjoining properties.

The two men felt both exhausted and vaguely depressed. They might have all the equipment they had asked for, but what were they going to do with it? The day's observation of the Arcilla boat had yielded no new information, and no plan had come to mind which might offer more. If the worst came to the worst they could always invite themselves aboard the *Tiburón Blanco* and see what happened, but such a tactic seemed unlikely to succeed, likely to be dangerous.

'It might look better in the morning,' Cafell said. 'I'm going to bed.'

Marker stayed up another half hour watching a soap on TV, and then reluctantly followed suit. But sleep wouldn't come, and he found himself drifting almost helplessly through angry memories of the last few days of his marriage. How long was this going to go on, he asked himself. Until he found someone else? Certainly after he slept with someone else – Tamara had been proof of that. He had never enjoyed such powerful sex in his life, and yet Penny seemed to loom even larger in his mind. He felt like an animal in a trap, whose struggles to break free only increased the pain.

Two women, he thought sleepily. Two men in a boat. Two submarines. The number three on the side.

Marker jerked himself up on to his elbows. That was it! That was how they did it. He levered himself into a sitting position on the side of the bed and reached for his shorts. He thought about waking Cafell but decided there was no point.

It was about five in the morning in Poole. He collected the keys to the boat, and walked across the sun terrace and up to the path which led to the jetty. The slimmest of crescent moons had risen in the last hour, and was throwing a thin line of yellow-cream light across the rippling water.

He recovered the PRC 319 from the locker in which it had been stowed, and climbed on to the cabin cruiser's roof. After getting an acknowledgement from the duty officer he applied his right index finger to the little keypad for several minutes, watching the letters slip past in the liquid crystal display. He told Colhoun what he had guessed, and suggested one possible source of confirmation. Finally, on the working assumption that he had guessed right, he asked the CO for another PRC 319, and a new, more specialized piece of equipment, to be flown out from England as soon as possible.

He then depressed the key which transmitted the

message in a single burst, carefully refolded the antenna, and packed up the small set.

He didn't go in immediately, preferring to sit awhile on the cabin cruiser's roof, staring out along the narrow swathe of moonlit ocean. For the first time in several days Marker felt a sense of well-being within himself, and he was not about to waste it in sleep.

10

Cafell took one look at his partner and wondered what had happened. Marker had not only made breakfast – fruit juice, pancakes, waffles and coffee – but had also shaved for the first time in four days. Since his last meeting with the Arcilla woman, in fact. He even had a smile on his face.

'What are you looking so cheerful about?' Cafell asked, picking up a glass of orange juice.

'Do you remember that moment on the SC1 course when they remind you that it's an officer's duty to have brilliant inspirations?'

'No. You just made it up.'

Marker grinned at him.

Cafell sighed and reached for the maple syrup. 'You've had one, I take it.'

'Let me ask you a question. Why would someone paint a large number three on something they only have one of?'

Cafell thought about it, his fork poised above the pancake. 'Good question,' he said. His eyes widened momentarily. 'Are you suggesting they have three of them?'

Marker smiled. 'No. You're looking at it the wrong way round.'

Cafell inserted a wodge of pancake between his lips and chewed. 'I don't . . .' he began to say, then his eyes widened again.

'Yeah,' Marker said. 'They have two of them, and they both have the same number. The whole point of the number is to make anyone watching believe that they're seeing the same submarine. As long as no one sees both submarines at once . . .'

'It's a great idea, but what proof do you have?'

'Absolutely none. But it fits, doesn't it. Who would know? There's only the Russian who brought them out here, and he got conveniently blown away . . .'

'And maybe that's what Nick Russell saw, that evening in the marina. Maybe someone overheard him talking about it in the bar. Or maybe someone saw him under the boat – that must be where they keep the second one.'

'Maybe. You remember *Thunderball*?'

'I saw the film.'

'Well, in the book – it must be in the film – the big villain's boat has an underwater hatch. Bond nearly got eaten by a barracuda checking it out.'

'Sounds familiar. But our chum Fidel would need a hell of a big hatch to take that sub of his. And if he has one then what could Russell have seen?'

'Good point. I hope you're right, because according to the master plan we need access to both subs.'

'Ah,' Cafell said, 'the master plan. Are you going to fill me in on the details by any chance?'

Marker looked at his watch. 'In a bit. The boss should be coming through in a few minutes. I called him last night with a couple of requests.'

I see,' Cafell said, following Marker out on to the terrace and watching as he prepared the PRC 319 for reception. 'Did anything else happen while I was asleep?'

'One of those supermodels came round to see you

– I didn't get her name. I told her you couldn't be disturbed.'

Cafell laughed.

Letters started marching across the liquid crystal display.

Marker acknowledged and waited for the Poole operator to send Colhoun's reply.

'Two, repeat two, submarines,' it began, 'missing Murmansk naval research. Fifty per cent reliable technical estimates suggest range 200 miles, subsurface max speed twenty knots. Items requested arrive Miami 18.15 hours. Contact airport FBI office Jim Brandon. Do you require reinforcements?'

Marker gave Cafell a questioning look.

'Not yet,' the younger man decided.

'Agreed,' Marker said, and sent the appropriate reply.

'So you were right,' Cafell said, as he watched him pack up the set.

'You doubted me?'

'The thought did cross my mind that you'd got everything confused with some film you'd seen.'

'Perish the thought.'

'So how about telling me the master plan? I already know what my role will be – I'll be doing the thinking, right?'

'Something like that. I . . .'

'Incidentally,' Cafell went on, 'I find those estimates hard to believe, particularly the speed. Our little beauty can hardly manage half that.'

'Maybe that's why Arcilla went to such trouble to get hold of them.'

'Yeah. And there's not much call for speed in treasure hunting . . .' He stopped suddenly, having just remembered something. 'What items have you requested?' he asked Marker.

'A second one of these,' he said, tapping the radio. 'And a tracking system . . .'

'More James Bond.'

Marker smiled. 'Come and take a look at the map,' he said.

Cafell followed him down the jetty and on to the *Slipstream Queen*.

'The way I work it out,' Marker said, opening up the map, 'the helicopter leaves Provo at around six-thirty in the evening – at least it has on its last two trips – picks up whatever it picks up en route and delivers it to the *Tiburón Blanco* sometime around eleven. The Muertos Cays are about seventy miles from here and another thirty or so from the mainland coast. At twenty knots the sub would have no trouble reaching either long before dawn.' He looked up at Cafell. 'So the radio's for us, because today you're taking the one we have to Frankie. The bugs are for Fidel's two submarines. The idea being that when Frankie sends word that the helicopter has left Provo we take the *Queen* out ten miles or so and wait for a little dot to appear on our screen. And then we follow it to wherever it's going.'

Cafell grinned at him. 'Now that's what I call a master plan.'

It was a hundred and ten miles to Miami, and Marker drove as fast as the traffic allowed, anxious that Cafell should not miss the only plane of the day to Providenciales.

The fifty-mile section between Marathon and Key Largo, which they had only previously traversed by night, was as attractive as the Keys' reputation claimed. Both ocean and bay were studded with pleasure boats, the motels seemed to strike the right balance between seedy nostalgia and soulless modernity, and the bright colours of the foliage blazed in the sunshine. Marker found himself thinking he would like to come back for a real holiday.

Two-thirds of the way down Key Largo the highway took an abrupt turn to the left and headed out along a causeway towards the mainland. As the ocean receded from sight the scenery grew less interesting, with only scrub and telephone poles breaking the flat horizon.

'OK,' Cafell said. 'Some questions. Do you know what the range of the tracking system is?'

'I'm not sure. I seem to remember that it's around thirty miles, but that may be optimistic.'

Cafell drew a rough circle on the map which was balanced on his knees. 'Even if you're right, and assuming the sub will head for the US mainland rather than the Bahamas, we'll have to narrow the angle a lot more than you suggested if we want to be certain of picking up the signal.'

'OK,' Marker said equably.

'Which leads to another question. How are we planning to follow these guys, in the *Queen* or the Vickers?'

'I think we have to play that by ear. If those estimates on the Soviet sub are even half right the Vickers is too slow to keep us in contact for more than an hour or so. And in any case, it only has a range of about seventy miles. We don't want to strand ourselves somewhere with no way of getting back to the boat.'

'Maybe one of us should stay in the boat. One man can handle those subs at a pinch.'

'At a pinch, maybe. I'd rather we were both in the same boat – literally – when we get to wherever it is we're going. It'll give us more flexibility.'

'You mean you want to jump out and have fun while I keep the motor running for you.'

Marker smiled.

'What about our gracious hosts?' Cafell asked. 'Do we tell them anything? They're likely to be pissed off if we don't.'

'Only if they find out. And anyway, as of this moment we still don't *know* that the trail will end on US soil.'

'Right,' Cafell agreed, as Marker sped past a camper in a no-passing section, 'and in the meantime at least you're giving their car a thorough test drive.'

They reached the airport with fifteen minutes to spare, and Cafell went straight through the international departures gate, carrying only the PRC 319 in a plastic bag. Marker checked the time of his partner's return from Provo and visited the British Airways desk for an update on the flight from London. It had taken off on time from Heathrow.

He went back out to the car and sat behind the wheel, wondering how best to spend the next six and a half hours. He would rather have done Cafell's job, but after the staged confrontation at the Ocean View hotel it didn't seem sensible for him to have any more contact with Worrell Franklin than was necessary.

'So go and see Miami,' he murmured to himself. At least he wasn't in a hire car, so the chances of being taken for a tourist and shot had to be better than fifty-fifty.

He followed the signs for Downtown out of the airport and found himself driving down an eight-lane freeway towards the usual clump of high-rise towers. Marker had been to America twice before – for a whole summer as a sixteen-year-old, when his parents were touring with a Shakespearian company, and for a couple of weeks in California with Penny about halfway through their eight-year marriage. There was a lot he had liked, and a lot that he hadn't. Sharing a concrete ribbon with a bunch of people who talked into their car phones as they swapped lanes at high speed came into the latter category. So did the idea of naming the damn thing the Dolphin Expressway. No dolphin of Marker's acquaintance would have been seen dead on it.

The clump of towers was appreciably nearer when an exit sign for Little Havana caught his attention. That was where Arcilla hung out when he was in Miami, which seemed to be most of the time. Marker took the ramp and dipped into his memory for the address which had been mentioned in the American briefing report. Calle Ocho, he remembered. Eighth Street. There hadn't been a number.

The street wasn't hard to find. He drove slowly down it, staring out at the thronging pavements and impressive buildings. Little Havana was an apt enough name – it certainly bore no resemblance to any part of America that Marker had seen before. Several of the buildings clearly dated from the art deco era, but over this Anglo-Saxon skeleton the Cuban exile community had draped their own flesh and blood. The faces were all black or Hispanic, the atmosphere an aggressive blend of Mediterranean and Caribbean. The signs all seemed to be in Spanish. In fact the only English word Marker could see was 'burger'.

A car pulling out into the traffic directly in front of him opened up a parking bay. He pulled over, inserted a couple of quarters in the meter, and walked on in the same direction until he found a coffee bar with tables by the window. He bought a cup of coffee just to get a seat, and found it was the most delicious he had ever tasted. He ordered another, this time with a roast beef sandwich, and sat there watching the Cuban-American world go by.

He was looking at the woman for a couple of seconds before he realized it was her. She had come out of a building on the other side of the street, and had stood outside the glass doors while the man with her finished saying something to someone inside.

She was wearing a short, primrose-coloured dress, a wide-brimmed hat of the same shade, and brown thong sandals. Marker felt an involuntary spasm in his groin as he looked at her.

He concentrated on the man. The photo they had seen at Poole hadn't really done Arcilla justice. Though the face looked much the same he looked taller than Marker had imagined. And there was an air of confidence about the man which no photograph could reproduce. The clothes were both well chosen and beautifully cut. Crockett and Tubbs would have been proud to wear them.

From Castro's version of borstal to this must have been a hell of a long journey, Marker thought. He remembered a history teacher at school arguing that most of humanity's woes could be traced to the widening gap between a caveman's emotions and modern man's ability to transform his environment. Mankind was still swinging a blunt club, only nowadays it was big enough to pulverize an entire rainforest.

And maybe the same principle held true for Arcilla and his sister. Between their Cuban origins and the world they now moved in there was no natural meeting ground. Something somewhere had been bound to get warped.

They were walking away. Marker slid off his stool and

left the café intent on pursuit, but before he had gone ten yards the couple disappeared through the door of a restaurant on the other side of the street. For a moment he felt disappointed, but as he thought about it the full stupidity of trying to follow them became apparent. If she had recognized him there would have been no way he could have explained his presence in Little Havana. At best their whole cover would have been blown; at worst he would have been bundled into a convenient alleyway, killed, and thrown in a skip.

In fact, coming to the area had been a mistake in itself. He was letting his cock do the thinking, rather than his brain. Feeling more than a little disappointed with himself, Marker walked quickly back to his car and took the first road heading east.

He spent the rest of his allotted hours behaving like a conventional tourist, taking a leisurely stroll through the art deco splendours of Miami Beach before taking a siesta on the beach itself. The evening rush hour was worse than he had expected, and the British Airways flight had already arrived when he finally reached the airport. Cafell was waiting for him in the agreed bar, and reported no problems in delivering the radio to Franklin. The ex-SAS man, according to Cafell, had 'looked like Fergie with a new toe to suck'. And he would be watching for helicopter departures from Arcilla's villa each evening until further notice.

The next job was to find the FBI office, which proved surprisingly simple. Agent Brandon, an enormous man dressed in white from head to foot, was expecting them, the bulky package prominent on his desk. Though obviously irritated by the fact that no one had considered it necessary to burden him with knowledge of what it contained, he signed the package over to them with no more than the usual surliness which Marker had come to expect from American law enforcers.

They carried it down to the subterranean parking lot and inspected the contents. The PRC 319 looked identical to the one Cafell had just delivered, the tracking system much as Marker remembered it from the technical aids workshop he had attended a couple of years before. He was relieved to see that Poole had included instructions for its use.

They drove south once more, this time with Cafell at the wheel. 'Are we going out in the *Queen* tonight?' he asked, as they crossed the bridge on to Key Largo.

'I'd say no,' Marker said. 'The first helicopter flight we know about was on a Thursday, and so was the second. It might just be coincidence . . . but if we assume the next one will be this coming Thursday, then tomorrow night seems a better bet for what we have to do. I'd like to be out all day, and give them the chance to get used to us being around. Sneaking up on them in the dark is more likely to make them wonder what the fuck we're doing.'

'I sometimes wonder that myself,' Cafell murmured.

It was just after two in the morning, and the compound on Tortuga seemed fast asleep. Russell was squatting underneath the trees outside his bungalow window, letting his eyes get accustomed to the dark. He could make out the silhouette of a guard standing in the ramshackle tower beside the gates, and there might well be sentries patrolling the outside of the perimeter wall, but within the compound no one seemed to be stirring.

He put his fingers into the dirt and scraped them across his face for camouflage, wishing he had remembered to do this properly before he came out. Well, there was no time now. He started making his way towards the building which housed Joutard's office, not using the path but setting a course which maximized the time spent in the darker shadows cast by the scattered palms.

Outside the barracks which housed the male orphans several were curled up on mattresses. They looked younger in sleep, Russell thought, and told himself to stop being sentimental.

The HQ building was almost directly in front of him now, the bare light-bulb glowing above the doors. Another light was glowing in the outer office where the night guard was stationed. The man was not in sight, but he was probably sitting at his desk, either dozing or reading one of the soft-porn cartoon books which were so popular among his colleagues.

Russell continued on his way, using the barracks on his left to shield him from the guard tower as he circled around to the back of the office. From that position he advanced along its side to the right-front corner and squatted on his haunches in the shadows to wait.

The previous night it had been exactly two-thirty when the guard emerged with the cup of coffee for the man in the watch-tower, but tonight that time went by without his emerging from the office. It was almost three, and Russell was beginning to fear that he had already missed his chance, when the screen door opened and the man emerged, steaming cup in his hand.

Russell watched him cross the parking space and disappear round the corner of the first barracks, waited a long two minutes, and then walked briskly towards the office doors, hoping that the guard's attention was now on his approaching refreshments. He passed inside and stopped, listening for any ominous sounds, either from elsewhere in the building or up on the distant tower.

There were none. He walked behind the desk and started memorizing the map that he had remembered was there from his only previous visit. If that night had been anything to go by he had another two minutes before the guard returned.

Almost thirty seconds were taken up in searching for the compound's location. A combination of logic, luck and the titbits of information which he had garnered from clinic patients finally enabled him to pinpoint it, and he spent the next minute studying the lie of the land between the compound and the island's southern coast. There seemed to be no roads, only paths connecting villages, and none of these crossed the range of hills, some nine hundred feet high, which ran east to west along the narrow island. He would have only five miles or so to travel, but they wouldn't be easy.

His time was up. He turned towards the door, just in time to catch sight of the guard coming back round the corner of the barracks.

He sank to his haunches, cursing under his breath, and then scuttled across the floor towards the passage which led down past Joutard's office. None of the doors was open.

He took a deep breath and opened one, stepped inside, and closed it behind him as quietly as he could. As his eyes adjusted he could see the thin light from the window shining on an iron bedstead and bare mattress. Otherwise the room was empty.

Russell blessed his luck and walked across to the open window. After unclasping the shutters he put a leg across the frame and levered himself out and down, landing in the dirt with what seemed like a deafening thud. He crouched there for a few minutes, decided it was safe to assume that no one had heard him, and made his way carefully back to his bungalow. There he spent the next ten minutes trying to recreate the details of the map he had examined.

It was amazing how much had stuck. SBS training, he told himself, remembering the agony of the film observation test almost fifteen years before. Once he had everything down on paper Russell went back to bed, and fell asleep counting oil drums as they were loaded on to the back of a lorry.

After rising early the following morning, Marker and Cafell were soon on their way. Franklin had made contact shortly after eight the previous evening with the news that the occupants of the Arcilla villa had apparently retired for the night, and that there had been no helicopter departure. If there was one during the coming evening then the SBS men would have to fix the tracking devices before the helicopter's arrival at the treasure boat, and then scurry back to the Keys for their own submarine. Leaving the area in the middle of the night would undoubtedly look suspicious, but a lot less so than towing the Vickers along behind them in full view of the *Tiburón Blanco*.

With any luck, Marker thought as he changed into his wetsuit, the opposition would stick to their Thursday pattern, and they would get another day's grace.

Once they were well beyond the reefs, and before they reached the shipping lane which ran down the centre of the Straits, Cafell cut the engines of the *Slipstream Queen* and let the boat drift. Marker went over the side and Cafell carefully lowered the electric torpedo down to him. Marker practised with the machine for the next fifteen minutes, taking it down around four fathoms and testing its manoeuvrability. He had used them often enough in the past, but not for several years, and in that time a number of modifications had been made.

Nothing basic had been changed though, and the practice session over, they resumed course for the Muertos Cays. This time they had decided on putting at least two miles between the *Slipstream Queen* and the *Tiburón Blanco*, reckoning that what they lost in observational clarity would be more than made up for by the enemy's assumption of their innocence. As luck would have it there were two other leisure fishing boats anchored within a mile and a half of the Arcilla boat, allowing them to set up shop slightly closer than they had expected.

The day proved long and hot. Once again they fished with an enthusiasm that was more apparent than real, and took occasional turns at the telescope. As far as they could tell the men on the *Tiburón Blanco* were following the same routine as before. The only obvious difference was that the man with the binoculars had more boats to keep a check on, and he seemed to be finding the larger of the two other craft by far the most interesting. Marker realized why when one of the two nymphets on board sat herself up, and began replastering her bare breasts with sunblock.

Both the other boats took off in a northerly direction during the hour before sundown, leaving the *Slipstream Queen* and the *Tiburón Blanco* with nothing else to look at but the sea, the sky and each other. The navigation lights grew brighter as darkness fell, and then fainter again as the crescent moon rose in the south-eastern sky, flooding the water with yellow light and turning the distant ship back into a discernible silhouette.

Marker and Cafell ate a light supper, played a few

hands of German whist on the galley table, and listened to a tape of early U2 songs which they had found in the Key Vaca house. They didn't drink any alcohol.

At eight o'clock Marker was ready on the roof for Franklin's incoming message, his body between the small radio and any watcher with a nightscope on the enemy's boat. To his relief the words 'not tonight, Josephine' skipped across the display.

Cafell was already asleep when Marker went back inside – he had always possessed the ability to turn himself off whenever it was convenient. A forte of the truly innocent, the older man thought. Either that or the truly obtuse.

He kept watch until twelve-thirty, then woke the other man so that he could have four hours' sleep himself. At four-thirty he was dreaming his way through playing Stanley Kowalski in *A Streetcar Named Desire* on Brighton Pier when Cafell brought him back to life.

The two men got into their diving suits in the dark, then checked the fastening on each other's breathing apparatus before crawling on their hands and knees out on to the deck. It didn't seem very likely that Arcilla's men would be keeping an all-night watch on the *Slipstream Queen* but Marker wasn't taking any chances. With the bulk of the cabin cruiser shielding them from the enemy the two men fixed goggles and put on their flippers. Cafell slipped over the side and Marker carefully lowered the electric torpedo into the water before joining him. The ocean seemed warmer than it had during the day.

Marker flipped the ignition switch on the electric torpedo, and the motor started up with a satisfyingly low purr. The two men took hold of the grab rail and Marker opened the throttle. They took themselves down about twenty feet and started in the direction of the *Tiburón Blanco*, Cafell doing the steering with the help of the luminous compass strapped to his wrist.

For the moment it was hardly necessary: the sinking moon shone above and behind them like an interrogator's lamp, flooding the water all around them with its ghostly yellow light. On the grey ocean floor plants waved at them eerily as in a nightmare.

But in ten minutes the moon would set, and they would have their window of darkness before the dawn.

Cafell looked as composed as ever, as if he didn't have a care in the world. Marker, on the other hand, could feel anxieties queuing up in his mind. First and foremost was the fear that the *Tiburón Blanco* would prove to have some kind of underwater hatch, and that they would be denied access to the second submarine. Second was the fear that there would be no second submarine, and that the whole business was an expensive waste of time. After all, there might be two subs missing, but they had no proof Arcilla had bought both of them. He might have just needed one for a bona fide treasure hunt; the other one could be anywhere.

But no, Marker told himself. Even if the treasure hunt was kosher it could still serve as a cover. A better cover, in fact.

Cafell tapped him on the hand holding the grab rail, and gestured off to the right where a large fish was watching them. The two similar dorsal fins gave it away as a sand tiger shark, one of the least aggressive members of the shark family. As if it suddenly realized as much, the fish turned lazily away and swam slowly out of their sight.

No other possible threats presented themselves during the remainder of the outward journey. The sea gradually darkened, but the compass was only needed for a few minutes before the navigation lights on the *Tiburón Blanco* were glimmering through the water and providing them with a new beacon. Using all his long experience of underwater operations to judge the distances, Cafell guided the electric torpedo in a long three-quarter circle to bring it around on the far side of their target. He then held the machine in five fathoms of water while Marker swam to the surface with the small hand periscope which had been devised at Poole for such situations.

Some hundred yards to the west Arcilla's boat sat on the near-motionless sea. Save for its navigation lights, the boat was still in darkness. There was no sentry visible on this, the starboard side, but Marker kept an eye glued to the periscope for several more minutes, searching for any tell-tale movement in the shadows. There was none.

He swam back down to where Cafell was treading water, and gave him the good news by means of the prearranged signal. A thumbs down would have meant the younger man returning straight to the *Slipstream Queen*, while Marker went in alone, and then swam the two miles back to their boat. The thumbs up meant they could both get closer without an appreciable risk of being observed.

Cafell put the electric torpedo back into gear and they headed towards the target, gaining depth as they did so. The navigation lights on the *Tiburón Blanco* dimmed and swung upwards until they seemed almost overhead, and at that moment the dark shape of the boat's keel loomed into sight slightly ahead and far above them. A thinner shape hung alongside it – the submarine that was stabled on the surface. If another one was attached to the keel they could not see it from where they were.

Cafell manoeuvred the torpedo until he was directly

underneath the boat, which would then assist in diffusing their oxygen bubbles.

Marker gave him a grin through the mask, waved a farewell, and swam slowly upwards.

It was there, as his instinct had told him it had to be. The submarine was held between two fin-like shields and attached to the keel by a customized system of clamps. There was an underwater hatch, but it was only big enough for divers. Even so, it clearly enabled them to exit the boat above and enter the submarine without any need for movement on the surface. An umbilical air-line was hooked up between the two craft, recycling the air while the sub was attached to the mother craft.

Marker swam from one end of the sub to the other, conscious that every moment increased the danger of discovery, but keen to find as inconspicuous a location as possible for the tracking bug. He settled on a niche inside the propeller casing, removed the two magnetic devices from his belt pocket and dropped one of them into place. Then he swam carefully around to where the other sub was gently tapping against the boat's port side, and fixed the other bug in the identical spot.

Swimming back down he found Cafell without difficulty, and gave him an even wider grin. They headed east once more before turning back in a long arc around the anchored *Tiburón Blanco*.

An hour later they were eating breakfast on the *Slipstream Queen*, watching the sun climb into the sky. By seven o'clock they had upped anchor and sailed off in a northerly direction, with Cafell at the wheel and Marker watching the signal from the tracking devices slowly fade as they slipped across the tiny screen.

They reached the villa on Key Vaca soon after eleven, reported the latest developments to Poole, and took to their beds for the rest of the daylight hours. Cafell was up around seven, and spent the best part of an hour checking and double-checking that anything and everything they might conceivably need was already on board the cabin cruiser. The only obvious omission, he thought, remembering what he had read in the guide book, was the set of beads they would need if they decided to buy the Everglades from the Seminoles.

Marker meanwhile had woken from a broken sleep, and lay on his bed feeling angry with himself. He knew the whole business with Tamara Arcilla was over – it even *felt* over – but it had been like an emotional tidal wave, and it seemed to have swept away almost everything in its path. Including his past with Penny.

He clenched his fist, unclenched it, and walked angrily into the adjoining bathroom. Standing under a cold shower took the edge off his rage, or at least gave it a new focus.

'Time to take control,' he murmured to himself. So far at least, Marker was pretty sure that the emotional turmoil he seemed unable to shake off during his unemployed hours was not affecting his active performance. But sooner or later, unless he found some way to snap out of it, it would. Already he was conscious of the occasional questioning look from Cafell.

He found his partner putting the microwave through its paces. They ate, copiously but less healthily than they would have wished, and then sat watching two dreadful TV sitcoms while they waited for Franklin's transmission. It came at eight, right on time. 'Chopper depart 18.35 hours, heading south.'

The two men looked at each other, eyes shining in the darkness.

'Bingo,' Cafell said.

On this Thursday evening the atmosphere in the Tortuga operating room seemed considerably more sober – and not merely in the alcoholic sense – than it had the week before. The loss of the girl the previous week had apparently disturbed Calderón, at least enough for him to tear a strip off Bodin. Or that was what Russell guessed: he couldn't think of any other reason why Bodin's breath should be so sweet or his temper so foul.

The four surgeons worked in virtual silence, each removing a pink kidney from the unconscious youth in their care. Bodin was the last to fill a plastic box, and Emelisse was almost finished sewing her patient back together before he reached the point of closure. She delegated the rest of the work to her nurse and bent over to examine Bodin's patient, provoking a vitriolic outburst in French. She ignored it, and came across to look at Russell's. 'Good,' she said, and went back to her own.

Russell finished closing his patient, stretched, and palmed the needle he had been using. In the washroom she waited for him, as if having a post-operative drink together was now part of the routine. He told her he was tired and felt like an early night.

'OK,' she said, in a tone which suggested it made no difference to her one way or the other.

He watched her go, feeling sorry that these days he felt awkward in her company.

Back at the bungalow he poured himself a modest shot of whisky, sat down at the table and removed one of the batteries from Dr Barlow's cassette recorder. Then he took the length of insulated wire he had acquired by shortening a light flex and coiled it carefully around the needle. This done, he held the two bare ends of the wire to the battery terminals for five minutes.

The bedsheet supplied him with a piece of thread, and he created a small loop in one end for the magnetized needle. Then he took the improvised compass out to the bungalow's veranda and put it to the test. At this latitude Polaris was too close to the horizon, and hidden by the intervening buildings and foliage, but Russell hadn't forgotten his celestial navigation. From the position of Cassiopeia and the other constellations which circled the North Star he was able to infer its position. The needle knew too.

'I thought you were going to bed,' she said, making him start.

'Changed my mind,' he said, more gruffly than he intended.

'I felt like some company,' she said simply.

He smiled. 'Come in,' he said, opening the door for her. 'Would you like a drink?' he asked, putting the compass down on the table beside the battery.

'Sure,' she said, examining the needle and thread. 'You're going, aren't you?'

He put a glass of whisky in her hand. 'Yes. I was going to tell you,' he added, 'and ask if you wanted to come.'

She shook her head. 'Thank you, no,' she said.

There was something in the way she said it which made him feel defensive. 'You don't have to pay such a price to help people,' he said.

She turned her lovely eyes on him. 'I don't know about other places,' she said, 'only here.'

He sighed and sat down. 'I don't know what's right,' he replied. 'Only . . . I don't know.'

She smiled. 'There's no right or wrong in this place. Except for what you feel here.' She tapped her breast above her heart.

'My heart tells me this is wrong.'

'Then follow it,' she said, almost coldly.

'I intend to.'

She put the glass down. 'When are you going?' she asked.

'I don't know yet. In a few days.'

She nodded. 'I shall miss you,' she said, the words sounding strangely out of sympathy with the coldness in her voice.

He didn't know what to say.

'Don't try the ocean,' she said from the doorway. 'The mainland is your best chance.'

And then she drained her glass and was gone.

11

The night was not as clear as its immediate predecessors, but the army of clouds that scudded across the star-laden sky, concealing and revealing the moon like the folds of a magician's cloak, more than made up in beauty for what had been lost to clarity. The breeze was stiffer too, ruffling the waters of the Florida Straits, and brushing Marker's hair across his eyes.

The *Slipstream Queen* was holding a position about forty miles south-east of Vaca Key, close to the centre of the Straits' shipping lane. It wasn't the most comfortable place to be – they had already twice been obliged to make way for passing oil tankers – but it marked the optimum position for picking up the signal from the tracking device.

On the map Cafell had drawn two lines connecting the position of the *Tiburón Blanco* with the two ends of the Florida keys archipelago. Assuming the submarine was headed straight for US territory its course had to lie inside the relevant segment. Cafell had then drawn a third line dissecting the segment, and found the point on that line which was thirty miles distant – the range of the tracking signal – from its outer edges. And just to be on the safe side he had moved the point forward a couple of miles.

And here they were, with at least another half an hour to wait, staring out across the shining sea.

'It doesn't get any better,' Marker murmured. The emotional knots of earlier that evening had untied themselves, or perhaps been untied by his guardian angel the sea. He felt the tingling sense of anticipation which had always accompanied action, be it a training exercise in Poole harbour, an anti-smuggling operation in the Hsi Chiang estuary or a terrorist alert on a North Sea oil rig.

The minutes ticked slowly by. All thirty of them, and then another ten, and another ten.

'Fuck,' Marker growled, turning away from the screen to stare at the ocean, as if willing the waters to yield up the missing submarine.

'Yes,' Cafell hissed happily beside him.

A faint signal was palpitating on the edge of the circular screen. Both men watched as it slowly took on substance, and worked its way millimetre by millimetre towards them.

'It's coming straight at us,' Marker said.

'Not quite,' Cafell cautioned.

Another ten minutes and it became apparent that if the submarine held to its present course – and there seemed no earthly reason why it should have plotted itself anything other than a straight line – it would pass about a mile or so to their west. 'If it's headed for the mainland I'd put my money on Channel Five,' Cafell said. 'It's between Fiesta and Craig Keys,' he added, pointing them out on the map. 'The water's just about deep enough for them.'

'How about getting there first?' Marker suggested. 'The longer we can keep ahead of them, the less distance we'll fall behind when we have to transfer to the Vickers.'

'OK, but what if they're heading for one of the Keys . . .'

'They aren't. There's too many people around, too many potential witnesses. They're heading for the Everglades. You could lose an army in there.'

'You're probably right,' Cafell agreed.

'We can always turn back,' Marker added.

'Sold.' Cafell engaged the cabin cruiser's engine and turned towards the north, matching its pace to the signal on the screen from the submarine behind them. 'It's doing nearly twenty knots,' he said, shaking his head.

'That's what the sneaky beaky said,' Marker muttered, using the Marine slang for Intelligence.

'Some boat,' Cafell said admiringly. 'It would make a lovely Christmas present for the boss.'

An hour passed by, the dark line of the Keys slowly emerging on the north-western horizon. They were back inside American territorial waters now, and someone was obviously watching, because a call came through on the emergency radio band demanding that they identify themselves and their destination. The former was easy enough, but they didn't know the latter, and given their current course they could hardly claim to be heading home to Key Vaca. After a quick glance at the map Cafell plumped for Naples on Florida's Gulf coast as the destination likely to cover the most eventualities.

'We could have asked them to talk to our friends in Key West,' Marker said, after they had been given a clean bill of health, 'but I didn't fancy having to spend most of the night explaining ourselves in triplicate.'

'Dead right,' said Cafell.

The bridge across Channel Five was now visible through the nightscope, but to the naked eye it was still buried in the dark background. Occasionally a vehicle's headlights would swoop up the long arc of the invisible causeway and down again, like twin planets in flight across the sky.

Another boat was passing under the bridge in their direction, and ten minutes later, as it passed fifty yards or so off their starboard bow, the voice of a silhouetted female could be heard shouting, 'We need another man.' Whether this was because they were numerically one short, or because they were not happy with the one they had, was not explained.

Cafell slowed the *Slipstream Queen* and concentrated on keeping to the deep-water channel under the bridge. Once they were through into the deeper waters of the bay he idled the engines and brought the boat to a drifting halt.

'She's still coming,' Marker said, his eyes on the screen. He looked at his watch. 'About forty-five minutes behind us.'

They settled down to wait, hoping that the Coast Guard was not observing the interruption with a suspicious mind. The palpitating dot on the screen inched slowly across the circular screen as the time passed.

'They're close to the bridge,' Cafell calculated. 'Now we'll see which way they're headed. My guess is that they'll hardly change course at all.'

As the next fifteen minutes went by it became apparent that he was right. They got the boat underway again and set off in pursuit, only slowing to match the submarine's pace when Cafell reckoned they were five minutes behind her. Traversing the bay took about an hour, and it was almost four o'clock when the leading boat approached the twelve-mile territorial limit off Cape Sable. Not much more than ninety minutes of darkness remained.

The submarine changed course slightly, moving in on a diagonal heading towards the coast.

Cafell studied the map. 'It has to be here,' he said, holding it in front of Marker and jabbing it with his finger. 'Lostman's River. It's the only channel into the Everglades which is deep enough.'

'Let's close the gap,' Marker suggested. Staring straight ahead at the dark line of the distant coast, he caught sight of something moving out of the corner of his eye. It didn't take more than a few seconds to make out what it was. 'Oh shit,' he muttered.

The Coast Guard cutter was on an interception course, and at maximum speed if the noise of the 210-foot vessel's engines was any guide. Its powerful searchlight was already on, waiting to bathe them in its glare.

The thought of attempting to outrun the pursuit flashed through Marker's mind, but was swiftly dismissed. For one thing he wasn't sure they could, and for another he knew the cutter carried both a radar-guided three-inch cannon on its foredeck and a fast helicopter on the helipad amidships.

'Heave to,' he told Cafell.

The cutter drew up alongside them, some twenty yards away, and the searchlight was turned full on the two SBS men. Another light picked out the submersible in the water behind them. A megaphone-amplified voice asked them to state their business in United States territorial waters. Shadows dancing on the cutter's deck looked suspiciously like a boarding party preparing itself.

'If they come across turn off the tracker,' Marker told Cafell quietly. Then he cupped his hand and shouted across the gap: 'We are British naval officers engaged in a police action against British citizens. We have clearance from the US Navy and US Coast Guard to operate in your waters. You should have the name of this boat on file. Our password is Key Limey.'

There was a pause, presumably for the Coast Guard officer to swallow his disbelief. 'Please stay in view,' he ordered them, with a hint of courtesy in his tone. 'We'll run a check.'

The two men waited in the searchlight's glare, conscious of the eyes watching them from the cutter's deck, not to mention the fingers that would be sweating on triggers. Five minutes passed, and then ten, without the officer reappearing.

'What the fuck's going on?' Cafell asked. 'We're going to lose the signal.'

'Someone in Key West can't believe their ears,' Marker guessed. 'They've probably decided to wake up Baskin or Jiménez for confirmation. Either that or they're wondering why we haven't shared any new discoveries with them.'

Another five minutes passed, and Marker was wondering whether throwing a tantrum would be counterproductive, when the searchlight abruptly went out. 'You're free to go,' the voice boomed through the megaphone. 'Sorry for the hold-up.'

Marker acknowledged the message with a wave, and tried to rub the light out of his eyes. 'Go,' he told Cafell.

The *Slipstream Queen* surged forward. Looking back, Marker watched the cutter beginning a long turn towards the south. At least it hadn't been given orders to follow them.

'We've lost the fucking signal,' Cafell said.

'Not for long. You said there was only one channel, right? Get in there.'

'And what if I'm wrong?'

'Then we'll have to turn the whole fucking Everglades upside down until we find them.'

The cabin cruiser headed north as fast as its engines and the towed submarine would allow. They were still about twenty-five miles from the mouth of Lostman's River when the signal reappeared, faintly at first but more strongly all the time. Marker took the wheel as Cafell transposed the dot's position from the screen to the map. 'They're about five miles up the river,' he said eventually. 'And they seem to have speeded up,' he added. 'The deep-water channel looks a bastard to navigate. I reckon they're running on the surface.'

'Why not?' Marker asked. 'It's still dark and there's no one in there to see them.'

'It won't be dark for long,' Cafell said, looking first at his watch and then at the eastern sky. Was that the first hint of light above the dark coastline or was he just imagining it?

He turned back to the tracking screen, and for the next half hour the dot's position hardly moved, reflecting the fact that they were travelling in roughly the same direction at roughly the same speed. When it did eventually move, it was to perform a slow U-turn. The distance between the two craft was shrinking. 'They've stopped,' said Cafell.

'Where?' Marker asked from the wheel.

Cafell took the map across. 'Somewhere on the northern shore of this lake,' he said, pointing it out. 'The closer we get, the better the fix we'll get. It's called Hell's Lake, by the way.'

'That figures,' Marker murmured. They were now approaching the mouth of the river, and the sky above the mangrove-covered banks was definitely lightening. As the land grew closer they could hear the swelling racket of the dawn chorus.

'How far up-river can we get?' Marker asked.

Cafell studied the charts again, and then the man-groves off the starboard bow. 'The water doesn't look low,' he said. 'So all the way, if we're careful.'

'I wouldn't like to sink our benefactor's boat,' Marker said.

'I wouldn't like to be in it when you do,' Cafell said, pointing a finger towards the nearer of the two banks. In the dawn twilight a long, dark shape was moving slowly across a flat stretch of grey mud beneath the overhanging trees. 'Are they crocodiles or alligators around here?' he asked.

'Both,' Marker replied, slapping at a mosquito on his neck.

They headed up the river, keeping to the deep-water channel, which mostly followed a line slightly closer to the southern bank than the northern. The river itself rapidly narrowed over the first couple of miles, and then its width stabilized at around a quarter of a mile. On both banks the mangroves looked and felt like walls: dense, impenetrable, almost uniform in height. And nothing rose up behind these walls, no taller trees, no hills, no signs of human occupancy. There was only one escape from this river, and that was the river itself.

There was no longer anything to be gained by speed – the submarine had reached its destination, the darkness was almost gone – but there was a lot that could be lost in waters as treacherous as these. Marker took it slowly according to the chart, with Cafell lending the use of his eyes from the bow in difficult-looking stretches.

Several miles went by, and the mosquitoes grew ever more annoying, but then the river began to widen once more, and the attacks abated. 'We're about two miles from Hell's Lake,' Cafell announced. 'And about half a mile short of what looks like a decent anchorage.'

'How far from there to the sub?'

'About four miles.'

'Sounds good.'

The sun had cleared the wall of mangrove now, and the river had widened to the extent of constituting a small lake. In the lee of a headland on the northern shore they found both Cafell's suggested anchorage and their second crocodile. The reptile ignored them at first, lying resolutely still on its patch of mud, but then it slowly started raising its upper jaw, as if it was miming Tower Bridge.

'They have no strength when it comes to opening their jaws,' Marker said conversationally, as they manoeuvred the submarine around to the side of the cabin cruiser. 'All the power is in the slamming shut.'

'So this one's just getting prepared.'

'I think it's ready,' Marker said. The crocodile's jaws were now at right angles to each other.

The two men concentrated on loading what was needed into the battery-operated Vickers, and then clambered one by one down through the hatch and on to the wooden floor of the submarine's belly. Despite the wide windows the interior felt decidedly cramped.

As Marker checked the dials and gauges on the pilot's console Cafell clanged shut the hatch and screwed the locking wheel tight. 'Ready to go,' he said.

Marker switched on the engines, which began to vibrate with an almost melodious hum. He then started the two propellers turning, the starboard slightly slower than the port, as he wanted to move off in a slight turn to starboard. The Vickers edged its way out towards deeper water.

The two men had decided that, for the first half of this short voyage, the risks involved in pranging some uncharted underwater obstruction greatly outweighed the risk that they might be spotted on the surface by unfriendly eyes.

The gamble paid off – only the eyes of several great white herons followed their progress eastward. A hundred yards short of Hell's Lake Marker brought the craft to a stop, and Cafell took a final reading on the exact location of Arcilla's submarine. 'There,' he said, pointing out the spot on the map. 'And here,' he added, pointing out another not too far away, 'looks like a good place to resurface.'

Marker nodded, and reached forward to open the vents. As the water swished into the tanks the submarine sank into the river, three feet, six feet . . . Marker closed the vents and turned on the outside lights. The craft was suspended between the river's bed and surface, with only a few feet to spare in either direction. He started the propellers again, and the Vickers moved forward into the slightly deeper waters of the lake.

The water was not particularly clear, but there was little doubt they would be visible from the air. The thought suddenly struck Marker that a helicopter might have been waiting for the sub, might even now be taking off and wheeling out across the lake . . .

No, he told himself. It would be heading east towards Miami or north towards Tampa.

'How are . . . ?' he started to say, when a dark shape exploded into view through the submarine's front windows, and just as quickly disappeared from view. The second approach, though, was slower. It was a dolphin, no, two dolphins, and they seemed to want to play.

For the next fifteen minutes, as Marker steered the Vickers across the wide lake, the two creatures kept them company, entertaining each other and the SBS men with an underwater display which included everything from looping the loop around their craft to close-up smiles in the observation windows. It was distracting, potentially dangerous, and downright wonderful. When the dolphins, apparently bored by their new friend's rigidity, finally took off for pastures new, the two men felt a rare sense of loss. Both knew that they had seen something few other humans would ever see: one intelligent species trying to play with another.

Cafell, meanwhile, was responsible for navigating them safely to their destination, and at times his powers of concentration were severely tested. But he stuck with it, not least because he knew that their surfacing in the wrong place might well prove fatal. There was no knowing what weaponry the enemy might have on hand, and there wouldn't be much chance of escaping in the submarine once their presence was discovered. Not in water this shallow, anyway.

Finally they neared the appointed spot. The bottom of the lake had been slowly rising for some time, which fitted in with Cafell's calculations. 'Another fifty yards,' he told Marker. 'But slow.'

They had moved forward around twenty yards when the slope of the lake bottom suddenly steepened. 'Here,' Cafell said.

Marker switched off the propellers, turned off the lights and stopped the engine. 'Here's hoping,' he said, and started emptying the tanks. The Vickers rose in the water, rocking gently from side to side. A dark and ragged line of vegetation swam into focus through the ruffled water, and then they were on the surface, and looking quickly round to see where they were.

Cafell's navigation had been spot on. The submarine was sitting in a small cove, surrounded on three sides by a wall of mangroves. Only the open lake was visible through the entrance to the cove. 'They're around that headland,' said Cafell. 'Probably only about three hundred yards as the crow flies.'

Marker did a quick calculation in his head. 'I shouldn't be more than an hour,' he told Cafell.

'Should I wait here or take her back down? If I take her down the noise of the engine might carry,' Cafell said.

'I guess you'd better just keep her where she is,' Marker replied. Having pulled the hood of the black wetsuit over his head he was now applying camouflage cream to his face. Next he double-checked that the camera was in the waterproof pouch at his belt, the silenced Browning High Power in the waterproof holster. He took one look at the Heckler & Koch MP5SD, which was still wrapped in its reinforced cling film, and decided that in this instance mobility was more important than fire-power.

'Ready,' he said.

Cafell was already unscrewing the hatch. 'Watch out for crocodiles,' he said seriously, as Marker clambered up and out on to the top of the submarine.

'Thanks for reminding me,' Marker said sarcastically. The only wildlife in sight was a black cormorant perched on a mangrove root some twenty yards away. 'Won't be long,' he said, and slid down into the water.

He only had to swim a few yards before the bottom came to meet him. He waded ashore, and found his path obstructed by the dense mangroves. 'Should have brought a fucking machete,' he muttered to himself.

He squeezed through a narrow gap, and then another, and another. It was like being trapped inside an enormous hedge, with the added complication that he was standing in three feet of water. Already the hour he had set himself was beginning to look optimistic.

A sudden movement in the water ahead stopped him in his tracks. The snake, striped like a tiger, only in dark brown and beige, swam away into a tangle of roots.

Marker breathed out heavily. Maybe this wasn't such a good idea, he thought. Maybe they should just tell the Yanks the whole story and head on home.

But first he had to find out whether Russell was here. With more than a little reluctance he started forward again.

His luck changed. The swamp and its wilderness of roots gave way to more solid ground and slightly sparser vegetation. Marker rechecked the compass on his wrist and walked on, his boots sinking into the moist soil, his eyes constantly sweeping both ground and foliage for snakes. According to the map it was only a hundred yards or so across this headland to the shores of a narrow creek.

It took almost fifteen minutes, and Marker's relief on catching his first sight of the creek was almost his undoing. He was just about to slide back into the water among the tangled roots when a strangely familiar sound halted him in his tracks.

He crouched down behind a gnarled trunk and found a small window on to the river in the wall of vegetation. He could hear the faint swish of a paddle being deftly wielded by an expert, and the canoe suddenly came into view. In the stern sat a man in jeans, T-shirt and felt hat. The feather in the latter went with the stereotypical Native American face, but the Walkman didn't. The leakage of noise from its earphones was providing the strangely familiar sound, one that Marker had last heard on a bus coming back from Bournemouth not ten days before. At this sort of volume, he reckoned, personal stereos would prove as dangerous to the Indians as white men or alcohol.

The sound faded into nothing, and Marker started making his way forward through the roots. He was within a couple of yards of open water when the view in front of him dramatically expanded. Across the thirty-yard width of the creek another wall of mangroves rose up, but a little way to his left the creek opened into Hell's Lake, and around the far headland, some two hundred yards in the distance, he could see the corner of a wooden jetty. As yet he could see no buildings, but logic put them close to the shore behind that jetty. His spirits, somewhat depressed by the struggle through the undergrowth, began to lift once more.

With only his head above the surface of the green-brown water he moved slowly out from behind the mangrove curtain. The musical canoeist had vanished from sight round the next bend in the creek, and there was no sign of his having a colleague. Marker pushed off through the torpid water towards the far bank.

Getting himself ashore proved as difficult as before. As he fought his way through the interwoven roots Marker promised himself that on his return the SBS would launch a multimillion-pound research programme into the problem of movement through mangroves. There had to be an easier way.

Fifteen minutes and fifteen yards later he was back on relatively dry ground. The trees here were taller and more varied – he was on a hummock, one of those slight humps in a flat land which acted as a magnet to wildlife. There certainly seemed to be more birds in the foliage, and there were flowering plants growing out of tree trunks and branches. Some of these were orchids, he realized. The place smelled like a perfumed Turkish bath-house.

He removed the Browning from its sealed holster, checked that the compass on his wrist tallied with his inbuilt sense of direction, and resumed his progress. He had not gone much further when the vegetation ahead of him began thinning out. Soon he could make out the straight lines of something man-made through the foliage.

It proved to be the roof of a large one-storey wooden building. Marker crawled forward until he could see the end which was facing him. It was about thirty-five feet wide, and boasted two big windows, both of which appeared screened and shuttered.

To his right, behind the building, an area the size of a tennis court had been painstakingly cleared and covered in tarmac, but there was no helicopter sitting on the pad. One had probably departed as soon as the contraband had been transferred from the sub.

To his left, through a gap between the corner of the lodge and the forest, he could see more of the jetty and the lake beyond. There was no cover in that direction. He removed the camera from its waterproof pouch and took several photographs, before moving further back into the trees and starting on a course that would take him around behind the helipad to the far side of the lodge-like building.

The going seemed easy after the mangroves, and it took only a few minutes to reach a spot from which he could study the back of the building. This was about sixty feet long, and contained eight shuttered windows and one door. It had been constructed as a wilderness lodge, Marker guessed, a place to bring boy scouts of all ages for canoeing, bird-watching, orchid picking, whatever.

There had to be at least a dozen rooms inside, and most of them were probably lined with bunk beds.

There was one separate outhouse to its right, and what looked like another closer to the lake shore. Maybe Russell was being held in one of them, Marker thought, though he couldn't think of a single reason why he should be.

He took more photographs, then resumed his march round the perimeter, making sure to keep out of sight inside the trees.

The second outhouse turned out to be a boat-house, built mostly of corrugated plastic sheets, with one side wall resting on dry land, another two on pilings in the lake. The fourth side looked open to the water from where Marker was standing.

He sat on his haunches among the trees, wondering what to do next. So far he hadn't seen a single occupant, but he had to reckon on there being at least two people inside the lodge – the submarine's crew. After a seven-hour voyage underwater it seemed likely that they would take a good long rest before heading back to the *Tiburón Blanco*. And in any case they would need darkness for the return passage through the shallow waters of the bay and the Keys.

They might be alone, though, and quite possibly sleeping.

At the very least, he had to check the outhouse, Marker decided. He carried on round the perimeter until he found the point of approach which offered the most cover, and began crawling out across the ten yards of open ground. There were no cries of discovery from the lodge.

The blind end of the outhouse lacked a window, so he was forced to risk the side facing the lake, which rendered him visible from the jetty and the front veranda of the lodge. One look in the window showed him the building was virtually empty, and certainly not a prison for Nick Russell. Marker turned away, and noticed with a leap of his heart what had previously been hidden from sight by the boat-house – there were two men on the jetty, both sitting in cheap plastic chairs.

Marker sank to the ground, thanking his lucky stars that the men had their backs to the shore. It made sense, since their task was presumably to frighten off unwelcome callers, and here in the western Everglades such visitors could only arrive by boat.

He studied the two men. One was Hispanic-looking and wore jeans, T-shirt and baseball cap. He was smoking a cigarette, and cradling what looked suspiciously like an Uzi sub-machine-gun in his lap. The other one, blond, was wearing a uniform which Marker didn't recognize but which he guessed was that of a Park Ranger. Both men were wearing wraparound sunglasses.

He took out his camera, and was about to take a picture of their backs when the uniformed man got to his feet. He stretched, turned, and said something which made the other guard laugh. Marker depressed the shutter release, and then watched the man walk back up the jetty and disappear behind the boat-house. About half a minute later the sound of a screen door slamming came from the direction of the lodge.

Marker crawled back into the safety of the trees and considered what to do next. He had already exceeded his stipulated hour, but Cafell would give him at least as much time again before he started to worry in earnest. Just the boat-house, Marker told himself, and then he would head home to the sub. The prospect of fighting his way back through the mangroves was not an enticing one.

It took him only a few minutes to come within spitting distance of the lake, but the configuration of the shoreline made it impossible for him to see what was inside the boat-house without leaving the shelter of the trees. Fortunately this didn't seem a risky proposition. There was only a short stretch of open ground between where Marker now stood and the top of the wooden steps which led down to the front of the boat-house. The view from the side windows of the lodge was obscured by the outhouse, and the line of sight of the guard on the jetty was blocked by the boat-house itself. Unless someone emerged from the front of the lodge at the exact moment Marker stepped out into the open there seemed little danger of his being seen.

He walked briskly across the space and on to the steps. The top one creaked slightly, and he took care to lighten his step as he descended the others. From the bottom a wooden walkway led in along the land wall of the boat-house. The Russian submarine and two canoes were tied up against it.

Marker had seen all that he needed to, but for a moment curiosity triumphed over caution, drawing him into the shadowed building for a better look at the submarine.

There was nothing much to see, of course. He would have to climb inside, study the controls, take the craft apart and put it back together again. One day, perhaps.

He crept back down the walkway, turned to ascend the steps, and heard a soft scraping sound from the path above. In the split second which passed before the man came into view Marker had braced his legs and brought the Browning into the classic two-handed firing position.

The Uzi was only halfway towards its target when Marker fired, pumping two bullets into the man's torso and a third through his brain, cancelling the message en route to the finger on the trigger.

The sub-machine-gun clattered noisily down the steps, while the guard sank slowly backwards on to the path.

Marker caught the Uzi on its third bounce, with the unconscious air of a conjuror making a difficult trick look easy. His ears were straining for evidence that someone had seen or heard what had just happened.

All he could hear was the singing of birds, the faint breeze in the trees, the slurping of water against the boat-house pilings. He climbed the steps, grabbed the dead man's feet, and half pulled, half slid him off the path and on to the top steps, where at least he was out of sight from the lodge veranda.

What to do? Marker stood there, his thoughts racing through the possibilities, and lingering for a moment over the memory of the only other man he had ever killed, a Chinese drug smuggler.

He shook his head angrily. There would be plenty of time to worry about his soul — first he had to get his body home.

There was still no sign of an alarm. It didn't look as if he would have any problem leaving by the same route he had used on his way in. Except, of course, that he couldn't take the dead man with him, and the discovery of his body would scupper any chances they had of finding Nick Russell and nailing Fidel Arcilla. The Cuban would put his operation on ice, close the pipeline down, hide away one of his submarines. As of now, they hadn't a shred of proof against any of his men, let alone Arcilla himself.

So how could he get rid of the dead man, and make

it look like an accident? With three bullet holes in him, there was no way they could afford an examination of the body. It had to disappear, either in the forest or the lake.

The canoes riding in the water beneath the jetty caught Marker's eye, and he tried to imagine he was looking down from above at the layout of lodge, boat-house and jetty. He decided that with any luck he could get to one of the canoes without ever putting himself in view from the lodge. It was risky, but no riskier than any alternative he could think of. And he wouldn't have to deal with the fucking mangroves.

He lowered the dead man down the steps and on to the walkway. There he removed the blood stained blue T-shirt and baseball cap, knotting the former around one thigh and stuffing the latter into his utility belt along with the dark glasses. He tangled the Uzi round the guard's wrist, lowered the body slowly into the water, and slid in beside it. Then be began swimming slowly towards the jetty some thirty yards distant, with one hand firmly grasping the dead man's wrist.

The canoe tethered at the near end was not visible from the lodge. With some difficulty Marker bundled the corpse over its side, and then clambered in himself. He took off his wetsuit hood and put on the blue T-shirt, the baseball cap and the sunglasses. The dead man was not that much smaller than he was, and sitting down in a canoe . . .

Marker decided that climbing up on to the jetty to untie the canoe would be riskier than leaving behind a rope that had clearly been cut. They would have no idea why the guard had gone out in the canoe, so how could they expect to understand how much of a hurry he had been in? He reached for his knife, sliced through the mooring rope, and used a hand to push himself off from the jetty.

With the skill acquired by long practice he manoeuvred the canoe around the end of the T-shaped jetty, and then moved it along the other side, with the wooden pilings effectively masking him from anyone watching on land. From the end of the jetty he would have to cross about a hundred and fifty yards in clear view, before the trees on the first headland screened him once more.

He paddled fast, as if he was in pursuit of someone, taking care to keep his face turned away from the lodge. If anyone shouted after him, he would just wave his arms excitedly and point in the direction of the hidden cove, where Cafell was hopefully waiting with the Vickers.

But no one shouted, and when he finally risked a look back all but the empty jetty was hidden from view. He took off the baseball cap and dark glasses, and let the boat drift while he pulled the sodden T-shirt over his head. Marker had no desire to test Cafell's reflexes by confronting him with what looked like a stranger in a canoe.

He rounded the headland beyond the creek, saw the Vickers in the distance and raised an arm in greeting. After what seemed like a long hesitation Cafell waved back.

The sardonic grin on the younger's man's face disappeared when he saw the corpse in the canoe. 'No time to explain,' Marker said. 'Find something to weigh him down with. And hurry.'

Cafell disappeared into the body of the submarine, and re-emerged less than a minute later. 'There's nothing,' he said.

'Shit. We'll have to take him with us,' Marker decided. He hauled the dead man up, and the two of them somehow contrived to lift him on to the roof of the vessel, before bundling him in through the hatchway.

After collecting the sunglasses, Uzi and clothes and passing them to Cafell, Marker leant down, overturned the canoe, and shoved it away from the submarine. There was still no sign of the enemy. 'Let's go,' he said.

Two minutes later they were submerged once more, and heading out across Hell's Lake towards the head of Lostman's River. As before, Marker took the controls and Cafell navigated. Neither man looked back at the body wedged behind them.

There was no sign of the dolphins on the return trip – perhaps they could sense the dead man on board, Marker thought – and the open-jawed crocodile had left his spot on the mudbank by the *Slipstream Queen*. There was no sign of it in the water either, but Cafell wasted no time as he waded the thirty feet which separated the boat from the nearby headland. There he found a heavy enough rock for their purposes.

It was too smooth for a rope attachment, so they wrapped the body in a blanket with the rock inside, and then secured both ends with rope, creating what looked like a human Christmas cracker.

Out in midstream once more, they dropped it into the deep-water channel and watched it sink.

Cafell caught the grim look on Marker's face. 'You had no choice,' he said firmly.

'I know. Let's get out of here.'

'OK.'

Marker went inside to find some fresh clothes, and emerged ten minutes later with a couple of cans. Cafell had one eye on the river, another on the chart, and one hand on the wheel. He reached out the other for the beer. 'So where do we go from here?' he asked.

'Home, I guess.'

'Not England?'

'No. Our villa in the Keys home.'

'And then what? After twenty-four hours' sleep, I mean.'

'Good question,' Marker said. 'Any answers?'

Cafell shrugged. 'I did have a few thoughts on the subject while you were out for your walk. And most of them were pretty depressing.'

'Like what?'

'Well, we may know how most of it works now, but we don't have a fucking thing that could be used in a court of law against Arcilla. We haven't any evidence that any crime has been committed at all. And worse, I haven't managed to think of any way we could get hold of any.' He put down his beer and ran a hand through his hair.

Marker waited for him to continue.

'There are two things we don't know. No, three. One is what they're smuggling, two is where they pick it up in the chopper, three is where it goes from the lodge back there. The obvious way to crack one is to follow the chopper when it leaves Provo, right? And the obvious way is to ask our friendly frigate to track it. But when we find out where it's going we're not really any further ahead. Say it's Haiti – well, the government's hardly going to sanction using the Royal Navy in Haitian waters, is it?'

'No, but . . .'

'Then there's the *Tiburón Blanco*,' Cafell went on. 'That at least is in international waters. We could try and board them during the transfer from chopper to sub, but what's to stop them throwing the drugs into the sea. And there goes our proof. There's no law against having two subs with the same number. The only other option is to intercept the sub with the stuff on board. Trouble is, the bloody thing's faster than we are. We'd have to catch it in a fucking great net or something. And that does sound more like James Bond than reality.'

'OK . . .'

'And one last thing,' Cafell insisted. 'Even if we do catch them with the goods, we still haven't implicated Arcilla. As it is he'll just say that his underlings were acting on their own, and using his treasure hunt as cover. He'll probably be indignant as hell.'

'Probably.' Marker gazed at the wall of mangroves sliding by, an idea beginning to form in his mind. He let his unconscious take over the task of bringing it to fruition. 'We have a more immediate problem,' he said.

'Which is?'

'Our hosts. They may have given us the green light last night, but I have the feeling that this morning they'll be expecting the explanation.'

Cafell laughed. 'Which is?'

'Fuck knows. If we tell them we were chasing a submarine they'll want to know where it went. If we say we lost it they'll think we're incompetent. Either way they'll want to take over.'

'These are their waters.'

'Yeah, but this is our op. They wanted us to nail Arcilla, and that's what we're trying to do. And I'm not sharing anything with the Yanks before I know for certain whose uniform that guy at the lodge was wearing.'

'OK,' Cafell said equably.

'And anyway,' Marker added, 'I always thought the idea of the sea belonging to anyone was a load of bollocks.'

'The Native Americans thought the same about the land,' Cafell volunteered. 'Are you sure the man you saw in the canoe was an Indian?'

'Nope, but he looked like Hollywood's idea of one.'

'Maybe he was just passing through.'

'Maybe.'

They stood in silence for a minute and more, watching the river widen to meet the open sea.

'How about – we were on our way to RV with a possible informant,' Cafell suggested. 'But he didn't show.'

'He was scared off by the Coast Guard cutter,' Marker added. 'I like it. It's thin, but so what – they aren't going to call us liars. Not to our faces anyway.'

'As long as they don't take the *Queen* back,' Cafell murmured.

'Right. We're going to need her for at least another week.' Marker lobbed his empty can into the bin that had thoughtfully been provided. 'And much as it pains me to say it, I think we're going to need reinforcements from Blighty. Two should do for what I have in mind.'

'And that is?'

Marker told him.

12

Neil Colhoun shut the door of his office behind him, propped the umbrella up against a wall, and dropped himself in the tattered chair. The only sound he could hear was the rain beating a tattoo on his windows. It was something of a change from home, where the members of his family were indulging their belief that God provided rainy Sunday afternoons for testing the volume controls on the house's three sound systems. Caught in the crossfire between his wife's country music, his younger daughter's new Björk single and his son's current favourites – the Crash Test Dummies – Colhoun had decided the office was the best place to consider an SBS invasion of the United States.

He picked up the transcription of the lengthy report Marker had sent by burst transmission on Friday afternoon, shortly after his and Cafell's return from their jaunt in the Everglades. And put it down again. By this time he could probably have recited the damn thing word for word.

He reached for the Admiralty and FO memos, which were almost as familiar. The Americans were not altogether happy with their British allies. In fact, they seemed to be a trifle hurt. In future it was hoped that cooperation in this particular endeavour could be more of a two-way street.

Fuck 'em, Colhoun thought sourly, and knew he was

being unfair. If SEALs were conducting themselves on British soil the way Marker and Cafell were behaving in Florida he would be outraged, and he knew it. But . . .

He started leafing through the computer-enhanced blow-ups which the Illustrators' Branch had generated from the pictures Marker had faxed. The quality wasn't that great, but the negatives would be arriving by express post on the following morning and better reproductions would then be possible. There was one picture in particular which Colhoun wanted to examine more closely. It showed the back of the lodge, and in the blown-up version some unusual-looking machines could be made out through the windows of the door. They seemed to be partly made of clear plastic, and their shape had touched a chord in Colhoun's memory. An unresponsive one, unfortunately.

He went on to the next picture, which showed the two men sitting on the wooden dock. The uniform, as Marker had suspected, was that of an Everglades National Park Ranger.

When it came down to it, Colhoun thought, he simply didn't trust the American authorities. He didn't trust their Special Forces to be efficient, and he had no faith in their security. If the man in the picture had been wearing a Coast Guard's uniform he wouldn't have been surprised.

Americans might be no more prone to corruption than Brits, but those working in Florida law enforcement certainly had more than their fair share of temptation to overcome. With so much drug money swilling around in the state the real surprise lay in the continued existence of honest and dedicated officials. The problem was in knowing who they were. Without such knowledge, enlisting American help was like entering a lottery. One in which the losers were apt to die.

It would be safer for all concerned to let Marker proceed with his plan. After all, Colhoun thought cynically, the four SBS men would simply constitute one more armed gang on American soil, and as far as the SBS CO knew, there was nothing against either carrying arms or gang membership in the US Constitution.

He tried to imagine selling this argument to the Foreign Office and failed. But then there was no reason why the FO should be told anything. As far as Colhoun was concerned he had been given carte blanche to sort this business out, and until such time as someone revoked his authority he intended to make the most of it.

Outside, the rain was still falling. He picked up the internal phone and called the duty office to tell them that he was on the premises. 'If anything comes in from London or the States, I want to see it right away,' he added.

'There's a fax here already,' the corporal replied.

Colhoun rolled his eyeballs at the ceiling. 'Send it over,' he said, and hung up.

It turned out to be the intelligence report he had been waiting for. One of the Washington MI6 contingent had done some local research in Florida, and come up with the name and owners of the property on Hell's Lake. Anhinga Lodge belonged to the Friends of Zion Health Care Trust, which ran hospitals in Miami, Fort Lauderdale, Fort Pierce and St Petersburg. It functioned as a weekend wilderness resort for the Trust's two thousand employees. There was a staff of ten on duty from noon on Friday to noon on Monday throughout the winter high season, and sporadically during the summer low season. There were two live-in caretakers. Staff, visitors and supplies were all flown in by one of the Trust's four helicopters.

Colhoun leant back in his chair, hands behind his head. There was something . . .

He had it!

He skimmed through the pages of his address book, found the number he was looking for, and reached for the phone.

'Can I speak to your dad?' he said when the child answered.

'You may,' the girl said primly, before apparently dropping the phone. A few moments later Dick Ferguson came on the line.

'Dick, it's Neil. I need to see you. Now, if possible.'

'We're just about to eat.'

'At four o'clock?'

'We eat late on Sunday, not that . . .'

'It'll only take a minute. I just need you to look at a photograph.'

'Come on over.'

Colhoun hung up, told the duty office he was leaving, and drove into Bournemouth. He had known Ferguson for five years now, since the doctor had performed the operation on his father-in-law. An initial prejudice against money-grabbing consultants had been eroded, if not completely removed, by a common Scots heritage, a mutual taste for malt whisky, and a love of rugby.

Ferguson opened the door himself, napkin still tucked inside his collar, and led Colhoun into the empty living room.

Colhoun handed him the blow-up. 'Those,' he said, pointing out the machines.

Ferguson stared at them. 'They look like Belzer-Kountz machines,' he said at last. 'I wouldn't want to stake my life on it, but that's what they look like.'

'And what are Belzer-Kountz machines?'

'They're for preserving human organs between removal and transplantation.'

Colhoun took back the photograph. 'Thanks,' he said.

'Is that it?'

'Aye, you can get back to your supper.'

'Lunch.'

Colhoun walked back to his car and sat behind the wheel, letting the pieces of the puzzle slip into place. The fact that a health trust owned the lodge, the fact that Russell, a paramedic, had been kidnapped rather than killed.

And Cafell had been right, he thought. It had to be Haiti – there was no way the necessary facilities could be hidden on one of the empty Bahamian keys.

Arcilla was smuggling human organs out of Haiti and into Florida, where desperate people were no doubt paying a fortune for something to which they had no earthly moral right. The more Colhoun thought about it, the angrier he felt.

He gunned the car's engine, and headed for home. He had already decided who Marker's reinforcements were going to be.

Fifteen miles away, Ian and Helen Dubery were parked in a New Forest lay-by, watching gusts of rain sweeping across the road. At least the weather was familiar, he thought unhappily. If this much wind and rain didn't make his wife feel more at home, then nothing would.

'I'm looking forward to seeing Mum,' she said,

confirming his suspicions. She always looked forward to her trips back home. He wondered if she ever told her family on Benbecula that she was looking forward to returning south. Some hope.

But why should she? Her friends were there, as well as her family. In Poole she had only him and a job she hated.

He had no doubt she loved him. After all, they had loved each other since they were about twelve. And he knew that loving him was enough to keep her here. But it wasn't enough to make her happy.

What could he do? He loved his work. Getting into the SBS had been like having every dream he had ever had come true, the realization of aspirations which had begun on the day his father first took him boating in the Sound of Monach. He was only four then, but the green sea and blue sky were still vivid in his memory.

What was he supposed to do – give it all up? For what? There was no work in the outer islands. The fishing fleets were a shadow of what they once had been. All the young people left, just like he and Helen had done.

For a moment he felt angry with her, but what was the point?

The shower was ending as abruptly as it had begun, the sun breaking through the overhanging trees. She turned towards him, a smile on her face. As always, he felt his anger melt away.

'Where now?' he asked.

'Home,' she said.

'Question twenty-nine,' the Scouse voice boomed through the amplifier. Silence settled on the Hardy

Arms. 'What is the average lifespan of an ostrich? That's an ostrich,' the Liverpudlian repeated. 'I'll give you five years either way.'

Three tables away, Stuart Finn leant forward and whispered 'fifty' to the team member who was writing in the answers.

'You sure?' one of his team-mates asked doubtfully. 'My budgie only lasted about six months.'

'That was because you breathed on it,' Finn retorted.

'Fifty does seem kind of old,' Dave muttered.

'How about forty,' his girlfriend Jean suggested.

'Jesus!' Finn said. 'Fifty's the right answer, leave it alone.'

'How come you're so sure of a thing like that?' Jean asked.

Finn smiled at the woman. 'I just am,' he said, placing a beer mat on the edge of the table. He flicked it up and caught it deftly with the same hand.

'The last question,' the quizmaster bellowed. 'That's number thirty to youse who can count. What was the name of the *Titanic*'s captain?'

Finn and the other six members of the Hounds of Heaven quiz team stared blankly at each other. 'What a fucking question,' Dave moaned. 'Finn, you're in the fucking navy,' someone else said.

'The *Titanic* wasn't a warship.'

'They're all boats, aren't they?'

Finn ignored him. The girl on the next table was staring at him again, and this time he just smiled at her. She smiled brazenly back at him for several seconds before turning away. Maybe, Finn thought, the man next to her was her brother or something.

She was going to the bar now, and Finn could see her legs for the first time. They were nice. Shame about the blouse, he thought, but then not everyone could have taste as good as his.

'I'm still not sure about the ostrich,' one of his team-mates lamented.

'I am,' Finn said, getting up, 'and if you change that answer I will go out and find a dead ostrich and stuff it up your arse.'

'He's always right about those things,' Jean said. 'It's depressing.'

'He certainly has a way with threats,' Dave said.

Finn grinned and went to the bar, squeezing in beside the woman. 'Can I buy you a drink?' he asked.

'No thanks,' she said, 'I'm buying one for my boy-friend.'

'Lucky man,' Finn said. 'So why were you staring at me?'

She handed a fiver to the barman. 'I work at the Institute for the Deaf in Bournemouth,' she said with a smile. 'As a lip-reading instructor. No one on our team knew what the average lifespan of an ostrich was.'

Finn was still smiling to himself the following morning, when he and Ian Dubery found themselves waiting for an audience with the CO. At first the summons had given Finn some cause for alarm – not that he could remember actually doing anything worthy of a reprimand – but his fellow-corporal's presence had reassured him. Ian Dubery was not the type to get keelhauled across the CO's carpet.

Colhoun lost no time in telling them what they were there for, and was pleased, if not surprised, by the eagerness on each man's face as he recounted the genesis of the operation and the developments to date. 'You'll be flying out from Heathrow this afternoon,' he said. 'One or both of the others will meet you at Miami Airport.'

'Uniform, boss?' Finn asked.

'No. And as far as US Immigration is concerned, you're just a couple of tourists come to do some diving on the reefs off the Florida Keys. So when they hand round the form on the plane, and you get to the question about purpose of visit, just tick "pleasure", don't write in "illicit military operations on US territory".'

The two men dutifully laughed.

'Captain Marker will brief you on what you'll actually be doing,' Colhoun continued. 'Any questions?'

'Aye,' Dubery said, almost apologetically. 'Do we know exactly what it is these people are smuggling into Florida?'

'Not for certain,' Colhoun admitted. 'But the door-to-door trip takes longer than ten hours, which apparently rules out hearts and livers. According to an expert I talked to last night the best bets are kidneys and corneas, and maybe bone tissue.'

'It must be a pretty expensive business,' said Finn, 'running two helicopters, two submarines, a treasure hunt and a wilderness lodge. They must be either getting an astronomic price or shifting a hell of a lot of kidneys.'

Colhoun checked the notes he had made while talking to Ferguson's friend at the School of Tropical Medicine in London. 'A kidney will fetch $20,000, a cornea about $7000,' he told them. 'A knee joint goes for about $2500. Three small ear bones – $750. You may find this hard to believe, but if you could extract an entire skeleton from a fresh corpse, and powder the bones, you would be talking nearly a quarter of a million.'

'Christ,' Dubery said.

222

'Looks like my Dad is going to leave me something after all,' Finn murmured.

Colhoun smiled despite himself. 'The reason's simple,' he said. 'Supply and demand. The queues keep getting longer, and for the best reasons. Since seat belts were introduced here and in America road deaths – and particularly brain deaths, which allow the organs to be removed from a technically living body – have declined dramatically. So there are less organs for transplant. When they raised the speed limit in some US states from fifty-five to sixty-five the death rate increased again, and the transplant surgeons thought it was Christmas. And then some states started imposing handgun controls, which tightened the supply again.'

'Sick,' Finn commented.

'Aye,' Dubery agreed. 'But if someone you loved was desperate for a new kidney ...' He shrugged. 'It's a hard call.'

'This smuggling is illegal in America, right?' Finn asked.

'Oh aye,' Colhoun said, checking his notes again. 'The National Organ Transplant Act of 1984 made it a criminal offence to buy or sell a human organ. But it's not illegal in a lot of Third World countries. In India it's quite common for families to sell a daughter's kidney. And even in places where it is technically illegal there seems to be a lot of it going on. In Russia loads of families can't afford to bury their dead unless they agree to sell off the profitable bits. And there was a case in London the other day of a Turkish immigrant caught selling his kidney to some man from Birmingham. In some places in Central America gangs just round up children and help themselves. Even at its nicest this is a very nasty business. And we have no way of knowing if the organs being smuggled into Florida have been donated voluntarily or not. For all we know some bastard warlord in Haiti could just be slaughtering people and cutting them up. Carefully.'

'I think we get the picture, boss,' Finn said soberly.

'Good. I don't want to find out that pieces of you two are on sale in half a dozen Florida hospitals.'

While waiting for the word from Poole on their request for reinforcements, Marker and Cafell found themselves with plenty of spare time on their hands.

This proved a mixed blessing as far as Marker was concerned. Usually there were few things he enjoyed more than simply messing around on or beside the sea, but on this occasion he found that the lack of a controlling purpose left his mind open for the demons to roam. He had hardly thought about Penny over the past couple of days, but now he seemed trapped once more by memories of his life with her.

One part of him wished he had left the Marine Corps, as she had wanted. They would probably have had a child by now, maybe even two. He would have been helping to bring new life into the world, rather than taking life away. He had no name for the man he had killed, and the only face he had seen had already been half obliterated by the bullet from the Browning.

Penny's face also seemed harder to visualize with each passing day, and once, when he tried to conjure it up, he found himself staring into the dead eyes of Tamara Arcilla. Maybe time would untangle these knots of grief, but Marker was no longer so sure. One thing he did know was that any future relationship would have to live and breathe in the shadow of both these women. The past, which had always seemed like a springboard to the future, now felt more like a set of emotional chains.

Rob Cafell had never killed anybody, but he too found himself dwelling on the man whose corpse was now rotting on the bed of Lostman's River. The trip back across Hell's Lake in the submarine had been like one of those black farces on TV, where a body keeps turning up despite the best efforts of all involved. Cafell had laughed at such programmes in the past, but he doubted if he would laugh at one again. And he wondered whether the authors of such pieces had ever seen death up close. For the first time he began to understand his father's lifelong reluctance to talk in any detail about his experiences in the war.

Russell was just finishing putting all the medicines back on the pharmacy shelves when Emelisse came into the room. 'I've got something to show you,' she said.

It was a copy of the *New York Times*.

'Where did that come from?' he asked.

'Oh, Calderón has the Tuesday edition sent up from Port au Prince every week. He likes to read the "Science Times" section. Keep up with developments.'

'I expect Dr Frankenstein was a regular subscriber,' said Russell.

She sighed and tapped the front page. 'Haitian Junta Faces Ultimatum' the headline read.

Russell skimmed through the report, which suggested, without offering any evidence in support, that American military intervention in Haiti was a couple of weeks away at most, and perhaps only a matter of days.

'Maybe it is not worth trying to escape,' she said softly.

'If the Americans bring back Aristide then Joutard's days are numbered.'

He put a hand on each of her shoulders. 'Emelisse,' he said, 'if law and order comes to Haiti it will come first to Port au Prince. And what do you think people like Joutard will do – wait for it to reach out for them?' He answered his own question. 'Of course not. They will cover their tracks, bury the evidence. And we are part of that evidence. All those young men and women with scars on their bodies are part of it.'

She took it in, and her eyes closed as in pain.

'Come with me,' he urged her.

She opened her eyes and looked at him. 'It frightens me,' she said, though as far as he could tell there was not a trace of fear in her eyes. 'But you are probably right.'

'You'll come?'

'Oh no, you don't understand. If you are right, then this is one more reason why I must stay.'

The burst transmission from Poole announcing the dispatch of reinforcements arrived at 09.00 hours on Monday morning. Both the decision and the selection were welcomed by the two recipients. Ian Dubery was as good a boat handler as anyone in the SBS, and Stuart Finn was known to be as effective in a crunch as he was insubordinate.

Marker had 'talked' to Franklin via the PRC 319 on their return from Hell's Lake, and now he composed another message, typed it out on the keypad, and sent it. In a way he felt sorry he couldn't offer the ex-SAS man a more active role, for Franklin had felt like an integral part of the team ever since their arrival in the Turks and Caicos.

Marker and Cafell decided that only one of them was needed to collect the incoming tourists that afternoon, and the younger man drew the short straw. Marker was left to go over the tactical plan once more, take a swim, and watch cartoons on TV. He felt in control again, and told himself that there would be time enough to sort out the meaning of sex, the universe and everything when they had Arcilla behind bars.

Cafell, meanwhile, arrived at Miami International with plenty of time to spare, parked the car, and started circumnavigating the now familiar sights. He bought and started reading a new paperback account of the Battle of Midway, and missed the on-screen announcement of the plane's arrival.

Hurrying down to the relevant gate, he caught sight of them through an open door, as they waited to be processed through Immigration. Dubery was the taller one, with dark, boyish good looks which reminded Cafell of the *Match of the Day* pundit who once played for Liverpool. Finn had lighter hair, swept back and heavily dosed with gel. He looked like one of the lads – Cafell's father would have called him a 'wide boy'. Standing in the Immigration queue, Finn seemed faintly amused by the whole business. Dubery, by contrast, looked slightly worried, as if conscious of how far he was from the presumed simplicities of life in the Outer Hebrides.

The two of them got through Immigration and Customs without any trouble, and Cafell hurried them down to the basement car park.

'Nice motor,' Finn commented.

'Wait till you see the boat,' Cafell told him.

They drove south out of Miami, setting sun to their right, rush-hour traffic all around them. Dubery gazed out of the window with interest, but Finn, happily spread across the two back seats, had apparently seen it all before.

'How many square feet of skin do you reckon you have, boss?'

'What?' Cafell exclaimed.

Finn repeated the question.

'He's been driving me mad all day,' Dubery lamented. 'He bought one of those mini-encyclopaedias at Heathrow, and he's been showing off ever since. When the hostess brought the meal on the plane he asked her when the microwave was invented.'

'And when was it?'

'Nineteen forty-seven,' Finn said from the back. 'And the average human has twenty square feet of skin.'

'I'll be able to sleep at night now,' Cafell said. The light was rapidly fading now, the lights of the oncoming cars like a river stretching into the distance.

'So what's the score, boss?' Dubery asked.

'Marker will tell you the plan. You've got the camcorder?'

'State of the art, according to the Illustrators,' Finn said from the back. 'The man said it would shoot in just about any light short of pitch-darkness. He said the Yanks use something like it for filming their drug busts.'

'Sounds ideal.'

'What are we going to be filming,' Finn asked, 'porno flicks with the boss and this Cuban guy's sister?'

Cafell suppressed a smiled. 'I wouldn't suggest that to Captain Marker if I were you,' he said. 'In fact I wouldn't mention the woman at all.'

'Left a nasty taste in the mouth, did she?' Finn asked mischievously.

'Something like that.'

'Why, was she really ugly or something?'

Cafell grunted. 'She was a stunner.'

'Then . . .'

'Don't ask me. And don't ask him either if you don't want your head bitten off.'

'OK, I get the message.'

They drove on, through Homestead and then on to the two-lane Keys section of Highway 1. As they went past Key Largo's Holiday Inn Cafell asked the other two if they had heard of *The African Queen*. Finn had, Dubery hadn't. Finn expressed his doubts as to whether they had flush toilets yet in the Outer Hebrides. These had been invented, he added gratuitously, in 1589, the year after the Spanish Armada.

For the next half hour Cafell treated the two corporals to a lecture on the defeat of the Armada, something he had studied and modelled in some depth.

'And you thought I was a know-all,' Finn said to Dubery as they arrived at Buena Vista.

Marker was waiting at the door to shake their hands. Supper was already heating in the microwave.

'Invented in 1947,' Cafell said, nodding at it.

'When else?' Marker agreed.

After eating, Finn and Dubery were shown over the *Slipstream Queen*, beers were retrieved from the fridge, and the four men sat in the boat's lounge as Marker went over his intended plan of action.

'My first idea was simply to take over the lodge and round up everyone as they arrived – the sub, the chopper, even the Indian in his canoe if he's part of the set-up. But there's one big problem with that. Either of you two see what it is?' he asked the newcomers.

They both thought for a moment. 'A lapful of kidneys,' Finn said eventually.

'Right. We can hardly expect the bad guys to go ahead and deliver them for us – they'd just make a run for it. And there's no way we could deliver them ourselves. We could just ignore the damn things, but after people have donated them – whether by choice or not – it seems like a terrible fucking waste not to let them go where they're needed.'

Marker looked from face to face. 'So this is what we're going to do instead . . .'

Russell strung the water bottle across his back and checked that he had everything else he needed. The food had been shared out between his pockets, the scalpel he had lifted from the surgery was stuffed in his right boot, inside a sheath made from paperback covers. The length of rope was wrapped around his neck.

It was one o'clock, the time he had decided offered an optimum balance of risks. Later would have been safer as regards escaping the compound, and earlier would have given him more time to get across the island.

Let's go, he told himself, and picked up the grappling-hook he had fashioned from bedsprings. After opening the front door he waited half a minute, watching the compound for any sign of movement, and then walked briskly through the trees and darkened bungalows to the southern perimeter wall.

The grappling-hook caught on the strands of barbed wire at the first attempt, and he quickly pulled himself up the face with the help of the twisted sheet rope. Once at the top he gathered together the sheet to make a cushion, and used it to roll across the barbs. He landed as well as he could have hoped in the bare dirt on the other side.

It had been too easy, he thought. If getting out of the compound was that easy, then getting off the island was likely to be a real bugger.

He stood up gingerly and took his first look at the outside world. It was not the way he had imagined it.

Away to his right a few tumbledown homes were gathered around the gate, and beyond them a line of tall palms followed what was probably a stream bed around the far side of the compound. But that was the extent of the cover. The forested hills he had expected were covered with low scrub up to about five hundred feet, and bare above that. It looked more like Provo than the Haiti he had imagined.

And the gibbous moon riding in the eastern sky was bathing the slopes in pale grey light.

Reckoning that the stream bed probably offered the easiest and most inconspicuous route up into the hills, Russell carefully threaded his way through the shacks beneath the watch-tower, keeping one eye on the guard above. Fortunately the man only seemed interested in what was going on inside the walls of the compound.

The stream bed was full of dry pebbles. Russell followed it uphill, slowly until he was sure he was out of earshot, then as fast as the terrain would allow. The moonlight ensured that he had no trouble finding his way, and until the stream bed petered out in an ocean of scrub he made good progress.

The last uphill stretch was a different matter, and it was almost four o'clock when he reached the ridge top, and found himself looking out across several miles of ocean channel at the distant Haitian mainland. Away to the west, he thought he could make out a few pinpricks of light where the town of Port de Paix was supposed to be.

Below and to his left, some two miles distant, a village was stretched along the sides of a small bay.

The downhill leg proved no easier. The southern slopes of the range were not so bare, and this time he had no stream bed to follow through the scrub. More than an hour had passed when he finally emerged into the cultivated fields above the village, and crawled to the crest of the last small rise overlooking the bay.

There were several small boats moored at a ram-shackle dock, and one large enough to serve as a public ferry. Russell was strongly tempted to walk straight down, steal a boat, and take his chances out on the water.

But it was gone five o'clock, and the chances of his reaching the far side of the strait before dawn were non-existent. He would have no time to pick and choose which boat to steal. And he would be a sitting duck if they caught him on the water.

On the other hand, he told himself, if he waited until the following night he could be sure of arriving on the mainland during the hours of darkness, and that would vastly increase his chances of finding some sort of sanctuary in Port de Paix before the local thugs found him.

He didn't much like it, but the smart money was on digging in for the day. He walked back through the cultivated fields, and into the scrub, where he dug out his first hide since the one above Port Stanley twelve years before. This one was blessed with natural cover, and didn't need to be constructed so professionally, but he was pleased with his work just the same.

Which was all to the good. Only a few minutes after incarcerating himself Russell heard the swelling drone of a helicopter. The search was underway.

13

On Russell's watch the second hand momentarily merged with the hour and minute hands. With butterflies dancing in his stomach and adrenalin coursing through his veins he started down the slope to the shoreline.

He had left the safety of the hide soon after dark, and surreptitiously worked his way down through the fields to the hilltop observation point he had reached the previous night. From there he had watched the last ferry arrive, the children dragged home to bed, the cooking fires doused, the kerosene glows dimmed one by one. Now only the two armed thugs were left, sitting on the beach end of the dock, their feet hanging just above the sand.

The four-hour wait had given Russell ample opportunity to both study their habits and work out the safest line of approach. The two men were each on their fourth beer, and though neither was showing any obvious signs of drunkenness – Haitian beer, as Russell knew from experience, was not the most potent in the world – the gaps between their visits to the end of the dock were growing noticeably shorter.

Why they should choose to walk all of fifty feet to piss in the sea when there was a perfectly good beach right next to them, only they could know. In Russell's experience such self-consciousness was refreshingly absent from most 'undeveloped' cultures. But maybe an inability to piss with someone watching was as crucial an indicator of development as cellular phones, microwaves and MTV. Not to mention transplant surgery.

Whatever the reason, he was grateful. It put a distance between the two men, and that would give him a chance.

He reached the shoreline about a hundred yards to the west of where they were sitting. They were talking with their backs to him, but every now and then one would turn his head, and Russell had no desire to play Creeping up on Grandma with two men toting Uzis. Instead he inched his way into the water, wishing the slope of the beach was steeper, but grateful for the noisy swish of the waves. Once the water was deep enough he began to swim, heading in a wide circle for the end of the dock.

The water was warmer than he'd expected, and dirtier too. Reaching his destination, he hauled himself in between the line of pilings and started pulling himself hand over hand towards the land end, where the four dangling feet were silhouetted against the sand. On his way he examined the boats which were tied up on either side, and realized with dismay that the outboard motors had been removed from those boats that normally carried them. He was going to have to row across the strait.

He provisionally picked out a red boat with the name Dolores, and moved on, reaching the point where the waves clawed at the sand about five yards from the four hanging legs. He could hear the two men talking quite clearly now – in Creole, he thought.

Russell lowered himself slowly on to his stomach in the gently breaking waves and began dragging himself slowly up the beach. When he was level with the waving feet he pulled himself up into a crouching position and waited. His breathing sounded far too loud, his heart was hammering like a road drill, and at any moment he expected one of the men to jump down on to the sand and smile at him over the barrel of his Uzi. Or simply blow him away.

But the minutes went by, the men kept talking, and occasionally flexing their feet. Every minute or so Russell would hear the sound of beer glugging out of a bottle and down a throat.

And then two legs suddenly disappeared, and the planks above his head shook with the feet walking away down the dock. Ten seconds, he thought, inching forward towards the still-hanging feet. Another two to get the dick out. And three more to reach mid-piss.

With both hands he grasped one of the offered ankles and pulled with all his might. A shriek split the night, and the man came crashing down on to the beach in front of him, landing head first in the sand. As Russell dived for the fallen gun another shout came from the far end of the dock, swiftly followed by the sound of running feet.

Russell's finger found the trigger and he turned, still on one knee, as the running man's silhouette loomed into view on the dock above. Both guns seemed to open fire at the same moment, but only Russell had a clear view of what he was aiming at. The Haitian was lifted into the air, and seemed to hang there for a moment, like a man bungling a backward somersault, before he crashed down with a sound of splintering wood into one of the small boats parked on the far side of the dock.

The other man, Russell discovered, had been knocked unconscious by the fall.

In the village a couple of lights had appeared, but no one ventured out to investigate, and within a few minutes the lights had been extinguished. Russell used his length of rope to tie up the unconscious man, and gagged him

with one of his own socks. Then he walked quickly down
the dock to the boat he had chosen, slipped its mooring,
jumped aboard, and picked up the oars.

He had more than five hours of darkness left, which
should give him all the time he needed. Soon the dock
was disappearing from view, swallowed up in the larger
silhouette of the hills behind the village.

Half an hour went by, and though the mainland hardly
seemed to grow any nearer, Russell felt happy with his
progress. With the moon shining down on the sea, the
heavens filled with stars, it was possible to forget for a
moment what might be waiting on the farther shore, and
what he had left behind in the compound on Tortuga.

It was through this precarious sense of well-being that
the first shouts of distress reached his ears, and for a
moment he thought it was his conscience playing tricks
with him.

But it was a boat, a small boat drifting towards him,
sitting unusually low in the water. At least two of its
occupants seemed to be shouting at him.

He rowed towards the other boat, and soon came
alongside. It wasn't much bigger than the *Dolores*, but
it was carrying a load more suited to a boat three times
the size. A huge mound of belongings filled its centre,
and seven people were wedged around its edges. One,
a middle-aged woman, was holding a baby in her lap.
The other five – two adults and three children all under
twelve – were baling for all they were worth.

In vain. The boat was already knee deep in water, the
tops of its sides only a few inches above the level of the
sea. It was sinking.

'America!' the woman with the baby shouted at him,
as if she thought he was waiting for a password.

Other eyes looked imploringly in his direction.

This was what they called instant karma, Russell thought. Someone up there was trying to tell him something.

He manoeuvred his boat alongside and gestured for the Haitian family to come aboard. The woman came first, and the baby was passed over to her. The children were next, and then the mother. With each new arrival Russell's boat let out a creak of alarm and sank lower into the sea.

The father was now beginning to transfer the pile of belongings from the sinking boat.

'No,' Russell told him, shaking his head for emphasis. The man gave him a look which seemed to say: Don't you understand, these things are our life?

Russell shook his head again. Already it was obvious that they wouldn't make it across the strait. He mimed to the Haitian that he could try towing the belongings, and at this the man's eyes lit up. He stepped nimbly into the stern of Russell's boat and reached out an arm for the bow of his own.

Russell turned the *Dolores* back towards Tortuga and begun rowing, conscious of the children's eyes staring up at him. The baby began to cry, and the mother started singing a soft Creole lullaby. Halfway to the shore he heard a despairing sigh behind him and knew that the other boat had taken the family's belongings to the bottom.

The child's wail seemed to grow stronger as they neared the beach, but it didn't matter. Russell's eyes had already picked out the men waiting on the dock.

The dark mangroves slid slowly by on either side, as the *Slipstream Queen* made its unhurried way up Lostman's River. The moon had risen an hour before, and was playing hide-and-seek with the fleet of clouds that were moving across the star-laden sky.. One moment the waters of the river would offer a shimmering carpet, the next a black mirror.

Dubery was at the wheel, Cafell reading the chart. Finn was sitting on the bow with the nightscope, looking out for any uncharted obstructions. Marker was in the lounge, checking through their equipment one last time.

They had been on the move for three hours now, since receiving Franklin's confirmatory message. This time they had secured advanced clearance for their passage through US territorial waters from the authorities in Key West, and had rashly promised a return on their American hosts' hospitality before the night was out. The US Customs Service Air Division at Homestead had been alerted to expect an incoming call sometime around dawn.

It was almost two o'clock now, and they were nearing the spot where they had anchored the cabin cruiser the previous week. As they passed it Cafell showed Dubery where the crocodile had lain, jaws at the ready. He didn't mention that they were passing over the spot where they had sunk the dead gunman.

In the lounge Marker heard both comment and omission, and decided that this team of four had gelled as smoothly as he could have hoped. He wasn't sure he had much in common with either of the two newcomers – Dubery was a bit on the earnest side, Finn still young enough to think the world revolved around him – but then Cafell wasn't exactly his idea of a soul mate either. The important thing was that they all felt confident enough in each other's abilities to make full use of their own, and after three days together Marker was pretty sure they did.

Any lingering doubts about team chemistry had been removed the previous evening. Emerging from his sleep shift Marker had come upon the other three practising cabrioles on the stern deck. Not that he knew them by that name. Finn's pocket encyclopaedia, it turned out, contained diagrams of the eight basic ballet steps, and his SBS comrades were practising number eight, leaping into the air with one arm outstretched, and two legs fluttering against the other. And laughing fit to burst.

Marker smiled at the memory and went forward to join the other two on the bridge. Hell's Lake was not much more than a mile ahead, and it was time to decide whether or not to douse the boat's lights. They were not intending to bring the vessel within three miles of the Anhinga Lodge, but it was always difficult to judge how far sound travelled across water. If the bad guys heard the boat, then it would be better if they could see it too.

'If we leave the lights on,' he suggested to Cafell and Dubery, 'then as far as they're concerned we'll just be one more boat cutting across the southern end of the lake on our way to the Everglades Waterway. There must be several boats a day doing just that.'

'In the daytime, yes,' Cafell said, 'but not in the middle of the night.'

'I don't think the noise will carry,' Dubery said quietly.

'Actually neither do I,' Cafell said.

Marker sighed. The engines seemed awfully loud to him, but maybe that was because he was listening to them. And it would be better not to raise any questions at all in the minds of the enemy. 'OK,' he said eventually, 'let's go for broke. But do your best to keep the engine noise down.'

'You got it,' Cafell said in a mock-American accent.

The entrance to the lake came into view, and a few minutes later the *Slipstream Queen* was venturing out on to the wide waters. Cafell kept them close to the southern shore, where, unless the enemy had acquired state-of-the-art thermal imaging since Marker's previous visit, they would be hidden in the dark line of mangroves.

Lights were already visible across the lake. With the aid of the nightscope Marker could make out two illuminated windows in the lodge, and what was probably a kerosene lamp burning on the end of the jetty.

The *Slipstream Queen* was now far enough away from the course the submarine would take. Marker gave Dubery the cutthroat gesture, and the Scot turned off the engines. In the bow Finn gently lowered the anchor into the lake.

The four men gathered in the lounge, and all but Dubery pulled on their wetsuit hoods. Using the pools of moonlight offered by the windows they applied the dark camouflage cream to the exposed parts of their faces and checked their equipment.

Satisfied, they went out on deck. Once the Kleppers had been quietly let down into the water, Finn and Cafell slid down the rungs and clambered aboard. Marker lowered the waterproof bag containing the camcorder and PRC 319 into the empty seat beside Cafell, and then climbed down to join Finn in the other canoe. Both crews pulled the spray-deck sheet over their heads, clamped it in place, and pulled the paddles from their pockets in the outer skin. Then with a wave of the hand from Marker they turned silently out towards the centre of the lake.

Standing on the deck, Dubery watched them go, frustrated at not being with them, but also remembering the day of his departure from Poole, and Helen telling him on the phone that she had no desire to be a widow at twenty-four.

Some six hundred miles to the south-east, Russell was wondering why he was still alive. When he had been returned to the camp that morning Joutard had made it clear that he would have one more chance to use his surgical skills, and that then he would be given the opportunity to experience the process from the patient's point of view.

But the operations were over, the helicopter long since gone, and he was still in the land of the living. Maybe there had not been enough time for Calderón to harvest both him and the man he had killed on the dock the previous night, several of whose bones, and both of whose corneas, had gone with the helicopter.

Maybe he had another week in hell, Russell thought. But at least he had saved that Haitian family, and he would be going out with a better opinion of himself than the one he had lately become used to. He had tried.

The quality of Joutard's hospitality had naturally dropped. Russell was back in the room where he had first seen Emelisse leaning over his face like an angel. And this time they had thought to board up the window from the outside, as well as lock the door.

He had been given one chance and blown it. And he had the distinct feeling that one was all he was going to get.

As the wilderness lodge grew nearer Marker left the paddling to Finn and devoted all his concentration to the nightscope. Before the angle became too obtuse he was able to pick out an occasional movement through one of the lighted windows, as if someone was walking across the room behind them. But there was no sign of enemy activity outside the lodge or on the jetty.

The mysterious disappearance of a colleague the week before had obviously been attributed to accident. They had found the upturned canoe and made the logical deduction as to the whereabouts of its former occupant.

In the lead Klepper Cafell veered away from the shoreline to pass an unusually ambitious root, and raised an arm to give the following canoe advanced warning. They had paddled about three miles now, on a course that hugged the lake's western shore, and were now not much more than half a mile from their destination. They had gambled on finding a suitable landing spot on this side of the lodge – Marker knew from experience that there were none on the other.

About a hundred yards from the boat-house they were forced to concede that there was none on this side either. At least they had no problem finding somewhere to tie up the canoes – there were about a thousand roots per square yard to choose from. The three men slipped quietly out into the waist-deep water and started wriggling and twisting their way towards dry land, passing the bag with the camcorder and satellite radio forward hand by hand in a leapfrogging sequence. All three men had experience of waterproof containers proving themselves otherwise.

They reached dry ground later than Cafell and Finn hoped but sooner than Marker expected. He unzipped the bag and gave the radio to Cafell, the camcorder to Finn, and kept the bag for himself. Then in single file they started slowly forward in the direction of the lodge. Soon they had their first glimpse of the light on the end of the jetty, and another few minutes brought them to a position just inside the trees which ringed the helipad behind the lodge. The helicopter – an Enstrom 280 FXA Shark – had already arrived.

Marker brought finger and thumb together in the prearranged signal for Finn to use the camcorder, and the corporal squirmed a couple of yards further forward to get a clear shot. Just in case, Marker also spent a few seconds memorizing the helicopter's number.

A raised voice suddenly disturbed the calm, causing all three men to freeze. The silence that followed lasted only a second, before a wail of laughter filled the air. It was only the men inside the lodge, having what sounded like a good time.

'Party animals,' Marker murmured to himself. And their party was about to get crashed.

It was about seventy-five yards from where they crouched to the front of the lodge, and most of it was in shadow. It was worth the chance, Marker decided, if only to check on the strength of the opposition. 'I'm going for a closer look,' he whispered to Cafell and Finn, and before the former could start an argument he was gone, darting over the open ground, along the side of the outhouse, and across the gap which separated it from the lodge.

An oblique look through the nearest window showed there were no curtains, only a mosquito screen. Marker moved away from the lodge, heading for a position in the shadows from which he could get a better look inside the room. Having found one, he took a single quick glance inside and sank to his haunches, letting his mind retrieve the image.

There were four men sitting around a table at one end of what looked like a games room. There was a table-tennis table behind them, and a pool table beyond that. Three of the men looked Hispanic, and none of them was older than thirty. The fourth man was sitting with his back to the window, but the hat and long hair looked more than familiar. It was the Indian he had seen on the creek.

One more look, Marker decided. Like many men with Special Forces experience he was a firm believer in the sixth sense – if you stared at anyone for long enough they became aware that they were being observed. The trick was to keep the vision peripheral, and just take it all in like a camera.

He rose slowly to his feet, took a second look, and sank back down. One of the Hispanics was wearing a shoulder holster, but there were no other weapons on display. If they had SMGs – and there was every reason to think they did – then they were probably leaning against the men's chairs, or maybe out near the main door. There was no way of knowing.

Satisfied he had seen all there was to safely see, Marker took the same route back to Cafell and Finn, and recounted in whispers what he had discovered.

'Can I go and take their pictures now?' Finn asked.

Marker grinned at him and looked at his watch. 'Time we were in position for phase two,' he said.

He collected the three MP5s, wrapped them in the bag which had carried the camcorder and radio, and rammed them into a convenient growth of ferns. Meanwhile, Cafell and Finn had both taken a ball of dark twine from their belts and tied one end around the trunk of the nearest tree. Marker and Finn then moved further back into the undergrowth and turned towards the lake, unrolling Finn's ball behind them. A few minutes later they reached the shoreline close to the spot from which Marker had first seen inside the boat-house, and started looking for the best camera angle.

Cafell had headed off in the opposite direction. According to the largest-scale map they had managed to find, the thick vegetation surrounding the lake rarely extended more than a hundred yards inland, and he was hoping to find a suitably open space in which to use the radio. His hundred yards of twine was nearly exhausted when the light began to brighten, almost imperceptibly at first, but then with increasing speed, as if a bright grey sun was rising. Cafell found himself standing on the edge of a sea of grass which stretched away under the stars as far as the eye could see. He stepped forward on to this strange plain, and found himself up to his knees in water.

He snorted at his own stupidity, and retreated to the dry ground of the hummock. After tying the end of the twine to a convenient tree he wedged the satellite set into a cleft between branches, and set off back through the trees, using the twine as a guide. At its end he transferred to Finn's line, and followed that down to where the other two had set themselves up behind a particularly tangled web of roots, with the camcorder's lens peeking out in the direction of the boat-house and jetty.

It was just after four o'clock, and they probably had the better part of two hours to wait. They did so mostly in silence, occasionally stretching cramped limbs, and intermittently scanning the dark lake for a sight of the submarine. Finn found himself thinking about the boating club on the River Lea where he had first discovered that escape was possible from the oppressive world of Hackney's high-rises. Crouching in a foot of water wondering where the water moccasins were wasn't exactly what he'd had in mind for a career, but he had no regrets. He might be halfway between the frying pan and the fire, but at least that meant he was out of the fucking frying pan. And who knew – he might land in a beautiful woman's lap. Eventually.

Cafell was thinking about his father, and what the old man would think to see him here. It wasn't the sort of war he had fought in, that was certain. But the days of the big boats were over, whether on the surface or beneath it. His dad thought that was sad, but Cafell, for all his love of naval history, didn't agree. In this sort of war, where canoes replaced battleships, the individual counted for more. Every man on this mission had real responsibility, whereas three-quarters of the men on his dad's nuclear sub were just there to keep the damn thing running.

Beside him, Marker was remembering a summer with his parents in one of the south coast resorts. Hastings, he thought it was. They had been playing in some murder mystery on the pier, and he had been given a small part himself, comprising a grand total of three lines. The third of these had been the last of the play: 'Mummy, where are they taking Daddy?'

He smiled to himself and wondered what they were doing now. Probably sitting at home in Highgate, watching themselves on TV, glasses of wine in hand, puffing away at their cigarettes. And here he was five thousand miles away, loitering among the mangrove roots. The whole family was half insane.

The minutes dragged by, and the setting of the moon deprived the lake of its silver sheen. Every now and then they heard laughter or good-natured shouting coming from the lodge. A single bird began to sing, and then another, and almost at once, or so it seemed, the rest of bird-kind was joining in. The sky above the lake's eastern shore began to lighten, bringing the small, dark shape of the submarine gradually into focus.

The men in the house had seen it too. There was the sound of a door slamming, the clump of feet on wood, and then three of them came into view around the wall of the boat-house. The two Hispanics clambered down the steps where Marker had shot their late comrade, one of them carrying the kerosene lamp, the other some sort of customized cradle. The Indian sat down on the top step and lit a cigarette.

Where's the fourth man? Marker wondered. The distant sound of rotor blades turning supplied the answer. He turned and gave the thumbs up to Cafell, who immediately melted away into the vegetation.

Finn looked enquiringly up at Marker, who shook his head. He wanted to be sure that the sound of the submarine's passage would drown out the whirr of the camcorder, and it was still a hundred yards away.

The two men on the walkway were talking to each other in Spanish, a language neither Marker nor Finn understood. Both were wearing open-necked shirts and slacks, and both were carrying handguns, one in a shoulder holster, the other in his belt. The Indian seemed unarmed.

The noise of the submarine was now loud enough, and Marker gave Finn the signal. The phrase 'you're on candid camera' floated out of some deep recess in his mind.

By this time Cafell had retrieved the PRC 319 and was wading out into the sawgrass swamp. The message, giving the helicopter's identification number, had already been keyed in. He sent it in a single burst. In the Poole operations room someone would be noting down the precise time the message was received, and using it as an approximate guide to the helicopter's time of departure. This, along with the location of the lodge and the helicopter's number, would then be phoned through to the waiting US Customs Service.

Back at the lake shore the submarine was being guided into the boat-house. Once it was secure, one of the crewmen clambered out into the yellow glow of the kerosene lamp, and stood there straddling walkway and submarine. His partner began passing out the Belzer-Kountz machines, and he handed them across to the men on the walkway, who placed them side by side in the carrying cradle. There were four of them, and two other containers of a different kind. Once they were all loaded in, the two Hispanics took hold of the rope handles at either end of the cradle and carried it off in the direction of the helicopter. The second crewmen followed the first on to the walkway, and handed a small package across to the now hovering Indian, who stuffed it inside the top of his trousers.

All three men headed up the steps, the Indian carrying the lamp. As they disappeared from view the distant whine of the rotor blades accelerated, and Marker thought he glimpsed a dark shape climbing up into the rapidly lightening sky. The plastic boxes would be delivered all right, and the waiting patients would get what they had paid for, but if the US Customs people were on the ball then there would be no escape for the people who had banked the cheques.

'Time to go,' Marker whispered.

He and Finn extricated themselves from the roots and followed the twine back to its source, where Cafell was already waiting for them. They removed the MP5s from the bag, and replaced them with the radio and camcorder.

Marker led the way to the edge of the trees, and stopped there for a full minute, watching for movement in the dawn twilight. Then all three men moved off at a loping run, Marker and Finn towards the back of the lodge, Cafell towards the front.

Marker had assumed that the door at the back would be in use whenever the helipad was, and therefore unlikely to be locked. In fact it was wide open.

He found himself in a narrow lobby, looking at the spare machines which Colhoun had picked out on the photographic blow-ups. Ahead of him a passageway extended for some ten yards before opening into the wide entrance lobby. In the distance he could see the front door, wide open.

He could hear voices ahead, and decided they were probably coming from the room in which he had witnessed the card game, and which he presumed must open on to the entrance lobby from the right. With any luck all five men would be in the same room.

He remembered his conversation with the captain of the *Argyll* about stun grenades, and allowed himself a bitter smile before advancing stealthily down the passageway to the threshold of the entrance lobby.

The Indian walked into view, his face turned back towards the room he had just left, as if he was listening to a parting comment.

At the same moment one of the two Hispanics walked out past him, took one stride across the lobby in ignorance, and then caught sight of the two SBS men. His eyes almost jumped out of their sockets, and his right hand flashed halfway towards his shoulder holster.

'Freeze!' Marker whispered fiercely, and the man's hand seemed to shift into slow motion as his brain registered the twin barrels of the two MP5s.

The Indian's head had spun around at the sound of Marker's voice, but either his brain was half asleep or he had somehow acquired – five hundred years of American history notwithstanding – a touching faith in the white man's reluctance to shoot unarmed red men in cold blood. Either way he made a break for the door, arriving at it just in time to impale his stomach on Cafell's MP5.

'*Qué pasa?*' the other Hispanic asked as he stepped out into the lobby like one more duck in a shooting gallery. He sounded more irritated than anxious.

By this time Marker had taken several quick steps forward, and there was no chance for the man to miss the menace of the MP5. He raised his hands in the air, and spat a torrent of Spanish in the direction of his fellow-caretaker. Marker yanked the automatic from the man's belt, and took a cautionary look around the corner of the door to the communal room. As he had hoped, the two submarine crewmen were simply standing there looking lost. This wasn't an eventuality they had prepared for.

The SBS men herded the Indian and the two caretakers back into the room to join them.

'OK, boss?' Cafell asked.

Marker nodded. 'And find some rope to tie this lot up with,' he shouted after his second in command.

Cafell disappeared through the front door. A few seconds later they heard the rushing sound of the flare being fired, and through the window Marker caught sight of the bright-green flash in the still lightening sky.

'We are taking you with us,' he told the five men. 'Because we have questions to ask you. Refuse to answer them or make any kind of trouble and you will end up where your friend did, at the bottom of the lake. That's right,' he added, noticing the look of comprehension on a couple of the faces, 'it wasn't an accident. This is not our first visit.'

They looked at each other, and then at the SBS men. The crewmen looked disgusted, the caretakers looked confused, the Indian looked depressed. No one said anything.

After a few minutes Cafell returned, carrying a coil of rope and the package which had dropped out of the Indian's belt. 'Presents,' he told Marker. 'Our stuff's on the jetty. Ian's on the way. I'll take one of the canoes and fetch the Kleppers.'

He disappeared again, and Marker kept the MP5 pointing steadily in the prisoners' direction as Finn went to work tying their wrists together behind their backs. Once all five were securely trussed, he left Finn keeping watch, took out his knife, and sliced open the end of the package. There were three small plastic bags inside, each containing white powder. He cut a slit in one of them, inserted a wet finger, and tasted the powder, just to be sure.

'Icing sugar, boss?' Finn asked.

'The very best,' Marker agreed. 'And just when we thought Comrade Arcilla had abandoned drug running in favour of spare parts.'

'Seems a bit weird,' Finn said. 'They could have brought in a hundred times as much.'

'True,' Marker agreed.

'And why give it to Sitting Bull here? Why not the helicopter?'

Marker looked at the Seminole. 'Maybe in payment,' he said, and a flicker in the man's eyes told him he had probably hit the mark.

It was almost full light outside now, and through the

window the *Slipstream Queen* could be seen approaching the jetty. He looked at his watch. Less than half an hour had passed since Cafell's transmission – they probably had as much time again before the American authorities could put in an appearance. They would probably be too busy tracking the helicopter's deliveries, but Marker was keen to avoid a potentially embarrassing argument over whose prisoners these were.

'Time to go, lads,' he told the five men, and led the way out of the lodge and down to the jetty, with Finn bringing up the rear. Dubery was easing the *Slipstream Queen* alongside, and Cafell was waiting to lift aboard the two Kleppers. Once this had been done the two men hurried round to the boat-house, where they loosed the submarine from its moorings and eased it carefully out on to the lake, before taking to the water themselves, and manoeuvring it across to the waiting tow-rope.

'All aboard,' Marker told the captives.

They filed on to the boat. One crewman and one caretaker were put in one of the two sleeping cabins beneath the stern deck, the remaining three men in the other. There were no locks on the doors, but there was only one narrow exit to the rest of the boat, and Finn was left to cover this with his MP5, just in case anyone had a brainstorm. So far Arcilla's men had seemed too stunned to offer resistance or attempt an escape, and Marker wasn't expecting any trouble in the near future. When the shock wore off they would still have nowhere to run.

As Dubery eased the *Slipstream Queen* away from the dock and took her back across the lake towards the Lostman's River egress, Marker and Cafell went through the questions they wanted answered. Once they had the list, one of the two crewman was brought forward to the lounge area. He was a dark-skinned Hispanic, probably in his late twenties. At first he refused to say anything, other than that he didn't speak English – 'No hablo inglés,' he repeated sullenly.

'OK then,' Marker told Cafell in a resigned voice, 'we'll have to do it the hard way. Go and get his partner up here, and then we'll throw this guy overboard. His partner will talk.'

Cafell had taken two steps towards the stern when the man rediscovered his flair for languages.

'My name is Miguel,' he said. 'What do you want to know?'

'What time are you expected back at the *Tiburón Blanco*?' Marker asked. 'We shall be asking your partner the same question,' he added as an incentive to truth.

'About four o'clock in the morning,' the man said. 'We leave from the lodge at nine.'

'Tonight?'

'*Sí.*'

Marker went on to extract a detailed breakdown of the *Tiburón Blanco*'s crew, and a sketch map of the boat itself. According to Miguel the two submarine crews greatly enjoyed the treasure-hunting side of their job and hated the long underwater voyages to and from Hell's Lake. Angel Socarras, the captain and head of the operation, was a complete bastard. Miguel had never heard of anyone called Fidel Arcilla.

Nor had his partner, another Cuban-American, whose name turned out to be Jorge. He too thought Socarras was the man in charge.

The two 'caretakers' had never heard of Arcilla either, but they took their orders from a man named Hector Chavez, who ran Anhinga Lodge for 'some corporation in Miami'. Their only job was to look after the place and scare off unwelcome visitors, particularly between

Thursday afternoon and Friday evening. They assumed the contraband organs were going to a hospital, but didn't know which or where. Once they had asked the helicopter pilot, merely out of curiosity, and been told in no uncertain terms to mind their own business.

The Seminole, who told them his name was Ricky Bowlegs, knew nothing of the wider picture. As Marker had suspected, the small shipment of cocaine was payment for services rendered – he and a few friends formed Anhinga Lodge's outer defences, watching and listening out for any hint of danger, either from the law, the Everglades Park authorities or their own people. One Seminole man had needed a strong warning, their captive said phlegmatically. And one Park Ranger had seen more than he should, but he had proved more than willing to jump on the bandwagon.

Marker showed him the photograph he had taken the week before.

The Seminole sighed. 'You boys are good,' he said.

'It's a gift,' Marker told him.

14

The joint operations undertaken by the US Customs Service and the Florida State Police on that summer Friday did not reach the ears or eyes of the press for several days. The hospital staff concerned were bound by confidentiality, the authorities by the hope that bigger fish would still fall into their net, and the donor recipients by sheer ignorance.

But there was no way of keeping the whole business under wraps indefinitely, and soon after four o'clock that afternoon Hector Chavez, the Cuban-American lawyer who had been acting as coordinator between the Health Trust and Arcilla's organization, received a phone call from a worried hospital executive. That afternoon the executive had arrived back from lunch to find the parking lot full of police cars. He had driven away again, and eventually gone home, only to find that there was a police car sitting outside his house. A phone call to a friend at the hospital had confirmed his fears that it all had something to do with the transplants, but he had been unable to get hold of any more specific information. What, he asked Chavez, should he do?

'Pray,' the lawyer told him, and hung up. Chavez then tried to reach his contacts at the other three hospitals in the Trust, but only one proved available, the consultant in St Petersburg, who denied that anything unusual had happened that day.

'Did you have a delivery today?' Chavez asked.

'No, it was . . .'

Chavez hung up on him too, and sat in his Miami office wondering whether he should call Arcilla.

Not yet, he decided. First he needed details. Half an hour and a dozen phone calls later he had set enough investigatory wheels in motion to satisfy a Congressional Committee. Before another hour had passed a picture had begun to emerge, one that was far from comforting. It was possible that the police had been tipped off by someone in the know at the first delivery point, and then followed the delivery boy to the other two hospitals. Possible, but a little too fortuitous, Chavez thought. More likely, and much more seriously, the delivery had been followed all the way from Anhinga Lodge.

He sat at his desk for a few minutes, building up the nerve to tell Arcilla, and finally picked up the phone. At almost the same moment a police detective pushed past his secretary, prised the receiver none too gently from his hand, and started to recite him his rights.

Marker was woken by the hand shaking his shoulder. 'Ten minutes, boss,' Finn told him.

'OK.'

He sighed, shifted his legs off the bunk, and sat on the edge rubbing his eyes and yawning. His watch said it was two-twenty in the morning. Mind and body were telling him that four hours' sleep in twenty-four hours was not enough.

The eighteen or so hours which had passed since the SBS team's hurried departure from Anhinga Lodge had been busy. They had conducted five interrogations, taken lessons in handling the Russian submarine and been through several conversations with Poole. They had sailed the *Slipstream Queen* through the Keys and out across the Straits to its current position some twenty miles south-west of the Muertos Cays. They had rendezvoused with the *Argyll*, and persuaded her captain to offer their prisoners the hospitality of the frigate's brig. He in turn had passed on some up-to-the-minute intelligence – American troops would be moving into Haiti within the next few days. Tuesday at dawn was the current best guess.

Which didn't bode well for Russell, Marker decided. Arcilla's man in Haiti would presumably be shutting up shop.

In fact the whole business was becoming a race against the clock. For all they knew the *Tiburón Blanco* had already received word that the operation was unravelling, and headed out into the wide blue yonder. Or was waiting, guns at the ready, for a visit from the SBS.

There was no way of knowing. The US authorities had promised Colhoun they would do their best to keep the lid on for twenty-four hours, but Marker didn't have the highest opinion of American security. It had also occurred to him, and perhaps the Americans too, that any communication between Arcilla and his captain at this juncture would make it harder for the former to claim ignorance of the *Tiburón Blanco*'s illicit activities. An American might reckon that was worth a couple of British casualties.

They would soon know. Marker got to his feet and walked forward to the lounge area, where Finn was sitting in his wetsuit, encyclopaedia in hand.

'Don't ask,' Marker told him. 'I can't cope with any more interesting facts.'

Finn grinned. 'Time to go?' he asked.

The two of them helped each other on with their

diving equipment, double-checked that everything was working, and went out on deck, where Cafell and Dubery were manoeuvring the Russian submarine along-side. They were dressed in the original crew's clothes, which fitted pretty well.

Marker walked forward into the bow and stood there for a few moments staring out into space. The sea stretched away, empty of other shipping, with only a few small and scattered cays to break the flat line of the horizon. The nearly full moon was almost overhead, and the Milky Way seemed to stream from its sides, north-west towards Florida, south-east towards Cuba. On nights like this Marker knew why men created gods.

It was time to go.

The four men synchronized their watches, and Cafell and Dubery clambered down through the hatch and into the submarine. Marker and Finn slung the cling-film-wrapped MP5s across their chests and lowered themselves on to the submarine's curving back, where they sat splay-legged and facing each other on either side of the protruding hatch, their hands grasping the loop of rope which had been thrown around it.

Inside the sub, Dubery started up the engine. The Russian craft was more uncomfortable than their own, and defiantly devoid of any cosmetic trimmings. But the controls were simple, it was wonderfully responsive, and its capacity for speed was almost unbelievable. Cafell thought he knew a bit about engineering, but he had no idea how the Russians had done it. If the sub survived this particular night the research lads back at Poole would be thinking Christmas was early this year.

Dubery steered them towards the north-east, aiming the submarine towards the easternmost of the three flat humps which made up the Muertos Cays. Assuming that the *Tiburón Blanco* had not shifted position during the last week, such a course should keep the cay between them and the enemy, blinding the latter's radar.

Perched on the submarine's back Marker was remembering the giant worm riders from *Dune*, one of his favourite books as a teenager. Dubery was keeping the sub to about fifteen knots, but the surface was calm, and they weren't in any danger of being thrown off. It was exhilarating, like one of those rides at seaside amusement parks. Whatever his childhood might have lacked, Marker thought, it hadn't been excitement.

The cay grew steadily nearer, the moonlit ocean floor visible beneath them. Dubery brought the submarine to a halt, and the two men on its back slid down into the water. While Finn untied the electric torpedo Marker and Cafell checked their watches again through the window.

They were now only a mile or so away from the *Tiburón Blanco*. Since their means of locomotion was considerably slower, Marker and Finn left earlier. The former steered them in an easterly direction for a couple of hundred yards, and then left Finn with the electric torpedo while he went up to the surface for a look through the small hand periscope. And there the boat was, exactly where they had left it ten days before.

He went back down, gave Finn a thumbs up, and they resumed their journey. The water was clear, and very shallow until they had left the cay far behind them. There seemed to be few fish, and Marker wondered whether the long presence of the *Tiburón Blanco* nearby had scared them away. If so, he was not sorry. The last thing they needed now was a run-in with an irritable barracuda.

None appeared, tetchy or otherwise. About fifteen minutes after leaving the sub they found themselves under the thick black square of the floating helipad, and Marker cut the electric torpedo's motor. After they had tethered the machine to one of the helipad's anchor lines the two men swam deeper before coming back up directly underneath the hull of the enemy's boat. Marker checked his watch. They had two minutes to spare before the sub arrived.

They hung there in the water, watching the bubbles bounce off the hull, Marker cursing the fact that he hadn't thought to wait under the helipad.

The seconds dragged by, but no divers came plunging through the surface. The submarine finally swam into view, and Marker could see the concentration on Dubery's face as the young Scot guided the craft into position just off the cabin cruiser's starboard side. He caught a glimpse of a thumbs up from Cafell as the submarine started rising towards the surface.

He and Finn moved to the other side, waited until the sub was no longer visible beyond the keel, and brought their heads up into the night air.

On the boat above them people were talking excitedly in Spanish. Cafell was presumably following the script and pretending to have trouble with the hatch.

Marker used the rungs on the boat's side to lift himself out of the water, and laboriously removed the cling film from the MP5 with his other hand. Then he advanced another two rungs and hung there while Finn followed the same procedure beneath him.

A tap on his foot told Marker the younger man was ready. He pushed his head up over the side of the boat, saw no one, and climbed over the rail and on to the deck. The voices on the other side of the boat was louder now, and more threatening. There seemed to be no one on the bridge.

Finn joined him, and the two men moved off at a brisk walk in the direction of the stern deck. They were only a few steps away when a cavalcade of noises – the clang of a hatch, the ping of bullet on metal, the reverberation of the shot – erupted from the other side of the boat.

Marker rounded the corner just as the man with the gun turned away from the rail in disgust. His brain registered the gun pointing loosely down, the empty hands of the other two men. 'Freeze,' he heard himself say, his finger poised to squeeze the trigger and send all three men backwards over the rail.

The gunman's hand twitched involuntarily, and then suddenly went limp by his side. The automatic hit the deck with a thud. Finn went forward, picked it up, and tossed it overboard.

Marker was wondering where the other submarine crew was. If they were on board the shot should have brought them out on deck. 'Look after this lot,' he told Finn, and made his way back along the deck to the lounge door. He slipped inside and held still for several seconds, listening for any sounds.

Then it suddenly occurred to him – there had been no submarine tethered beneath the boat. He went swiftly through the rest of the cabins, and came up as empty as he had expected. Back on deck he found Cafell and Dubery trussing up the new prisoners while Finn kept them covered. At this rate, Marker thought, they should go into business as bounty-hunters.

'Take them inside,' he told Finn, and then waited until they were out of earshot before whispering new instructions to Cafell and Dubery. Both men smiled.

While Cafell disappeared down the deck, Marker and

Dubery followed the others inside. 'Where is the second submarine?' he asked the man in the captain's cap.

The man said nothing.

'Your name is Angel Socarras,' Marker told him. 'You work for Fidel Arcilla as a treasure hunter and a smuggler of human spare parts. I will happily feed you to the sharks.'

Socarras shrugged. 'Do what you wish,' he said.

Marker looked at him, sighed, and nodded to Dubery and Finn. The latter looked surprised, but joined Dubery in taking hold of one of the captain's arms. 'Off the stern,' Marker added, and the two SBS men bundled the man out into the night. A few seconds later the men in the cabin heard the beginnings of a struggle, as it belatedly dawned on Socarras that Marker wasn't bluffing. A few more seconds, and there was a loud splash.

'Where is the other submarine?' Marker asked the man who had held the gun.

The man's mouth was gaping open. 'It is gone to Florida,' he said quickly.

'With another shipment?'

'Yes, they go every night now. Because the Americans invade Haiti,' he added unnecessarily.

It was even worse than Marker had feared – Arcilla's man in Haiti was upping production to make the most of the little time he had left. He thought about the cargo that was now heading towards Anhinga Lodge – kidneys probably. They had been taken from someone, but the chances of their finding a new home were distinctly remote. And when the submarine arrived at the lodge the shit would hit the fan . . .

The crew would have to be intercepted. He would have to radio the American authorities.

Every night now, the man had said. 'The helicopter, what time does it arrive?' Marker asked.

The man shrugged. 'Around eleven.'

'See what you can make of their radio,' Marker told Cafell. 'We need to call the Yanks and the *Argyll*.'

Dubery arrived back in the doorway.

'How's the captain?' Marker asked.

'Still out old.'

'What did you throw overboard?'

'A chest full of fishing tackle.'

The gunman's mouth was gaping again.

'The oldest tricks are always the best,' Marker told him.

The following twenty hours were much like the previous twenty. The four men slept in shifts, and devoted their waking hours to the jobs that needed doing. Dubery and Finn went off in the Russian submarine to collect the *Slipstream Queen*, which they then used for transferring the new prisoners to the *Argyll*. The frigate, on station some fifty miles to the east, came to meet them, but the captain failed to show his face.

'Fucking brass,' Finn said. 'They spend weeks sailing their little ships round in circles, and when someone asks them to do something useful they get pissed off.'

'Maybe he didn't join the navy to be a prison governor,' Dubery observed.

Back on the *Tiburón Blanco*, and now relieved of the need to guard their captives, Marker and Cafell contacted Poole via the satellite radio. According to Colhoun the American authorities had so far been successful in keeping the lid on their end of the operation. And Arcilla, who was being watched from a discreet distance, had displayed no awareness of anything being amiss. As far as the Turks and Caicos were concerned, two men from the Attorney-General's office were en route from London with all the necessary powers. They would be there that evening.

The sun went down, and Dubery was entrusted with the task of moving the *Slipstream Queen* a reasonable distance away from the *Tiburón Blanco*. The hours dragged by. At ten-thirty Cafell switched on the helipad's perimeter lighting, and the three men sat out on the bow deck, ears cocked for the sound of an approaching helicopter.

At one minute past eleven they heard it, and soon the dark shape was growing in the south-eastern sky. The pilot landed without difficulty on the barely moving helipad, cut the engine, and jumped down from the cockpit, shouting something in Spanish at the waiting SBS men. Marker advanced towards him in the captain's hat, but the pilot was not so easily fooled. He stared for several seconds, then shouted out a question in Spanish, and finally lunged for the safety of his cockpit. Marker caught him by the legs, pulled him back out again, and showed him his Browning High Power.

'Shit,' the man said, but he seemed more surprised than upset.

Behind him Cafell was examining the plastic boxes, and the organs suspended within them. 'What are we going to do with these?' he asked.

'Feed them to the fish,' Marker said.

There was something in his voice which made Cafell reluctant to argue.

They took the pilot aboard the *Tiburón Blanco*, and sat him down in the saloon cabin. He was not much older than twenty-five, good-looking, and with at least an air of intelligence. And he was certainly pleased with himself – even in these circumstances he had a hard job to keep from smiling.

'Right,' Marker said. 'You understand English?'

'Of course,' the man replied indignantly.

'Good. Your name?'

'Felix Córdoba.'

'OK, Felix. You have two choices. Cooperate with us for twenty-four hours and we'll let you go. Refuse to cooperate, and we'll hand you over to the authorities on Provo, and make damn sure you serve at least ten years in prison. So choose now.'

The man looked at Marker, disbelief on his face. 'Ten years? And you will really let me go?'

'Yes,' Marker said. 'If you help us.'

There was another long pause.

'Felix . . .'

'OK, OK, I cooperate. What do I lose?'

'Not a lot.'

Felix laughed, as if the misfortune belonged to someone else. 'So what you want to know?'

'First off, where do you fly from here?'

'Back to Provo.'

'OK, then that's where we're going.'

'First we must refuel.'

Marker turned to Cafell. 'Tell Colhoun what's happening, and ask him to contact the people Whitehall has sent out to Provo. We need to make sure the people at Arcilla's villa are in custody before we get back.'

'OK, boss.'

'Let's fill up the chopper,' Marker told Finn and Felix.

The helicopter came to rest on the tarmac at Provo's tiny airport soon after four in the morning. To Marker's relief the men from London were not there to meet them. Jet lag had presumably taken its toll, and the hapless Sergeant Oswald had been obliged to form the entire welcoming committee.

There were rooms waiting for the SBS quartet at the Club Med-Turkoise, he said. Marker told him they needed the use of a room here in the airport building for the interrogation of their captive.

Oswald found them one in the west wing, which was not used during the tourist low season. A windowless storeroom next door could be used as a detention room for their captive. Marker thanked the sergeant and gently shut the door on him.

Felix asked if he could have a few hours' sleep.

'Not yet,' Marker told him. 'Questions first, and then you can have some sleep.'

'OK,' Felix agreed good-naturedly.

'Where do you make the pick-up?'

The pilot looked surprised that they didn't know. 'Tortuga,' he said.

'Where on Tortuga?' Cafell asked, pushing a map in front of him.

'Here,' Felix said, pointing with his finger.

'And what is it?' Marker asked.

'What do you mean?'

'Is it a house like the one here on Provo?'

'No, no. It is a camp, a soldiers' camp, but with many civilians. It is Colonel Joutard's camp.'

'How many soldiers?' Marker asked.

'Hard to say. Ten, fifteen, maybe twenty even. They are not army, you understand. More like Ton-Ton. Private soldiers.'

'Armed thugs,' Cafell suggested.

'*Sí.*'

Marker stretched his back in the chair. 'OK, Felix, now we want to know every single thing you can remember about this place – where everything is, where the soldiers are and the civilians are, where this Joutard will be.' Marker grinned at him. 'And the better your memory, the more future you'll probably have, because this evening you'll be taking us in there, and your chances of getting out again are probably going to depend on how well we do once we're on the ground.'

Felix murmured something unhappy in Spanish, but he didn't bother to argue, and for the best part of an hour he answered the questions Marker and Cafell put to him. He knew there were doctors in the camp, but he had not seen them himself, and couldn't confirm that one of them was English. He hadn't been around the camp either, but he had seen it from the air, albeit always in darkness, each time he made a pick-up. And as Marker jogged the pilot's memory with questions, Cafell's diagram of the camp acquired more and more useful detail.

Eventually the well of information ran dry.

'Round up some cushions for our friend here,' Marker told Dubery. 'And you and Finn should get some sleep as well.'

Once the pilot had been locked in the storeroom, Finn said he had a question.

Marker gave him an enquiring look.

'Are we going to get away with this? I mean, isn't HMG going to jump on us from a great height when they find out we've been invading a foreign country?'

'We're going in after one of our own,' Cafell retorted. 'The CO will back us up. He . . .'

'He will,' Marker agreed, 'but it's still a good question.' He ran a hand through his hair. 'And I guess the only answer is – what choice do we have? The good news is that if we fuck up then we probably won't be around to care, and if we don't the most we can expect is a rap on the wrist.' He looked at Finn. 'But if you feel you don't want . . .'

'Fuck, no,' Finn said, looking offended. 'I'm coming. I just like knowing exactly where, if you see what I mean.'

'Up shit creek,' Cafell told him cheerily.

'But with a paddle,' Marker said. He got to his feet. 'Thing that worries me is someone trying to stop us. Like these guys from the Attorney-General's office or wherever it is they really come from. So before they come looking for our guide I think I'll go looking for them. Take them our video, tell them about the prisoners on the *Argyll*. That should keep them happy for a couple of hours.'

'You can tell them to go collect the Americans' boat,' Cafell suggested.

Marker grinned. 'You know, I'd completely forgotten about that.'

'I expect the *Argyll* wants her submarine and Kleppers back too,' Finn suggested.

'You never saw James Bond going round collecting all the equipment he'd abandoned,' Cafell said. 'No wonder Q always looked pissed off.'

Marker's fears of interference from the new arrivals were soon laid to rest. Taking morning coffee with them on the terrace of their luxury hotel, he formed the strong impression that the less the two men from London had to do with him and his men the better they would like it.

They would look at the video in due time, and planned to interview the prisoners on the *Argyll*, probably on the following day. In the meantime, they were waiting for a plenipotentiary from Miami. Nothing could be done, as one of them explained, until they had discussed the ramifications of the whole business with the Americans, and settled any 'potential disputes over jurisdiction'. The man looked across at Marker as if wondering whether he needed to use words with fewer syllables.

Marker left them drinking their coffee, gazing out across the turquoise sea, and probably discussing a convivial round of golf. Back at the airport he woke Dubery, and fell almost instantly asleep on the line of sequestered cushions.

Soon after he and Tamara returned from church, at around ten on that Sunday morning, Fidel Arcilla received a call from a well-wisher in the Dade County Police Department. Two hours, and several phone calls later, he was able to gauge the full extent of the disaster which had befallen his operation.

He lit a rare cigar, and sat back in his orthopaedic office chair.

If the Florida and Provo ends were both blown, he realized, then there was no chance that the *Tiburón Blanco* had escaped. Joutard on Haiti was probably immune, at least until such time as US forces went ashore.

Arcilla picked up the phone to summon his radio operator, then put it down again. Making contact with Joutard in these circumstances might not be the wisest of moves.

He walked out on to the roof garden and leaned over the parapet, looking down at the Sunday promenaders on Calle Ocho. To his right the towers of Downtown split the blue sky, and between them he could see Miami Beach and the distant sparkle of the sun on the sea.

He was not used to set-backs, not any more. He would have to think this through with care, and not let anger get the better of him.

The operation had not been important, or at least not in the financial sense. He could do without such profits fifty times over. The problems were merely legal, and as far as he could tell not particularly acute. He had been careful to interpose numerous cut-outs between himself and the operation, and those who had actually worked in the business would happily go to prison for him, secure in the knowledge that they and their families would all be well rewarded.

The British might try and extradite him, but in a case like this, where the law could be endlessly muddled with moral issues, the process could be delayed for years. US laws had been broken too, but his friends in the CIA would ensure that any legal action against him here would be deferred indefinitely. With Castro's regime crumbling at home they knew they might be needing him at a moment's notice.

No, there was nothing much to worry about. The only obvious crimes had been committed in Haiti, and there was no way he could be held accountable for them.

Still, he thought, turning away from the Miami skyline and grinding the cigar beneath his foot, he would have no more contact with Haiti. There was no point in taking unnecessary risks for a psycho like Toussaint Joutard.

Worrell Franklin arrived at the airport around five o'clock, and made no bones about what his priorities were. 'I'm coming,' he told Marker belligerently.

The SBS man sighed. 'How the hell did you know we were here? And going somewhere?'

'I gave him a call,' Cafell said apologetically.

Marker opened his mouth to say something, closed it again, and eyed his partner with a tolerance born of affection.

'I want to come,' Franklin said.

'Who's stopping you?' Marker said. The ex-SAS man had been in on this business from the beginning, and Marker had no fears he would let the side down. In fact, if Joutard had twenty men, he would narrow the odds from 5–1 to 4–1.

Franklin, who had been expecting more of an argument, looked at Marker, surprise written all over his face. 'My wife would like to,' he said, and then smiled ruefully. 'No, that's not really true. She wants to help Nick. She's just scared I won't come back.'

'I can't guarantee it,' Marker said quietly.

'I can't guarantee surviving my next fucking drive on the Leeward Highway,' Franklin said.

In the Tortuga camp office Joutard handed Calderón a small glass of rum. The doctor raised an eyebrow.

'This is the last night,' Joutard explained. 'I want you to start half an hour earlier. When you've finished the usual, the Englishman will be killed. And the woman too.'

'The woman,' Calderón echoed, but he didn't object.

'She will talk,' Joutard said, as if the doctor had. And because she once spat in my face, he added to himself. It had only been her indispensability that had kept her alive that day. The thought of taking her that evening crossed his mind, but he let the idea go. There would be no pleasure in it. Certainly nothing to compare with the profit her body would bring him on the operating table.

'How will they be killed?' Calderón was asking.

'Head shots?'

Calderón nodded. 'That is best . . .'

'And after you've taken what you can from them, I want you and Bodin to take out the other kidneys,' Joutard decided. There were already two many people in camp bearing the tell-tale scar.

Calderón finished his rum and left. Joutard called in his number two. 'Once they've started with the operations I want you to bring me a girl,' he told the man. 'The one with the perfect body – her name is Françoise, I think. You know the one I mean?'

'The orphan Françoise?' the man said doubtfully.

'Of course the orphan,' Joutard said. Emelisse Alabri's hold over him was a thing of the past, and he could now take whom and whatever he wanted.

Forty minutes after leaving Provo the Haitian coast hove into view. 'Remember, anyone carrying a gun is to be taken out,' Marker shouted over the noise of the rotors. 'And don't wait for them to pull the trigger first. This isn't Tombstone.'

The other four men nodded their agreement.

Marker could now see the cliffs rising from the sandy beach, and the walled compound above them. Beside him Cafell was waiting to check his diagram against the reality.

Felix lifted the chopper a little higher, and they could see the mosaic of buildings, trees and open spaces which lay inside the walls. It was not well lit, Marker noticed with relief. There was electric lighting in some of the buildings, and a few fires outside them, but darkness was the rule. If the watch-tower on the landward side was equipped with a searchlight it hadn't yet been turned on.

The helicopter was coming down now, aimed at a stretch of open ground surrounded by several small fires. At first Marker thought a square had been marked out as a landing sight, but then realized he was looking at a baseball diamond. As the helicopter sank towards the hard dirt surface Cafell made frantic alterations to the diagram.

Two men stood waiting close to one of the fires, both armed with sub-machine-guns. The chopper was still a foot from the ground as Marker stepped off, rather in the manner of a man leaving a moving London bus, and fired a concentrated burst from his silenced MP5. Both men collapsed, sending little clouds of firelit dust into the night air.

The other five men piled out, Felix with rather less enthusiasm than the others. 'This way,' Cafell said, and they were all off at a run, heading for a gap between a long, low building and a stand of royal palms. So far no one else seemed aware of their presence.

Reaching a path Cafell stopped for a moment. 'Is that Joutard's office?' he asked Felix, pointing at a one-storey building a hundred yards or so to their right.

'Yes.'

'The gate's this way,' Cafell told Marker.

'Good luck,' Marker told him, and the group split up, with Finn following Cafell at a run, the others the team leader.

Marker's group sped along the tree-lined path, conscious of the darkened windows in the buildings to either side, and came to the edge of an open space. On the far side was a line of three identical buildings, which would have looked like barracks but for the full-length verandas. According to Felix, the middle one of these contained Joutard's office and living quarters.

Marker paused in the shadows before gesturing the others to follow, and they were only about ten yards short of the veranda when a shout came out of the dark to their right. The SBS men sank instantly to the ground, and their eyes were still seeking out the shout's source when a short burst from an SMG exploded in their ears, and knocked down the still-standing Felix.

Suddenly two men were running towards them like idiots, only to be hurled backwards by the silent power of the MP5s.

The new silence seemed less natural than the old. For a few seconds the birds and the cicadas seemed to hold their breath, and during that time the SBS team could hear music coming from inside the building. To Marker's astonishment it sounded like Elvis Presley.

He managed a quick look at Felix, and realized his wounds were not life-threatening. 'I'm going in. You two get him under the steps,' he whispered, just before another burst of fire erupted out of the night, longer this time, but also wilder.

Dubery and Franklin scrambled for the ground beneath the raised veranda, as Marker leapt up the three steps and hurled himself bodily at the office door. Crashing through, he found himself flying across the room inside, and landing almost at the feet of a running man.

The man's surprise was greater than Marker's, and the SBS man managed to grab an ankle and flip his opponent towards the duty desk, which he hit head first.

As the man slid motionless to the floor the first door in the passage swung open, and Marker had a momentary picture of a naked man looking out, and a naked girl sitting up somewhere behind him, before the door was slammed back shut. He strode swiftly across the intervening yards, raised his right foot, and rammed its sole against the door, sinking down on to his left knee almost in the same motion. The naked man was waiting with pistol raised, but the only shot he had time for went over Marker's head, and the burst from the MP5 stitched a line of momentary agony across his chest. He sank back on to the girl behind him, who lay there whimpering in terror. 'Is your heart filled with pain?' Elvis was asking. 'Shall I come back again, tell me, dear, are you lonesome tonight?'

In the operating room everyone had heard the gunshots, but had done nothing beyond share questioning glances. The Americans couldn't be here already, Russell thought, as he snipped carefully through one of the minor arterial links. It was probably just Joutard's goons entertaining each other. Still . . .

He looked across at Emelisse, whose skin seemed stretched even tighter across her lovely cheek-bones than usual. 'Just keep on going,' she murmured, so softly that he couldn't be sure whether she was talking to him or herself.

Marker put an eye round the corner of the office door, just as another burst of automatic fire ripped across the front of the building. A splinter caught in his cheek, drawing blood. He waited a few seconds and then swung himself through the rail and down to the ground, before rolling instantly back into the shelter of the veranda.

'Hi,' Cafell said casually.

'How's the gate?' Marker asked him.

'It's ours. One man climbed over it and disappeared,

276

but we had to take out the guy in the tower. Finn's in occupation now. No one'll get past him without learning an interesting fact.'

Marker grinned. 'Good,' he said. 'And Joutard's dead,' he added. 'At least, I think it must have been him. That makes about eight of them accounted for – still a few to go. I think we'd better get to the hospital before anyone gets the idea of taking hostages. Then we can clear up. Frankie, you and Ian keep the bastards busy.'

'OK, boss.'

Marker and Cafell crawled along the front of the veranda to its end, turned the corner and scrambled to their feet. To their right they could see several curtained windows, each with lines of brilliant light seeping through. 'Let's go,' Marker murmured.

They were halfway down the side of the building when someone came running round the far corner. Seeing the two SBS men he had the presence of mind to throw himself on the ground and cover his head with his hands. Marker left him for Cafell, and headed straight for what seemed the only entrance to the hospital building. He was only a few feet from the door when a bullet whizzed past his head and zipped into the vegetation beyond.

He ran even faster, hurling himself through the door as another shot echoed in his ears, and a cry of pain came out of the room ahead.

Russell's head spun round just in time to see Calderón's dead body hit the ground. The kidney he had been holding slithered bloodily across the white floor, and Marker came tumbling in through the open doorway.

For a second no one moved.

'Dr Russell, I presume,' Marker said.

An hour later the compound was secure. Joutard and six of his men had been killed, another ten had wounds of varying severity. The remaining few had escaped across the walls.

Emelisse had spoken to the orphans, many of whom were now wandering around the compound as if they finally owned it. The doctor herself, as Russell told Marker, was back in the operating theatre, sewing the surviving three kidneys back into their donors. 'The tissue match couldn't be better,' he added wryly.

'Some woman,' Marker murmured.

'Yeah,' Russell agreed. 'And I'd better go and see if she needs any help.'

Marker walked slowly down to where Cafell, Dubery, Franklin and Finn were sitting with a bottle of Joutard's rum. But despite the drink, despite the fact that they all had survived, the mood was far from cheerful. The enormity of what had happened in this place was still sinking in.

Marker accepted a glass, but after a while he got up again and walked on alone to where a gap in the cliff-top wall allowed a view out across the shining water. He sat there, remembering the look of terror on the girl's face, and Elvis asking if her heart was filled with pain.

He thought about the other orphans, who had paid with their own flesh for the things which he had always taken for granted, and about the Americans who were no longer slaves to dialysis because of this devil's bargain.

He remembered the haunted loneliness in Tamara Arcilla's eyes, and the hunger in himself which he hadn't even known was there.

He thought about Penny, and knew she was finally gone.

And he stared out across the moonlit sea, drawing on its strength and beauty, so that the healing might begin.

OTHER TITLES IN SERIES FROM 22 BOOKS

Available now at newsagents and booksellers or use the order form provided

continued overleaf . . .

All at £4.99 net

All 22 Books are available at your bookshop, or can be ordered from:

22 Books
Mail Order Department
Little, Brown and Company
Brettenham House
Lancaster Place
London WC2E 7EN

Alternatively, you may fax your order to the above address. Fax number: 0171 911 8100.

Payments can be made by cheque or postal order, payable to Little, Brown and Company (UK), or by credit card (Visa/Access). Do not send cash or currency. UK, BFPO and Eire customers, please allow 75p per item for postage and packing, to a maximum of £7.50. Overseas customers, please allow £1 per item.

While every effort is made to keep prices low, it is sometimes necessary to increase cover prices at short notice. 22 Books reserves the right to show new retail prices on covers which may differ from those previously advertised in the books or elsewhere.

NAME ....

ADDRESS...

....

....

☐ I enclose my remittance for £_____
☐ I wish to pay by Access/Visa

Card number
☐☐☐☐ ☐☐☐☐ ☐☐☐☐ ☐☐☐☐

Card expiry date
☐☐ ☐☐

Please allow 28 days for delivery. Please tick box if you do not wish to receive any additional information ☐